BOOKS BY
ALEXANDER McCALL SMITH

BLUE SHOES AND HAPPINESS

BLUE SHOES
AND HAPPINESS

Alexander McCall Smith

Pantheon Books

New York

Copyright © 2006 by Alexander McCall Smith
All rights reserved. Published in the United States by Pantheon Books,
a division of Random House, Inc., New York. Published simultaneously
in Canada by Alfred A. Knopf Canada, a division of Random House of
Canada Limited, Toronto. Originally published in Great Britain by
Polygon, an imprint of Birlinn, Ltd., Edinburgh.

Pantheon Books and colophon are registered trademarks
of Random House, Inc.

Library of Congress Cataloging-in-Publication Data
McCall Smith, Alexander, [date]
Blue shoes and happiness / Alexander McCall Smith.
p. cm.—(The No. 1 Ladies' Detective Agency series)
ISBN 0-375-42272-2
1. Ramotswe, Precious (Fictitious character)—Fiction. 2. No. 1 Ladies'
Detective Agency (Imaginary organization)—Fiction. 3. Women private
investigators—Botswana—Fiction. 4. Botswana—Fiction. I. Title.
PR6063.C326B58 2006   823'.914—dc22   2005052122

www.pantheonbooks.com
Printed in the United States of America
First American Edition
2 4 6 8 9 7 5 3 1

This book is for
Bernard Ditau in Botswana
and
Kenneth and Pravina King in Scotland

BLUE SHOES AND HAPPINESS

CHAPTER ONE

AUNTY EMANG,
SOLVER OF PROBLEMS

WHEN YOU ARE JUST the right age, as Mma Ramotswe was, and when you have seen a bit of life, as Mma Ramotswe certainly had, then there are some things that you just know. And one of the things that was well known to Mma Ramotswe, only begetter of the No. 1 Ladies' Detective Agency (Botswana's only ladies' detective agency), was that there were two sorts of problems in this life. Firstly, there were those problems—and they were major ones—about which one could do very little, other than to hope, of course. These were the problems of the land, of fields that were too rocky, of soil that blew away in the wind, or of places where crops would just not thrive for some sickness that lurked in the very earth. But looming greater than anything else there was the problem of drought. It was a familiar feeling in Botswana, this waiting for rain, which often simply did not come, or came too late to save the crops. And then the land, scarred and exhausted, would dry and crack under the relentless sun, and it would seem that nothing short of a miracle would ever bring it to life. But that miracle would eventually arrive, as it always had, and the landscape would turn from brown to green within hours under the kiss of the rain. And there were other colours that would follow the green; yellows, blues, reds would appear in patches across the veld as if great cakes of dye had been crumbled and scattered by an unseen hand. These were the colours of the wild flowers that had been lurking there, throughout the dry season, waiting for the first drops of moisture to awaken them. So at least that sort of problem had its solution, although one often had to wait long, dry months for that solution to arrive.

The other sorts of problems were those which people made for themselves. These were very common, and Mma Ramotswe had seen many of them in the course of her work. Ever since she had set up this agency, armed only with a copy of Clovis Andersen's *The Principles of Private Detection*—and a great deal of common sense—scarcely a day had gone by without her encountering some problem which people had brought upon themselves. Unlike the first sort of problem—drought and the like—these were difficulties that could have been avoided. If people were only more careful, or behaved themselves as they should, then they would not find themselves faced with problems of this sort. But of course people never behaved themselves as they should. "We are all human beings," Mma Ramotswe had once observed to Mma Makutsi, "and human beings can't really help themselves. Have you noticed that, Mma? We can't really help ourselves from doing things that land us in all sorts of trouble."

Mma Makutsi pondered this for a few moments. In general, she thought that Mma Ramotswe was right about matters of this sort, but she felt that this particular proposition needed a little bit more thought. She knew that there were some people who were unable to make of their lives what they wanted them to be, but then there were many others who were quite capable of keeping themselves under control. In her own case, she thought that she was able to resist temptation quite effectively. She did not consider herself to be particularly strong, but at the same time she did not seem to be markedly weak. She did not drink, nor did she over-indulge in food, or chocolate or anything of that sort. No, Mma Ramotswe's observation was just a little bit too sweeping and she would have to disagree. But then the thought struck her: Could she resist a fine new pair of shoes, even if she knew that she had plenty of shoes already (which was not the case)?

"I think you're right, Mma," she said. "Everybody has a weakness, and most of us are not strong enough to resist it."

Mma Ramotswe looked at her assistant. She had an idea what Mma Makutsi's weakness might be, and indeed there might even be more than one.

"Take Mr J.L.B. Matekoni, for example," said Mma Ramotswe.

"All men are weak," said Mma Makutsi. "That is well known." She paused. Now that Mma Ramotswe and Mr J.L.B. Matekoni were married, it was possible that Mma Ramotswe had discovered new weaknesses in him. The mechanic was a quiet man, but it was often the mildest-looking people who did the most colourful things, in secret of course. What could Mr J.L.B. Matekoni get up to? It would be very interesting to hear.

"Cake," said Mma Ramotswe quickly. "That is Mr J.L.B. Matekoni's great weakness. He cannot help himself when it comes to cake. He can be manipulated very easily if he has a plate of cake in his hand."

Mma Makutsi laughed. "Mma Potokwane knows that, doesn't she?" she said. "I have seen her getting Mr J.L.B. Matekoni to do all sorts of things for her just by offering him pieces of that fruit cake of hers."

Mma Ramotswe rolled her eyes up towards the ceiling. Mma Potokwane, the matron of the orphan farm, was her friend, and when all was said and done she was a good woman, but she was quite ruthless when it came to getting things for the children in her care. She it was who had cajoled Mr J.L.B. Matekoni into

fostering the two children who now lived in their house; that had
been a good thing, of course, and the children were dearly loved,
but Mr J.L.B. Matekoni had not thought the thing through and
had failed even to consult Mma Ramotswe about the whole matter. And then there were the numerous occasions on which she
had prevailed upon him to spend hours of his time fixing that
unreliable old water pump at the orphan farm—a pump which
dated back to the days of the Protectorate and which should have
been retired and put into a museum long ago. And Mma Potokwane achieved all of this because she had a profound understanding of how men worked and what their weaknesses were;
that was the secret of so many successful women—they knew
about the weaknesses of men.

That conversation with Mma Makutsi had taken place some
days before. Now Mma Ramotswe was sitting on the verandah of
her house on Zebra Drive, late on a Saturday afternoon, reading
the paper. She was the only person in the house at the time,
which was unusual for a Saturday. The children were both out:
Motholeli had gone to spend the weekend with a friend whose
family lived out at Mogiditishane. This friend's mother had picked
her up in her small truck and had stored the wheelchair in the
back with some large balls of string that had aroused Mma
Ramotswe's interest but which she had not felt it her place to ask
about. What could anybody want with such a quantity of string?
she wondered. Most people needed very little string, if any, in
their lives, but this woman, who was a beautician, seemed to need
a great deal. Did beauticians have a special use for string that the
rest of us knew nothing about? Mma Ramotswe asked herself.
People spoke about face-lifts; did string come into face-lifts?

Puso, the boy, who had caused them such concern over his
unpredictable behaviour but who had recently become much
more settled, had gone off with Mr J.L.B. Matekoni to see an

important football match at the stadium. Mma Ramotswe did not consider it important in the least—she had no interest in football, and she could not see how it could possibly matter in the slightest who succeeded in kicking the ball into the goal the most times—but Mr J.L.B. Matekoni clearly thought differently. He was a close follower and supporter of the Zebras, and tried to get to the stadium whenever they were playing. Fortunately the Zebras were doing well at the moment, and this, thought Mma Ramotswe, was a good thing: it was quite possible, she felt, that Mr J.L.B. Matekoni's depression, from which he had made a good recovery, could recur if he, or the Zebras, were to suffer any serious set-back.

So now she was alone in the house, and it seemed very quiet to her. She had made a cup of bush tea and had drunk that thoughtfully, gazing out over the rim of her cup onto the garden to the front of the house. The sausage fruit tree, the moporoto, to which she had never paid much attention, had taken it upon itself to produce abundant fruit this year, and four heavy sausage-shaped pods had appeared at the end of a branch, bending that limb of the tree under their weight. She would have to do something about that, she thought. People knew that it was dangerous to sit under such trees, as the heavy fruit could crack open a skull if it chose to fall when a person was below. That had happened to a friend of her father's many years ago, and the blow that he had received had cracked his skull and damaged his brain, making it difficult for him to speak. She remembered him when she was a child, struggling to make himself understood, and her father had explained that he had sat under a sausage tree and had gone to sleep, and this was the result.

She made a mental note to warn the children and to get Mr J.L.B. Matekoni to knock the fruit down with a pole before anybody was hurt. And then she turned back to her cup of tea and to her perusal of the copy of *The Daily News,* which she had unfolded on her lap. She had read the first four pages of the paper, and had gone through the small advertisements with her usual care. There was much to be learned from the small advertisements, with their offers of irrigation pipes for farmers, used vans, jobs of various sorts, plots of land with house construction permission, and bargain furniture. Not only could one keep up to date with what things cost, but there was also a great deal of social detail to be garnered from this source. That day, for instance, there was a statement by a Mr Herbert Motimedi that he would not be responsible for any debts incurred by Mrs Boipelo Motimedi, which effectively informed the public that Herbert and Boipelo were no longer on close terms—which did not surprise Mma Ramotswe, as it happened, because she had always felt that that particular marriage was not a good idea, in view of the fact that Boipelo Motimedi had gone through three husbands before she found Herbert, and two of these previous husbands had been declared bankrupt. She smiled at that and skimmed over the remaining advertisements before turning the page and getting to the column that interested her more than anything else in the newspaper.

Some months earlier, the newspaper had announced to its readers that it would be starting a new feature. "If you have any problems," the paper said, "then you should write to our new exclusive columnist, Aunty Emang, who will give you advice on what to do. Not only is Aunty Emang a BA from the University of Botswana, but she also has the wisdom of one who has lived fifty-eight years and knows all about life." This advance notice brought in a flood of letters, and the paper had expanded the amount of space available for Aunty Emang's sound advice. Soon she had become so popular that she was viewed as something of a national institution and was even named in Parliament when an opposition member brought the house down with the suggestion that the policy proposed by some hapless minister would never have been approved of by Aunty Emang.

Mma Ramotswe had chuckled over that, as she now chuckled over the plight of a young student who had written a passionate love letter to a girl and had delivered it, by mistake, to her sister. "I am not sure what to do," he had written to Aunty Emang. "I think that the sister is very pleased with what I wrote to her as she is smiling at me all the time. Her sister, the girl I really like, does not know that I like her and maybe her own sister has told her about the letter which she has received from me. So she thinks now that I am in love with her sister, and does not know that I am in love with her. How can I get out of this difficult situation?" And Aunty Emang, with her typical robustness, had written: "Dear Anxious in Molepolole: The simple answer to your question is that you cannot get out of this. If you tell one of the girls that she has received a letter intended for her sister, then she will become very sad. Her sister (the one you really wanted to write to in the first place) will then think that you have been unkind to her sister and made her upset. She will not like you for this. The answer is that you must give up seeing both of these girls and you should spend your time working harder on your examinations. When you have a good job and are earning some money, then you can find another girl to fall in love with. But make sure that you address any letter to that girl very carefully."

There were two other letters. One was from a boy of fourteen who had been moved to write to Aunty Emang about being picked upon by his teacher. "I am a hard-working boy," he wrote. "I do all my schoolwork very carefully and neatly. I never shout in the class or push people about (like most other boys). When my teacher talks, I always pay attention and smile at him. I do not trouble the girls (like most other boys). I am a very good boy in every sense. Yet my teacher always blames me for anything that goes wrong and gives me low marks in my work. I am very unhappy. The more I try to please this teacher, the more he dislikes me. What am I doing wrong?"

Everything, thought Mma Ramotswe. That's what you are doing wrong: everything. But how could one explain to a fourteen-year-old boy that one should not *try* too hard; which was what he was doing and which irritated his teacher. It was better, she thought, to be a little bit bad in this life, and not too perfect. If you were too perfect, then you invited exactly this sort of reaction, even if teachers should be above that sort of thing. But what, she wondered, would Aunty Emang say?

"Dear Boy," wrote Aunty Emang. "Teachers do not like boys like you. You should not say you are not like other boys, or people will think that you are like a girl." And that is all that Aunty Emang seemed prepared to say on the subject—which was a bit dismissive, thought Mma Ramotswe, and now that poor, over-anxious boy would think that not only did his teacher not like him, but neither did Aunty Emang. But perhaps there was not enough space in the newspaper to go into the matter in any great depth because there was the final letter to be printed, which was not a short one.

"Dear Aunty Emang," the letter ran. "Four years ago my wife gave birth to our first born. We had been trying for this baby for a long time and we were very happy when he arrived. When it came to choosing a name for this child, my wife suggested that we should call him after my brother, who lives in Mahalapye but who comes to see us every month. She said that this would be a good thing, as my brother does not have a wife himself and it would be good to have a name from a member of the family. I was happy with this and agreed.

"As my son has been growing up, my brother has been very

kind to him. He has given him many presents and packets of sweets when he comes to see him. The boy likes his uncle very much and always listens very carefully to the stories that he tells him. My wife thinks that this is a good thing—that a boy should love his kind uncle like this.

"Then somebody said to me: *Your son looks very like his uncle. It is almost as if he is his own son.* And that made me think for the first time: Is my brother the father of my son? I looked at the two of them when they were sitting together and I thought that too. They are very alike.

"I am very fond of my brother. He is my twin, and we have done everything together all our lives. But I do not like the thought that he is the father of my son. I would like to talk to him about this, but I do not want to say anything that may cause trouble in the family. You are a wise lady, Aunty: What do you think I should do?"

Mma Ramotswe finished reading the letter and thought: surely a twin should know how funny this sounds—after all, *they are twins.* If Aunty Emang had laughed on reading this letter, then it was not apparent in her answer.

"I am very sorry that you are worrying about this," she wrote. "Look at yourself in the mirror. Do you look like your brother?" And once again that was all she had to say on the subject.

Mma Ramotswe reflected on what she had read. It seemed to her that she and Aunty Emang had at least something in common. Both of them dealt with the problems of others and both were expected by those others to provide some solution to their difficulties. But there the similarity ended. Aunty Emang had the easier role: she merely had to give a pithy response to the facts presented to her. In Mma Ramotswe's case, important facts were often unknown and required to be coaxed out of obscurity. And once she had done that, then she had to do rather more than make a clever or dismissive suggestion. She had to see matters through to their conclusion, and these conclusions were not always as simple as somebody like Aunty Emang might imagine.

It would be tempting, she thought, to write to Aunty Emang when next she had a particularly intractable problem to deal with. She would write and ask her what she would do in the circumstances. *Here, Aunty Emang, just you solve this one!* Yes, it would be interesting to do that, she thought, but completely unprofessional. If you were a private detective, as Mma Ramotswe was, you could not reveal your client's problem to the world; indeed, Clovis Andersen had something to say on this subject. "Keep your mouth shut," he had written in *The Principles of Private Detection*. "Keep your mouth shut at all times, but at the same time encourage others to do precisely the opposite."

Mma Ramotswe had remembered this advice, and had to agree that even if it sounded like hypocrisy (if it was indeed hypocrisy to do one thing and encourage others to do the opposite), it was at the heart of good detection to get other people to talk. People loved to talk, especially in Botswana, and if you only gave them the chance they would tell you everything that you needed to know. Mma Ramotswe had found this to be true in so many of her cases. If you want the answer to something, then ask somebody. It always worked.

She put the paper aside and marshalled her thoughts. It was all very well sitting there on her verandah thinking about the problems of others, but it was getting late in the afternoon and there were things to do. In the kitchen at the back of the house there was a packet of green beans that needed to be washed and chopped. There was a pumpkin that was not going to cook itself. There were onions to be put in a pan of boiling water and cooked until soft. That was part of being a woman, she thought; one never reached the end. Even if one could sit down and drink a cup of bush tea, or even two cups, one always knew that at the end of the tea somebody was waiting for something. Children or men were waiting to be fed; a dirty floor cried out to be washed; a crumpled skirt called for the iron. And so it would continue. Tea was just a temporary solution to the cares of the world, although it certainly helped. Perhaps she should write and tell Aunty Emang that. Most problems could be diminished by the drinking of tea and the thinking through of things that could be done while tea was being drunk. And even if that did not solve problems, at least it could put them off for a little while, which we sometimes needed to do, we really did.

CHAPTER TWO

CORRECT AND INCORRECT WAYS OF

DEALING WITH A SNAKE

THE FOLLOWING MONDAY MORNING, the performance of the Zebras in the game against Zambia on Saturday afternoon was the first topic of discussion, at least among the men.

"I knew that we would win," said Charlie, the elder apprentice. "I knew it all the time. And we did. We won."

Mr J.L.B. Matekoni smiled. He was not given to triumphalism, unlike his two apprentices, who always revelled in the defeat of any opposing team. He realised that if you looked at the overall results, the occasional victory tended to be overshadowed by a line of defeats. It was difficult, being a small country—at least in terms of numbers of people—to compete with more populous lands. If the Kenyans wanted to select a football team, then they had many millions of people to choose from, and the same was true, and even more so, of the South Africans. But Botswana, even if it was a land as wide as the sky and even if it was blessed by those great sunburned spaces, had fewer than two million people from whom to select a football team. That made it difficult to stand up to the big countries, no matter how hard they tried. That applied only to sport, of course. When it came to everything else, then he knew, and was made proud by the knowledge, that Botswana could hold its own—and more. It owed no money; it broke no rules. But of course it was not perfect; every country has done some things of which its people might feel shame. But at least people knew what these things were and could talk about them openly, which made a difference.

But football was special.

"Yes," said Mr J.L.B. Matekoni. "The Zebras played very well. I felt very proud."

"Ow!" exclaimed the younger apprentice, reaching for the lever that would expose the engine of a car that had been brought in for service. "Ow! Did you see those people from Lusaka crying outside the stadium?"

"Anybody can lose," cautioned Mr J.L.B. Matekoni. "You need to remember that every time you win." He thought of adding, *and anybody can cry, even a man*, but knew that this would be wasted on the apprentices.

"But we didn't lose, Boss," said Charlie. "We won."

Mr J.L.B. Matekoni sighed. He had been tempted to abandon the task of teaching these apprentices anything about life, but persisted nonetheless. He took the view that an apprentice-master should do more than show his apprentices how to change an oil filter and repair brakes. He should show them, preferably by example, how to behave as honourable mechanics. Anybody can be taught to fix a car—did the Japanese not have machines which could build cars without anybody being there to operate them?—but not everybody could meet the standards of an honourable mechanic. Such a person could give advice to the owner of a car; such a person would tell the truth about what was wrong with a car; such a person would think about the best interests of the owner and act accordingly. That was something which had to be passed on from generation to generation of mechanics, and it was not always easy to do that.

He looked at the apprentices. They were due to go off for another spell of training at the Automotive Trades College, but he wondered if it did them any good. He received reports from the college as to how they performed in the academic parts of their training. These reports did not make good reading; although they passed the examinations—just—their lack of seriousness, and their sloppiness, was always commented upon. What have I done to deserve apprentices like this? Mr J.L.B. Matekoni asked himself. He had friends who also took on apprentices, and they often commented on how lucky they were to get young men who very quickly developed sufficient skill to earn their pay, and more. Indeed, one of these friends, who had taken on a young man from Lobatse, had freely admitted that this young man now knew more than he did about cars and was also very good with the customers. It struck Mr J.L.B. Matekoni as very bad luck that he should get two incompetent apprentices at the same time. To get one would have been understandable bad luck; to get two seemed to be a singular misfortune.

Mr J.L.B. Matekoni looked at his watch. There was no point in wasting time thinking about how things might be if the world were otherwise. There was work to be done that day, and he had an errand which would take him away for much of the morning. Mma Ramotswe and Mma Makutsi had gone off to the post office and the bank and would not be back for a while. It was the end of the month and the banks were always far too busy at such times. It would be better, he thought, if people's pay days were staggered. Some could be paid at the end of the month, as was traditional, but others could get their wages at other times. He had even thought of writing to the Chamber of Commerce about this, but had decided that there was very little point; there were some things that seemed to be so set in stone that nothing would ever change them. Pay day, he thought, was one of those.

He glanced at his watch again. He would have to go off shortly for a meeting with a man who was thinking of selling his inspection ramp. Tlokweng Road Speedy Motors already had one of these, but Mr J.L.B. Matekoni thought that it would be useful to have a second one, particularly if he could get it at a good price. But if he went off on this errand, then the apprentices would be left in sole charge of the garage until Mma Ramotswe and Mma Makutsi arrived. That might be all right, but it might not, and Mr J.L.B. Matekoni was worried about it.

He looked at the car which was being slowly raised on the ramp. It was a large white car which belonged to Trevor Mwamba, who had just been appointed Anglican Bishop of Botswana. Mr J.L.B. Matekoni knew the new bishop well—it was he who had married Mma Ramotswe to him under that tree at the orphan farm, with the choir singing and the sky so high and empty—and would not normally have let the apprentices loose on his car, but it seemed that there was very little choice now. The bishop wanted his car back that afternoon if at all possible, as he had a meeting to attend in Molepolole. There was nothing seriously wrong with the car, which had been brought in for a routine service, but he always liked to check the brakes of any vehicle before he returned it, and there might be some work to be done there. Brakes were the most important part of a car, in Mr J.L.B. Matekoni's view. If an engine did not work at all, then admittedly that was annoying, but it was not actually dangerous. You could hardly hurt yourself if you were stationary, but you could certainly hurt yourself if you were going at fifty miles an hour and were unable to stop. And the Molepolole road, as everybody knew, had a problem with cattle straying onto it. The cattle were meant to stay on the other side of the fence—that was the rule—but cattle were a law unto themselves and always seemed to think that there was better grass to be had on the other side of the road.

Mr J.L.B. Matekoni decided that he would have to leave the bishop's car to the mercies of the apprentices but that he would check up on their work when he came back just before lunchtime. He called the older apprentice over and gave him instructions.

"Be very careful now," he said. "That is Bishop Mwamba's car. I do not want slapdash work done on it. I want everything done very carefully."

Charlie stared down at the ground. "I am always careful, Boss," he muttered resentfully. "When did you ever see me being careless?"

Mr J.L.B. Matekoni opened his mouth to speak, but then thought better of it. It was no use engaging with these boys, he decided. Whatever he said would be no use; they simply would not take it in. He turned away and tore off a piece of paper towel on which to wipe his hands.

"Mma Ramotswe will be here soon," he said. "She and Mma Makutsi are off on some business or other. But until they come in, you are in charge. Is that all right? You look after everything."

Charlie smiled. "A-one, Boss," he said. "Trust me."

Mr J.L.B. Matekoni raised an eyebrow. "Mmm," he began, but said no more. Running a business involved anxieties—that was inevitable. It was bad enough worrying about two feckless young employees; how much more difficult it must be to run a very large company with hundreds of people working for you. Or running a country—that must be a terribly demanding job, and Mr J.L.B. Matekoni wondered how it was possible for people such as prime ministers and presidents to sleep at night with all the problems of the world weighing down upon them. It could not be an easy job being President of Botswana, and if Mr J.L.B. Matekoni had a choice between living in State House or being the proprietor of Tlokweng Road Speedy Motors, he was in no doubt about which one of these options he would choose. That is not to say that it would be uncomfortable occupying State House, with its cool rooms and its shaded gardens. That would be a very pleasant existence, but how difficult it must be for the President when everybody who came to see you, or almost everybody, wanted something: please do this, sir; please do that; please allow this, that, or the next thing. Mind you, his own existence was not all that different; just about everybody he saw wanted him to fix their car, preferably that very day. Mma Potokwane was an example of that, with her constant requests to attend to bits and pieces of malfunctioning machinery out at the orphan farm. Mr J.L.B. Matekoni thought that if he could not resist Mma Potokwane and her demands, then he would not be a very good candidate for the presidency of Botswana. Of course, the President had probably not met Mma Potokwane, and even he might find it a bit difficult to stand up to that most forceful of ladies, with her fruit cake and her way of wheedling things out of people.

The apprentices did not have long to themselves that morning. Shortly after Mr J.L.B. Matekoni had left, they had found themselves comfortable seats on two old upturned oil drums from which they were able to observe the passers-by on the road outside. Young women who walked past, aware of the eyes upon them, might look away or affect a lack of interest, but would hear the young men's appreciative comments nonetheless. This was fine sport for the apprentices, and they were disappointed by the sudden appearance of Mma Ramotswe's tiny white van only ten minutes or so after the departure of Mr J.L.B. Matekoni.

"What were you doing sitting about like that?" shouted out Mma Makutsi, as she climbed out of the passenger seat. "Don't think we didn't see you."

Charlie looked at her with an expression of injured innocence.

"We are as entitled to a tea break as much as anybody else," he replied. "You don't work all the time, do you? You drink tea too. I've seen you."

"It's a little bit early for your tea break," suggested Mma Ramotswe mildly, looking at her wrist-watch. "But no matter. I'm sure that you have lots of work to do now."

"They're so lazy," muttered Mma Makutsi, under her breath. "The moment Mr J.L.B. Matekoni goes anywhere, they down tools."

Mma Ramotswe smiled. "They're still very young," she said. "They still need supervision. All young men are like that."

"Especially useless ones like these," said Mma Makutsi, as they entered the office. "And to think that when they finish their apprenticeships—whenever that will be—they will be let loose on the public. Imagine that, Mma. Imagine Charlie with his own business. Imagine driving into a garage and finding Charlie in control!"

Mma Ramotswe said nothing. She had tried to persuade Mma Makutsi to be a bit more tolerant of the two young men, but it seemed that her assistant had something of a blind spot. As far as she was concerned, the apprentices could do no right, and nothing could be said to convince her otherwise.

The two went into the office. Mma Ramotswe walked over to the window behind her desk and opened it wide. It was a warm day, and already the heat had built up in the small room; the window at least allowed the movement of air, even if the air itself was the hot breath of the Kalahari. While Mma Ramotswe stood before the window, gazing up into the cloudless sky, Mma Makutsi filled the kettle for the first cup of tea of the morning. She then turned round and began to pull her chair out from where she had tucked it under her desk. And that was the point at which she screamed— a scream that cut through the air and sent a small white gecko scuttling for its life across the ceiling boards.

Mma Ramotswe spun round, to see the other woman standing quite still, her face frozen in fear.

"Sn . . . ," she stuttered, and then, "Snake, Mma Ramotswe!
Snake!"

For a moment Mma Ramotswe did nothing. All those years
ago in Mochudi, she had been taught by her father that with
snakes the important thing to do was not to make sudden movements. A sudden movement, only too natural of course, could
frighten a snake into striking, which most snakes, he said, were
reluctant to do.

"They do not want to waste their venom," he had told her.
"And remember that they are as frightened of us as we are of
them—possibly even more so."

But no snake could have been as terrified as was Mma
Makutsi when she saw the hood of the cobra at her feet sway
slowly from side to side. She knew that she should avert her eyes,
as such snakes can spit their venom into the eyes of their target
with uncanny accuracy; she knew that, but she still found her
gaze fixed to the small black eyes of the snake, so tiny and so
filled with menace.

"A cobra," she whispered to Mma Ramotswe. "Under my
desk. A cobra."

Mma Ramotswe moved slowly away from the window. As she
did so, she picked up the telephone directory that had been lying
on her desk. It was the closest thing to hand, and she could, if
necessary, throw it at the snake to distract it from Mma Makutsi.
This was not to prove necessary. Sensing the vibration made by
the footfall, the snake suddenly lowered its hood and slid away
from Mma Makutsi's desk, heading for a large waste-paper bin
which stood at the far side of the room. This was the signal for
Mma Makutsi to recover her power of movement, and she threw
herself towards the door. Mma Ramotswe followed, and soon

the two women were safely outside the office door, which they slammed behind them.

The two apprentices looked up from their work on Bishop Mwamba's car.

"There's a snake in there," screamed Mma Makutsi. "A very big snake."

The two young men ran across from the car to join the shaken women.

"What sort of snake?" asked Charlie, wiping his hands on a piece of waste. "A mamba?"

"No," said Mma Makutsi. "A cobra. With a big hood—this big. Right at my feet. Ready to strike."

"You are very lucky, Mma," said the younger apprentice. "If that snake had struck, then you might be late by now. The late Mma Makutsi."

Mma Makutsi looked at him scornfully. "I know that," she said. "But I did not panic, you see. I stood quite still."

"That was the right thing to do, Mma," said Charlie. "But now we can go in there and kill this snake. In a couple of minutes your office will be safe again."

He turned to the other apprentice, who had picked up a couple of large spanners and who was now reaching out to hand one to him. Armed with these tools, they slowly approached the door and edged it open.

"Be careful," shouted Mma Makutsi. "It was a very big snake."

"Look near the waste-paper basket," added Mma Ramotswe. "It's over there somewhere."

Charlie peered into the office. He was standing at the half-open door and could not see the whole room, but he could see the basket and the floor about it and, yes, he could make out something curved around its base, something that moved slightly even as his eye fell upon it.

"There," he whispered to the other apprentice. "Over there."

The young man craned his neck forward and saw the shape upon the floor. Letting out a curious half-yell, he hurled the spanner across the room, missing the target, but hitting the wall immediately behind the basket. As the spanner fell to the ground, the snake reared up, its hood again extended, facing the source of the danger. Charlie now threw his spanner, which also struck the wall but in this case fell in such a way that it hit the end of the snake's tail. The tail whipped round as the snake struggled to find its balance. Again the head swayed menacingly, the tongue darting in and out as the reptile sought to make sense of the noise and danger of its surroundings.

Mma Ramotswe clutched Mma Makutsi's arm. "I'm not sure if these boys . . ."

She did not finish the sentence. In their excitement they had not noticed a vehicle draw up and a sunburned young man with fair hair step out.

"Well, Mma Ramotswe," said the man. "What's going on here?"

Mma Ramotswe turned to face their visitor. "Oh, Mr Whitson," she said. "You have come just in time. There is a snake in there. The apprentices are trying to kill it."

Neil Whitson shook his head. "There's no need to kill snakes," he said. "Let me take a look."

He walked up to the door of the office and nodded to the apprentices to stand aside.

"Don't frighten it," he said. "It just makes it worse if you frighten it."

"It is a very large snake," said Charlie resentfully. "We have to kill it, Rra."

Neil looked in through the door and saw the cobra curled at the foot of the waste-paper basket. He turned to Charlie.

"Do you have a stick here?" he said. "Any stick will do. Just a stick."

The younger apprentice went off, while Charlie and Neil continued to watch the snake.

"We will have to kill it," Charlie said. "We cannot have a snake here. What if it bites those ladies over there? What if it bites Mma Ramotswe?"

"It'll only bite Mma Ramotswe if it feels threatened," said Neil. "And snakes only feel threatened if people tread on them or . . . ," he paused, before adding, "or throw things at them."

The younger apprentice now returned with a longish stick from the jacaranda tree which grew at the edge of the garage plot. Neil took this from him and edged his way slowly into the office. The snake watched him, part of its body raised, the hood half up. With a sudden movement, Neil flipped the stick over the snake's back and pressed the neck of the snake down against the floor. Then, leaning forward, he gripped the writhing cobra behind the head and picked it up. The lashing tail, searching for purchase, was soon firmly held in his other hand.

"There," he said. "Now, Charlie, a sack is what we need. You must have a sack somewhere."

WHEN MR J.L.B. MATEKONI returned an hour later, he was in a good mood. The inspection ramp which he had viewed was in excellent condition and the owner was not asking very much for it. It was, in fact, a bargain, and Mr J.L.B. Matekoni had already paid a deposit on the purchase. His pleasure in his transaction was evident from his smile, but this was hardly noticed by the apprentices as they greeted him in the workshop.

"We've had big excitement here, Boss," said Charlie. "A snake got into Mma Ramotswe's office. A very large snake, with a head like this. Yes, this big."

Mr J.L.B. Matekoni gave a start. "Mma Ramotswe's office," he stuttered. "Is she all right?"

"Oh, she's all right," said Charlie. "She was lucky that we were around. If we hadn't been here, then I don't know . . ."

Mr J.L.B. Matekoni looked at the younger apprentice, as if for confirmation.

"Yes, Rra," said the young man. "It is a good thing that we were here. We were able to deal with the snake."

"And where is it?" asked Mr J.L.B. Matekoni. "Where have you thrown it? You must know that if you leave one of these snakes lying around, its mate will come to seek it out. Then we will have trouble."

The younger apprentice glanced at Charlie. "We have had it taken away," said Charlie. "That man from Mokolodi, the one you trade engine parts with. He has taken it away."

"Mr Whitson?" asked Mr J.L.B. Matekoni. "He has taken it?"

Charlie nodded. "You don't need to kill snakes," he said. "It is best just to let them loose. You know that, don't you, Boss?"

Mr J.L.B. Matekoni did not reply. Striding across to the office door, he knocked and entered. Inside, seated at their desks, Mma Ramotswe and Mma Makutsi looked up at him expectantly.

"You have heard about it?" asked Mma Ramotswe. "You heard about the snake?"

Mr J.L.B. Matekoni nodded. "I have heard all about it," he said. "I am only happy that you have not been hurt, Mma Ramotswe. That is all that I am interested in."

"And me?" asked Mma Makutsi from her desk. "What about me, Rra?"

"Oh, I am pleased that you were not bitten, Mma," said Mr

J.L.B. Matekoni. "I am very pleased about that. I would not want either of you to be bitten by a snake."

Mma Ramotswe shook her head. "It was a very close thing for Mma Makutsi," she said. "And we were very lucky that your friend happened to come by. He is a man who knows all about snakes. You should have seen him pick it up, Mr J.L.B. Matekoni. He picked it up just as if it were a tshongololo or something like that."

Mr J.L.B. Matekoni looked confused. "But I thought that the boys dealt with it," he said. "Charlie told me that . . ."

Mma Makutsi let out a peal of laughter. "Them? Oh, Rra, you should have seen them. They threw spanners at it and made it all angry. They were no use at all. No use."

Mma Ramotswe smiled at her husband. "They did their best, of course, but . . ." She broke off. Nobody was perfect, she thought, and she herself had not handled the situation very well. None of us knows how we will cope with snakes until the moment arises, and then most of us find out that we do not do it very well. Snakes were one of the tests which life sent for us, and there was no telling how we might respond until the moment arrived. Snakes and men. These were the things sent to try women, and the outcome was not always what we might want it to be.

CHAPTER THREE

FREE FOOD MAKES YOU FAT

I T TOOK EVERYBODY some time to settle down after the incident with the cobra. The apprentices, convinced that they had played a vital role in dealing with the snake, were full of themselves for the rest of the day, embroidering the truth at every opportunity as they told the story in detail to every caller at the garage. Mr Polopetsi, the new employee whom Mr J.L.B. Matekoni had taken on at the garage—on the understanding that he could also help out, when required, in the No. 1 Ladies' Detective Agency—heard all about it when he arrived an hour or so later. He had been sent by Mr J.L.B. Matekoni to collect tyres from a depot on the other side of town, a job which often required a long wait. Now, returning in the truck which was used for garage business, he was regaled with an account of the event by Charlie, who this time was careful to mention the presence of the manager of the Mokolodi Game Reserve, even if only in a supporting role.

"Mma Makutsi was very lucky," he said once Charlie had finished the tale. "Those snakes strike like lightning. That quick. You cannot dodge them if they decide to strike."

"Charlie was too quick for it," said the younger apprentice.

"He saved Mma Makutsi's life." He paused, and then added, "Not that she thanked him for it."

Mr Polopetsi smiled. "I am sure that she is very grateful," he said. "But you boys should remember that nobody is too quick for a snake. Keep out of their way. I saw some very bad snake-bite cases when I was working at the hospital. Very bad." And he remembered, as he spoke, the woman who had been brought in from Otse; the woman who had been bitten by a puff-adder when she had rolled over in the night and disturbed the fat, languid snake that had slid into her one-room hut for the warmth. He had been on duty in the pharmacy and had been standing outside the entrance to the emergency department when she had been carried out of the government ambulance, and he had seen her leg, which had swollen so much that the skin had split. And then he had heard the next day that she had not lived and that there were three children and no father or grandmother to look after them; he had thought then of all the children there were in Africa who now had no parents and of what it must be like for them, not to have somebody who loved you as your parents loved you. He looked at the apprentices. They did not think of things like that, and who could expect them to? They were young men, and as a young man one was immortal, no matter what the evidence to the contrary.

At a garage there is no time for thinking such thoughts; there is work to do. Mr Polopetsi unloaded the new tyres, with their pristine treads and their chalk markings; Mr J.L.B. Matekoni attended to the delicate task of adjusting the timing on an old French station wagon—a car he did not like, which always went wrong and which in his view should have been given a decent burial a long time ago; and the two apprentices finished the servicing of Bishop Mwamba's well-behaved white car. Inside the

adjoining office of the No. 1 Ladies' Detective Agency, Mma
Ramotswe and Mma Makutsi shuffled papers about their desks.
They had very little real work to do, as it was a slack period for the
agency, and so they took the opportunity to do some filing, a task
in which Mma Makutsi took the lead, on account of her training
at the Botswana Secretarial College.

"They used to say that good filing was the key to a successful
business," she said to Mma Ramotswe as she looked through a
pile of old receipts.

"Oh yes," said Mma Ramotswe, not with great interest. She
had heard Mma Makutsi on the subject of filing on a number of
occasions before and she felt that there was very little more to be
said on the subject. The important thing, in her mind, was not
the theory behind filing but the simple question of whether it
worked or not. A good filing system enabled one to retrieve a
piece of paper; a bad filing system did not.

But it seemed that there was more to be said. "You can file
things by date," Mma Makutsi went on, as if lecturing to a
class. "Or you can file them by the name of the person to whom
the document relates. Those are the two main systems. Date or
person."

Mma Ramotswe shot a glance across the room. It seemed
odd that one could not file according to what the paper was all
about. She herself had no office training, let alone a diploma from
the Botswana Secretarial College, but surely a subject-based system was possible too. "What about subject matter?" she asked.

"There is that too," Mma Makutsi added quickly. "I had forgotten about that. Subject matter too."

Mma Ramotswe thought for a moment. In her office they
filed papers under the name of the client, which she thought was
a perfectly reasonable system, but it would be interesting, she

thought, to set up a system of cross-referencing according to the subject matter of the case. There would be a large file for adultery, in which she could put all the cases which dealt with that troublesome issue, although it would probably be necessary to subdivide in that case. There could be a section for suspicious husbands and one for suspicious wives, perhaps, and even one for male menopause cases now that she came to think about it. Many of the women who came to see her were worried about their middle-aged husbands, and Mma Ramotswe had read somewhere about the male menopause and all the troubles to which it gave rise. She could certainly add her own views on that, if anybody should ask her.

MMA RAMOTSWE and Mr J.L.B. Matekoni went home for lunch at Zebra Drive, something they enjoyed doing when work at the garage permitted. Mma Ramotswe liked to lie down for twenty minutes or so after the midday meal. On occasion she would drop off to sleep for a short while, but usually she just read the newspaper or a magazine. Mr J.L.B. Matekoni would not lie down, but liked to walk out in the garden under the shade netting, looking at his vegetables. Although he was a mechanic, like most people in Botswana he was, at heart, a farmer, and he took great pleasure in this small patch of vegetables that he coaxed out of the dry soil. One day, when he retired, they would move out to a village, perhaps to Mochudi, and find land to plough and cattle to tend. Then at last there would be time to sit outside on the stoep with Mma Ramotswe and watch the life of the village unfold before them. That would be a good way of spending such days as remained to one; in peace, happy, among the people and cattle of home. It would be good to die among one's cattle, he thought;

with their sweet breath on one's face and their dark, gentle eyes watching right up to the end of one's journey, right up to the edge of the river.

MMA RAMOTSWE returned from the lunch break to find Mma Makutsi waiting for her at the office door. The younger woman seemed agitated.

"There's a woman waiting inside."

Mma Ramotswe nodded. "Has she said what she wants, Mma?" she asked.

Mma Makutsi looked rather annoyed. "She is insisting on talking to you, Mma. I offered to listen to her, but she said that she wanted the senior lady. That is what she said. The senior lady. That's you."

Noticing Mma Makutsi's look of disapproval, Mma Ramotswe suppressed a smile. Her assistant was always irritated when this sort of thing happened. People would phone and ask to be put through to the boss, provoking from Mma Makutsi an indignant request for an explanation of what the query was about.

"I do not see why they cannot talk to me first," she said peevishly. "Then I can put them through to you after I have told you who they are and what it's about."

"But that means they might have to repeat themselves," Mma Ramotswe pointed out. "They might think it better to wait until . . ." She broke off. Mma Makutsi was unlikely to be convinced by this argument.

And this woman waiting for her in the office was another of these people who had been unwilling to tell Mma Makutsi what her business was. Well, one had to be understanding; it was often a big step to go and see a private detective about some private trouble, and one had to be gentle with people. She was not sure whether she herself would have the courage to consult a perfect stranger about something intimate. If Mr J.L.B. Matekoni were to begin misbehaving, for example—and it was inconceivable that he should—would she be able to go and talk to somebody about it, or would she suffer in silence? She rather thought that she might suffer in silence; that was her reaction, but others were different, of course. Some people were only too happy to pour out their most private problems into the ear of anybody who would listen. Mma Ramotswe had once sat next to such a woman on a bus; and this woman had told her, in the time that it takes to travel down the road from Gaborone to Lobatse, all about her feelings towards her mother-in-law, her concerns for her son, who was doing very well at school but who had met a girl who had turned his head and taken his mind quite off his schoolwork, and about her prying neighbour whom she had seen on several occasions looking into her bedroom through a pair of binoculars. Perhaps such people felt better if they talked, but it could be trying for those chosen to be their audience.

The woman sitting in the office looked up as Mma Ramotswe came into the room. They exchanged polite greetings—in the prescribed form—while Mma Ramotswe settled herself behind her desk.

"You are Mma Ramotswe?" asked the woman.

Mma Ramotswe inclined her head, taking in the little details that would allow her to place this woman. She was thirty-five, perhaps; of traditional build, like Mma Ramotswe herself (perhaps even more traditional); and, judging from the ring on her finger, married to a man who was able to afford a generously sized gold band. *Clothing*, said Clovis Andersen in *The Principles of Private Detection, provides more clues than virtually anything else (other than a pocket book or wallet!). Look at the clothing. It talks.*

Mma Ramotswe looked at the woman's clothing. Her skirt, which was tightly stretched across her traditional thighs, was made of a reasonably good material and was of a neutral grey colour. It said nothing, thought Mma Ramotswe, other than that the woman cared about her clothes and had a bit of money to spend on them. Above the skirt, the blouse was white and . . . She paused. There on one sleeve, just below the elbow, was a red-brown stain. Something had been dribbled down the sleeve, a sauce perhaps.

"Are you a cook, Mma?" asked Mma Ramotswe.

The woman nodded. "Yes," she said, and was about to say something else when she stopped herself and frowned in puzzlement. "How did you know that, Mma? Have we met one another before?"

Mma Ramotswe waved a hand in the air. "No," she said. "We have not met, but I have this feeling that you are a cook."

"Well, I am," said the woman. "You must be a very clever woman to work that out. I suppose that is why you do the job you do."

"People's jobs tell us a lot about them," said Mma Ramotswe. "You are a cook, perhaps, because . . . Now let me think. Is it because you like eating? No, that cannot be. That would be too simple. You are a cook, then, because . . . You are married to a cook. Am I right?"

The woman let out a whistle of surprise. "I cannot believe that you know all this," she exclaimed. "This is very strange."

For a moment Mma Ramotswe said nothing. It was tempting to take undeserved credit, but she decided that she could not.

"The reason why I know all this, Mma," she said, "is because I read the papers. Three weeks ago—or was it four?—your photograph was in the paper. You were winner of the Pick-and-Pay cooking competition. And the paper said that you were a cook at a college here in Gaborone and that your husband was a cook at the

President Hotel." She smiled. "And so that, Mma, is how I know these things."

The disclosure was greeted by a burst of laughter from Mma Makutsi. "So you see, Mma," she said, "we knew these things the moment you walked in here. I did not need to talk to you at all!"

Mma Ramotswe cast a warning glance in Mma Makutsi's direction. She had to watch her with the clients; she could sometimes be rude to them if she thought that they were treating her with inadequate respect. It was a strange tendency, stemming, thought Mma Ramotswe, from this ninety-seven per cent business. She would have to talk to her about it some day and refer her, perhaps, to the relevant section of Clovis Andersen's book in which he described proper relations with clients. One should never seek to score a point at the expense of a client, warned Clovis Andersen. The detective who tries to look smart at the expense of the client is really not smart at all—anything but.

Mma Ramotswe signalled to Mma Makutsi for a cup of tea. Tea helped clients to talk, and this woman looked ill at ease and needed to relax.

"May I ask you your name, Mma?" Mma Ramotswe began.

"It is Poppy," the woman said. "Poppy Maope. I am normally just called Poppy."

"It is a very pretty name, Mma. I should like to be called Poppy."

The compliment drew a smile. "I used to be embarrassed about it," said Poppy. "I used to try to hide my name from people. I thought it was a very silly name."

Mma Ramotswe shook her head. There was nothing embarrassing about the name Poppy, but there was no telling what names people would find embarrassing. Take Mr J.L.B. Matekoni, for instance. Very few people, if any, knew what his initials stood for. He had told her, of course, as he was then her fiancé, but nobody else seemed to know; certainly not Mma Makutsi, who had asked her outright and had been informed that unfortunately she could not be told.

"Some names are private," Mma Ramotswe had said. "This is the case with Mr J.L.B. Matekoni. He has always been known as Mr J.L.B. Matekoni, and that is the way he wishes it to be."

The tea made, Mma Makutsi brought two cups over and placed them on the desk. As she put them down, Mma Ramotswe saw her looking at the client, as if preparing to say something, and threw her a warning glance.

"I have come to see you on a very private matter," Poppy began. "It is very hard to talk about it."

Mma Ramotswe stretched out a hand across the desk, just far enough to touch Poppy lightly on the forearm. It is a marriage matter, she thought, and these are never easy to talk about; they often bring tears and sorrow, just at the talking of them.

"If it is a marriage question, Mma," said Mma Ramotswe gently, "just remember that we—that is, Mma Makutsi over there and myself—we have heard everything that there is to be said on such matters. There is nothing we have not heard."

"Nothing," confirmed Mma Makutsi, sipping at her tea. And she thought of that client, a man, who had come in the previous week and told them that extraordinary story and how difficult it had been for both of them not to laugh when he had described how . . . Oh, it was important not to think of that, or one would begin to laugh all over again.

Poppy shook her head vehemently. "It is not a marriage matter," she said. "My husband is a good man. We are very happily married."

Mma Ramotswe folded her arms. "I am happy to hear that," she said. "How many people can say that in these troubled times? Ever since women allowed men to think that they did not need to get married, everything has gone wrong. That is what I think, Mma."

Poppy thought for a moment. "I think you may be right," she said. "Look at the mess. Look at what all this unfaithfulness has done. People are dying because of that, aren't they? Many people are dying."

For a moment the three of them were silent. There was no gainsaying what Poppy had said. It was just true. Just true.

"But I have not come to talk about that," said Poppy. "I have come because I am very frightened. I am frightened that I am going to lose my job, and if I do, then how are we going to pay for the house we have bought? All my wages go on the payments for that, Mma. Every thebe. So if I lose my job we shall have to move, and you know how difficult it is to get somewhere nice to live. There are just not enough houses."

Mma Ramotswe took up a pen from her desk and twined her fingers about it. Yes, this woman was right. She, Mma Ramotswe, was fortunate in owning her house in Zebra Drive. If she had to try to buy it today it would be impossible. How did people survive when housing was so expensive? It was a bit of a mystery to her.

Poppy was looking at her.

"Please go on, Mma," said Mma Ramotswe. "I hope you don't mind if I fiddle with this pen. I am still listening to you. It is easier to listen if one has something to do with one's hands."

Poppy made a gesture of assent. "I do not mind, Mma. You can fiddle. I will carry on talking and will tell you why I am frightened. But first I must tell you a little bit about my job, as you must know this if you are to help me.

"I was always interested in cooking, Mma. When I was a girl I was always the one in the kitchen, cooking all the food for the family. My grandmother was the one who taught me. She had always cooked and she could make very simple food taste very good. Maize meal. Sorghum. Those very plain things tasted very good when my grandmother had added her herbs to them. Herbs or a little bit of meat if we were lucky, or even chopped-up Mopani worms. Oh, those were very good. I cannot resist Mopani worms, Mma. Can you?"

"No Motswana can resist them," said Mma Ramotswe, smiling. "I would love to have some right now, but I'm sorry, Mma . . ."

Poppy took a sip of her tea. "Yes, Mopani worms! Anyway, I went off to do a catering course in South Africa. I was very lucky to get a place on it, and a scholarship too. It was one whole year and I learned a very great deal about cooking while I was on it. I learned how to cook for one hundred, two hundred people, as easily as we cook for four or five people. It is not all that difficult, you know, Mma Ramotswe, as long as you get the quantities right.

"I came back to Botswana and got my first job up at one of the diamond mines, the one at Orapa. They have canteens for the miners there, and I was assistant to one of the chefs in charge of that. It was very hard work and those miners were very hungry! But I learned more and more, and I also met my husband, who was a senior cook up there. He cooked in the guest house that the mining company had for their visitors. They liked to give these visitors good food and the man I married was the cook who did that.

"My husband decided one day that he had had enough of living up at the diamond mine. 'There is nothing to do here,' he said. 'There is just dust and more dust.'

"I said to him that we should not move until we had made more money, but he was fed up and wanted to come to Gaborone. Fortunately, he got a job very easily through somebody who had stayed in the guest house and who knew that the President Hotel was looking for another chef. So he came down here, and I soon found a job at that college, the big new one which they built over that way—you know the place, Mma. I was very happy with this job and I was happy that we were able to live in Gaborone, where everything is happening and where it is not just dust, dust, dust.

"And everything went very well. I was not the senior cook—there is another woman who has that job. She is called Mma Tsau. She was very good to me and she made sure that I got a pay-rise after I had been there one year. I was very happy, until I discovered something bad that was going on.

"Mma Tsau has a husband, whom I had seen about the place once or twice. One day, one of the cleaning ladies said to me, 'That man is eating all the food, you know. He is eating all the best food.'

"I had no idea what this lady meant, and so I asked her which man she was talking about. She told me that it was Mma Tsau's husband and that there was a storeroom in the college where he came for a meal from time to time and was given all the best meat by his wife. On other days, she said, Mma Tsau would take home packets of the best meat to cook for her husband at their house. This food belonged to the college, she said, but it went straight into the mouth of Mma Tsau's husband, who was getting fatter and fatter as a result of all these good meals he was having.

"I did not believe this at first. I had noticed that he was a very fat man, but I had thought that this must be because he was married to a good cook. The husbands of good cooks are often fatter than other men—and that is natural, I suppose.

"I decided one day to see whether what the cleaning lady had told me was true. I had noticed that at lunchtimes Mma Tsau used to leave the kitchen from time to time, but I was always so busy that I hardly paid any attention to it. There is always something happening in a busy kitchen, and there are many reasons why the head cook may need to leave the stoves for a short time. There are supplies to be checked up on. There are telephones to answer. There are assistants to chase up.

"On that day I kept an eye on Mma Tsau. She went outside at one point to call one of the helpers, who was standing outside in the sun and not doing enough work. I looked out of the window and saw her shaking a finger at this woman and shouting at her, but I did not hear what she said. I had a good idea of it, though.

"Then, a few minutes later, I noticed that she went to the door of one of the warming ovens and took out a covered dish. It was an oven that we never used, as we had too much capacity in that kitchen. She took this dish, which was covered by a metal plate, and went out of the kitchen. I moved over to a window and saw her walking towards a small block near the kitchen. There was an old office there, which was not used any more, and a storeroom. She went in, was inside for a few moments, and then came out again, without the dish, but wiping her hands on her apron.

"I waited a few minutes. Mma Tsau was now busy supervising the assistants who were dishing out the stew to the students. She was telling them that they should not give helpings that were too generous, or there would not be enough for the students who came in for their lunch a bit later. I overheard her telling one of them that they should not give more food to those students whom they liked, who smiled at them when they reached the head of the line, or who were related to them. I could not believe that I was hearing that, if what I thought I had just seen was true. I think that you should not say one thing and then do exactly the opposite yourself, should you, Mma Ramotswe? No. That is what I thought too.

"This was now the best time for me to leave the kitchen, while Mma Tsau was lecturing the assistant. I went outside and ran across to the block which I had seen her enter. I had decided that the best thing to do would be to pretend to be looking for something, and so I did not knock on the door, but just pushed it open. There was a man inside, that fat man, the husband of Mma Tsau. He was sitting at a small table with a large plate of steak in front of him. There were vegetables too—some potatoes with gravy on them and a pile of carrots. He had a bottle of tomato sauce on the table in front of him and a copy of *The Daily News*, which he was reading as he ate.

"I pretended to be surprised, although what I saw was exactly what I had expected to see. So I greeted him and said that I was sorry to have disturbed his lunch. He smiled and said that it did not matter, and that I should look for whatever it was that I was searching for. Then he went back to eating his steak, which smelled very good in the small space of that room."

As the story progressed, Mma Ramotswe's mouth opened wider and wider with astonishment. Mma Makutsi also seemed transfixed by the tale which their client was telling, and was sitting quite still at her desk, hanging on every word.

Poppy now paused. "I hope that you do not think that I was being too nosy," she said. "I know that you should not look into things that are not your business."

Mma Ramotswe shook her head. "But it *was* your business, Mma," she said. "It was surely your business. It is always the business of people who work in a place that somebody else in that place is stealing. That is everybody's business."

Poppy looked relieved. "I am glad you said that, Mma. I would not like you to think that I was one of those nosy people. I was worried . . ."

"So," interrupted Mma Ramotswe. "You have to decide what to do. Is that why you have come to see me today?"

This conclusion seemed reasonable to Mma Ramotswe, but Poppy held up her hands in denial. "No, Mma," she said. "I decided what to do straightaway. I went to Mma Tsau the next day and asked her about her husband. I said, 'Why is your husband eating all this college food? Do you not have enough food of your own?'

"She was inspecting a pot at the time, and when I asked her this question she dropped it, she was so surprised. Then she looked closely at me and told me that she did not know what I was talking about and that I should not make up wild stories like that in case anybody believed that what I said was true.

"'But I saw him myself,' I told her. 'I saw him in the store-room over there eating steaks from the college kitchen. I saw him, Mma.'"

Mma Makutsi, who had been silent, could no longer contain herself. "Surely she did not try to deny that, Mma," she said. "That wicked woman! Taking the meat from the students and giving it to that fat husband of hers! And our taxes paying for that meat too!"

Poppy and Mma Ramotswe both looked at Mma Makutsi. Her outrage was palpable.

"Well, she didn't," Poppy continued. "Once I had told her that I had seen what was going on, she just became silent for a while. But she was watching me with her eyes narrowed—like this. Then she said that if I told anybody about it, she would make sure that I lost my job. She explained to me that this would be easy for her to do. She said that she would simply tell the college managers that I was not up to the job and that they would have to get somebody else. She said that they would believe her and that there would be nothing I could do."

"I hope that you went straight to the police," said Mma Makutsi indignantly.

Poppy snorted. "How could I do that? I had no proof to give the police, and they would believe her rather than me. She is the senior cook, remember. I am just a junior person."

Mma Ramotswe looked up at the ceiling. She had recently read an article about this sort of problem and she was trying to remember the word which was used to describe it. Whistle-blowing! Yes, that was it. The article had described how difficult it was for whistle-blowers when they saw something illegal being done at work. In some countries, it had said, there were laws to protect the whistle-blower—in some countries, but she was not sure whether this was true of Botswana. There was very little corruption in Botswana, but she was still not sure whether life was made any easier for whistle-blowers.

"Whistle-blowing," she said aloud. "That's what it is—whistle-blowing."

Poppy looked at her blankly. "Who is blowing a whistle?" she asked.

"You are," said Mma Ramotswe. "Or you could blow a whistle."

"I do not see what whistles have to do with it," said Poppy.

"If you went to the police you would be a whistle-blower," explained Mma Ramotswe. "It's a way of describing a person who lets others know about what is going on behind the scenes."

"Behind what scenes?" asked Poppy.

Mma Ramotswe decided to change tack. There were some people who were rather literal in their understanding of things, and Poppy, it seemed, was one of these.

"Well, let us not think too much about whistles and such things," she said. "The important thing is this: you want us to do something about this woman and her stealing. Is that right?"

The suggestion seemed to alarm Poppy. "No," she said. "I do not want that, Mma. You must wait until I finish telling you my story."

Mma Ramotswe made an apologetic gesture, and Poppy began to speak again.

"I was frightened, Mma. I could not face losing my job and so I did nothing. I did not like the thought of that man eating all that government food, but then I thought of what it would be like not to have a house, and so I just bit my tongue. But then, three days ago, Mma Tsau came to me just as I was about to leave work to go home. My husband has a car and was waiting for me at the end of the road. I could see him sitting in the car, looking up at the sky, as he likes to do. When you are a chef all you see is the kitchen ceiling and clouds of steam. When you are outside, you like to look at the sky.

"Mma Tsau drew me aside. She was shaking with anger and I thought that I had made some very bad mistake in my work. But it was not that. She gripped me by the arm and leaned forward to speak to me. 'You think you're clever,' she said. 'You think that you can get me to give you money not to say anything about my husband. You think that, don't you?'

"I had no idea what she was talking about. I told her that, but she just laughed at me. She said that she had torn up the letter I had written. Then she said that on the very first opportunity that she could find, she would get rid of me. She said that it might take a few months, but she would make very sure that I would lose my job."

Poppy stopped. Towards the end of her tale, her voice had risen, and by the time that she finished, the words were coming in gasps. Mma Ramotswe leaned forward and took her hand. "Do not be upset, Mma," she said gently. "She is just making threats. Often these people don't do what they threaten to do, isn't that right, Mma Makutsi?"

Mma Makutsi glanced at Mma Ramotswe before she answered. She thought that people like that often did exactly what they threatened to do—and worse—but now was not the time to express such doubts. "Hot air," she said. "You would think that in Botswana we had enough hot air, with the Kalahari just over there, but there are still people like this Mma Tsau who add to the hot air. And you do not need to worry about hot air, Mma."

Poppy looked over towards Mma Makutsi and smiled weakly. "I hope that you're right, Mma," she said. "But I am not sure. And anyway, what was this letter? I did not write to her about it."

Mma Ramotswe rose from her seat and walked to the window. Poppy had spoken about how chefs liked to look at the sky when they had the chance; well, so did private detectives, she thought; ladies and private detectives. Indeed, everybody should look at the sky when they could, because the sky had many answers, provided one knew how to see them. And now, as she looked at the sky, over the tops of the acacia trees and up into that echoing emptiness, it seemed to her so very obvious that Poppy was not the only person who knew about the food and that the other person who knew—who, again so obviously, must have been the cleaning woman—was taking the opportunity to blackmail Mma Tsau. Unfortunately for Poppy, she was getting the blame, but that was quite typical of life, was it not? The wrong people often got the blame, the wrong people suffered for what the right people did. And the sky in all this, the sky which had seen so much of it, was neutral, absolutely neutral.

The problem with blackmail, thought Mma Ramotswe, is this: the victim is often a wrongdoer, but, once blackmailed, attracts our sympathy. But why should we feel sorry for somebody who is simply being made to pay for the wrong that he did? It occurred to Mma Ramotswe that this was a problem that deserved serious consideration. Perhaps it was even a question to put to Aunty Emang. Aunty Emang . . .

CHAPTER FOUR

WHAT FEMINISTS HAVE IN
MIND FOR MEN

MMA MAKUTSI made the evening meal that night for Mr Phuti Radiphuti, her newly acquired fiancé. Phuti Radiphuti was the son of the elder Mr Radiphuti, successful businessman, farmer, and proprietor of the Double Comfort Furniture Shop. She had met Phuti at the dancing classes which they had both attended at the Academy of Dance and Movement. This was not a real academy, in that it had no buildings and indeed had no staff other than the woman who took the money and the instructor, Mr Fano Fanope, an accomplished dancer who had danced, successfully, in Johannesburg and Nairobi. Word of the engagement had spread round the dance class, and Mr Fanope himself had made an official announcement at the end of one evening that the academy was proud to have brought the couple together.

"Dancing is about contact between people," he had said in his speech. "When you dance with somebody you are talking to him, even if you do not open your mouth. Your movements can show what is in your heart. That is very important. And that is why so many happy couples meet through dancing. And that is another reason why if you have not already booked your place on our next

course, you should do so now. Ladies, you could be like Grace
Makutsi and find a good husband here; gentlemen, look at Mr
Phuti Radiphuti, who has found this fine lady. May they be very
happy together! May they have many happy hours on the dance
floor and elsewhere!"

Mma Makutsi had been touched by this speech, in spite of
the blatant reference to advance bookings. She liked Mr Fanope,
and she knew that he was genuinely pleased about the engagement. She knew, too, that this pleasure was shared by many of
the other members of the class, even if not by all. One of the
other women, a person by the name of Violet, who had been at
the Botswana Secretarial College with her, had smirked during
Mr Fanope's speech and had muttered something to the man
standing next to her, who had suppressed a laugh. Mma Makutsi
had exchanged words with this woman at an earlier session, when
Violet had made a disparaging remark about Mma Makutsi's
green shoes (of which she was very proud) and had effectively
sneered at Phuti Radiphuti. By a supreme effort of will, Mma
Makutsi had replied to her courteously and had even gone out of
her way to compliment her. This had been difficult indeed, as
Violet had achieved a bare pass mark at the Botswana Secretarial
College—somewhere around fifty per cent—and was clearly only
interested in finding the richest husband available.

As she witnessed the smirk, for a delicious moment Mma
Makutsi imagined what she might say to Violet if the opportunity
presented itself. And in fact it did, at the end of that evening,
when Violet sidled up to her and said, "Well, Mma, that's a kind
thing you've done. It's very good of you to look after Mr Radiphuti
like that. It must have been very hard for him to find a wife and
now you have agreed to marry him. You are a really kind person.
But I always knew that, of course."

Mma Makutsi had looked at her enemy. At the back of her

mind were the memories of those days at the Botswana Secretarial College when the glamorous girls, of whom Violet was more or
less the leader, would sit at the back of the class and discuss their
social triumphs and snigger when Mma Makutsi or one of the
other hard workers was complimented by the instructor. She had
said nothing then, and she really should say nothing now, but the
temptation was just too great.

"Thank you, Mma," she had said. "But I am the lucky one,
you know. It's not every girl can get a husband like that." She
paused before continuing, "But I hope that you have some of
my luck in the future. Who knows?" And with that she smiled
sweetly.

Violet's eyes widened. "Lucky? Oh, I don't know about that,
Grace Makutsi! I'm not so sure that it's lucky to be landed with a
man like that. Anyway, I hope that it works out well for you. And
it might." And then she herself added, "Who knows?"

Mma Makutsi felt her heart beating fast within her. It was
time for the coup de grâce. "But I am lucky, Mma," she said. "I
think that any girl who marries into that family will be very lucky.
And rich too."

Violet faltered. "Rich?"

"Ssh," said Grace Makutsi, putting a finger to her lips. "It's
not polite to talk about it. So I won't mention the Double Comfort Furniture Shop, which is one of the businesses my fiancé
owns, you know. I must not talk about that. But do you know the
store, Mma? If you save up, you should come in some day and
buy a chair."

Violet opened her mouth to speak, but said nothing. And
then Mr Fanope had appeared and had shaken Mma Makutsi's
hand and led her away to speak to another member of the class
who wanted to congratulate her. Mma Makutsi had glanced
back at Violet, who was fiddling with her handbag, but who looked

up and caught her eye and could not conceal her envy. There was so much history there; a history of shame, and poverty, and struggle, and she could hear Mma Ramotswe's voice in her head now. "That was not a very kind thing to do, Mma Makutsi," Mma Ramotswe said. "You should not have done that."

"I know," Mma Makutsi answered, mentally. "But I just couldn't help it, Mma."

And the voice of Mma Ramotswe immediately softened. "I know too," she said. "I know." And she did, because although she was kind, Mma Ramotswe was also human, and appreciated that there were times when it was impossible to resist a small triumph, especially one that could make one smile when one remembered it later; smile for hours and hours.

MMA MAKUTSI and Phuti Radiphuti had slipped comfortably into an arrangement. On four days of the week, including Monday, Phuti came for his evening meal at Mma Makutsi's house; on the other three days he ate in turn with his senior aunt, his sister and her husband, and, on Sunday evening, with his aged father. The dinners with his father were sometimes trying for him, as his father's memory was not what it used to be and he frequently repeated himself, especially when talking about cattle. But Phuti was dutiful, and he would sit for hours while his father went over and over the same ground: Did Phuti remember that fine bull that he had sold to that man who lived at Mahalapye? Could Phuti remember how much they had paid for that Brahmin cow that they had bought from that Boer farmer down at Zeerust? That had been a fine cow, but when did she die? Did Phuti remember which year it was? And what about that bull that went to Mahalapye? Did Phuti remember that one? Was he sure?

On occasion, Mma Makutsi would join him for these meals

at his father's house, and she would sit through the same conversations, trying hard not to nod off during the narratives or the
questions that interspersed them. What were the cattle like up at
Bobonong this year? Were they thin? Were they different from
the cattle down in the south? She noticed that when he was with
his father, Phuti's stammer became more acute. During the dinners that they had at her house, it was barely noticeable now,
which spoke to the confidence which she had succeeded in
building up in him. In her company, he was now quite capable of
uttering long and involved sentences, either in Setswana or in
English, without any hesitation or stumbling. This new-found
fluency, of which he was so proud, enabled him to say things that
he had been unable to say for years, and the words flowed out of
him; words about childhood, about being a boy; words about the
furniture business and the comfort, or otherwise, of the various
sorts of chairs; and words about the pleasure, the sheer pleasure,
of having found somebody with whom he would now start to
share his life. It was as if a drought had ended—a drought that
had made for expanses of silence, as drought will dry up a salt pan
and render it white and powdery—and the words were like
longed-for rain, turning the land green at last.

She soon found out what Phuti liked to eat, and she made
sure that she always cooked these dishes for him. He liked meat,
of course, and T-bone steaks in particular, which he would pick
up and gnaw at with gusto. He liked marrow and broad green
beans doused in melted butter, and he liked chopped-up biltong
soaked in gravy and then served over mashed potato. All of these
dishes she did for him, and each time he complimented her en-
thusiastically on her cooking as if it were the first time that he
had said anything about it. She loved these compliments, and the
nice things he said about her appearance. In her mind she had
been no more than a woman with large glasses and a difficult

skin; now she found herself described as one of the prettiest women in Botswana, with a nose that reminded him of . . . and here he mumbled and she did not catch what it was that her nose reminded him of, but it was surely a positive association and so she did not mind not knowing what it was.

That evening, after the drama with the snake, Mma Makutsi regaled Phuti with a full account of what had turned into a memorable day. She told him of the apprentices' ridiculous account of their role in the removal of the snake, and he laughed at that. Then she told him about Poppy's visit and her curious tale of the theft of the food and the threat of dismissal.

After Mma Makutsi had finished, Phuti sat in silence for a few minutes. "So?" he said at last. "So what can you do to help this woman? I don't see how you're going to save her job for her. What can you do?"

"We could make sure that the chef—that other woman—is the one to lose her job," said Mma Makutsi. "She's the one who should be fired."

Phuti looked doubtful. "Maybe. But I don't see how you could make that happen. Anyway, where would you start with a case like this? What can you do?"

Mma Makutsi helped him to another portion of mashed potato. "We could find out who is blackmailing Mma Tsau. Then we could tell Mma Tsau that it is not Poppy."

Phuti thought that this was a perfectly sound suggestion, but then a better idea occurred, and he outlined this to Mma Makutsi as he began to eat his mashed potato. "Of course it would be easier, wouldn't it, to tell Mma Tsau that if she fires Poppy, then *we* shall tell the college that she has been stealing. Surely that would be simpler."

Mma Makutsi stared at him. "But that in itself is blackmail," she pointed out. "You can't go round threatening people like that."

"I don't see what's wrong with it," said Phuti, wiping a small speck of mashed potato from his chin. "We're not getting anything from her. It can't be blackmail if you're not getting anything yourself."

Mma Makutsi pondered this. Perhaps Phuti had a point, and yet Mma Ramotswe had always stressed to her that the end did not justify the means, and that one should not commit a wrong to set right another. And yet, Mma Ramotswe herself had been known to tell the occasional lie while trying to get at the truth. She had obtained information from a government clerk by quoting a non-existent regulation; she had pretended to be somebody she was not when looking into a family dispute for a former minister; the list was really quite long when one came to think of it. In every case, she had done this in her attempts to help somebody who needed help, and it was also true that they were not large lies, but they were lies nonetheless, and so she wondered whether Mma Ramotswe was entirely consistent on this point. She would have to ask her about it, but for the moment it was perhaps better to move on to another topic. So she looked up from her plate and asked Phuti Radiphuti what had happened at the furniture store that day.

He was pleased to leave the philosophical complexities of blackmail, and launched with alacrity into an account of a difficulty they had encountered with the delivery of a table that had only three legs. The factory was adamant that it had left their premises with four, but his warehouse man was equally firm in his view that it had only three on arrival.

"Perhaps that is another one for Mma Ramotswe," said Mma Makutsi. "She is very good at finding out things like that."

Phuti smiled at the suggestion. "There are bigger things for Mma Ramotswe to do," he said. "She has big crimes to solve."

Mma Makutsi had heard of this popular misconception. It

flattered her to think that the reputation of the No. 1 Ladies' Detective Agency had been so inflated, but she could not allow Phuti, her own fiancé, to remain in ignorance about what they actually did.

"No," she said. "Mma Ramotswe does not solve crimes. She deals with very small things." To portray the smallness, Mma Makutsi put a thumb and forefinger within a whisker of one another. "But," she went on, "these small things are important for people. Mma Ramotswe has often told me that our lives are made up of small things. And I think she is right."

Phuti thought she was right too. He was slightly disappointed to be disabused of the notion that the No. 1 Ladies' Detective Agency dealt with major crimes. It had been pleasing enough for him to have a fiancée at all, let alone a fiancée who pursued so glamorous a profession, and he had boasted to friends that he was engaged to a well-known detective. And of course that was strictly speaking true—Mma Makutsi was indeed a detective, and it did not matter too much that she concerned herself with mundane matters. In fact, this was probably all for the good. The other sort of detective might be exposed to danger, and that was not what he had in mind for his wife-to-be. There was little danger in the furniture business, and there would always be a place for her there should she decide to abandon detection. He wondered whether he should mention this to her, but decided against it. He did not want her to think that marriage to him would involve her submitting to his plans; he had heard that women were reluctant to accept that sort of thing these days—and a good thing too, he thought. For far too long men had assumed that women would do their bidding, and if women were now questioning that, then he was quite happy to agree with them. Not that he was sympathetic to those people who called themselves feminists: he had heard one of those ladies on the radio and had been shocked by her aggressiveness towards the man who was interviewing her. This woman had more or less accused the reporter of arrogance when he had questioned her statement that men had, in general, fewer abilities than women. She had said that his time was "over" and that men like him would be swept aside by feminism. But if men were to be swept aside, wondered Phuti Radiphuti, then where would men be put? Would there be special homes for them, where they could be given small tasks to perform while women got on with the important business of running things? Would men be allowed out of these homes on selected outings (accompanied, of course)? For some days after he had listened to the interview, Phuti Radiphuti had worried about being swept aside, and had experienced a vivid and uncomfortable dream—a nightmare, really—in which he was indeed swept aside by a large feminist with a broom. It was an unpleasant experience, tumbling head over heels, covered with a cloud of dust, in the face of the frightening woman's aggressive brush-strokes.

He looked at Mma Makutsi as she cut at a piece of meat on her plate. She wielded the knife expertly, pushing the cut meat onto her fork. Then the fork was before her mouth, which opened wide to receive the food before the teeth came together. She smiled at him and nodded to his plate, encouraging him to get on with his meal.

Phuti looked down at his plate. It had just occurred to him that Mma Makutsi might be a feminist. He did not know why he should think this. She had never threatened to sweep him away, but there was no doubt about who had been in charge when they had danced together at the Academy of Dance and Movement. Mr Fano Fanope had explained that it was always the men who led in ballroom dancing, but Phuti had found himself quite unable to lead and had willingly followed the firm promptings of Mma Makutsi's hands planted on his shoulders and in the small of his back. Did this make her a feminist, or merely one who could tell when a man had no idea of how to take the lead in dancing? He raised his eyes from his plate and looked at Mma Makutsi. He saw his reflection in the lenses of her large round glasses, and he saw the smile about her lips. Perhaps it would be best to ask her, he thought.

"Mma Makutsi," he began, "there is something I should like to ask you."

Mma Makutsi put down her knife and fork and smiled at him. "You may ask me anything," she said. "I am your fiancée."

He swallowed. It would be best to be direct. "Are you a feminist?" he blurted out. His nervousness made him stumble slightly on the word "feminist," making the letter "f" sound doubled or even tripled. His stammer had been vastly improved since his meeting with Mma Makutsi and her agreeing to marry him, but occasions of stress might still bring it out.

Mma Makutsi looked a bit taken aback by the question. She had not been expecting the topic to arise, but now that she had been asked there was only one answer to give.

"Of course I am," she said simply. Her answer given, she stared at him through her large, round glasses; again she smiled. "These days most ladies are feminists. Did you not know that?"

Phuti Radiphuti was unable to answer. He opened his mouth to speak, but words, which had recently been so forthcoming, seemed to have deserted him. It was an old, familiar feeling for him; a struggle to articulate the thoughts that were in mind through a voice that would not come, or came in fits and starts. He had imagined a future of tenderness and mutual cherishing; now it seemed to him that he would face stridency and conflict. He would be swept aside, as he had been swept aside in that dream; but there would be no waking up this time.

He looked at Mma Makutsi. How could he, who was so

cautious, have been so wrong about somebody? It was typical of his luck; he had never been noticed by women—it would never be given to him to be admired, to be looked up to; rather, he would be the target of criticism and upbraiding, for that is what he imagined feminists did to men. They put them in their place; they emasculated them; they derided them. All of this now lay ahead of Phuti Radiphuti as he stared glumly at his fiancée and then down again at his plate, where the last scraps of food, a mess of potage in a sense, lay cooling and untouched.

CHAPTER FIVE

MORE CONVERSATIONS WITH SHOES

THIS IS A VERY BUSY DAY," said Mr J.L.B. Matekoni, wiping his hands on a small piece of lint. "There are so many things that I have to do and which I will not have the time to do. It is very hard." He raised his eyes up to the sky, but not before casting a glance in the direction of Mma Ramotswe.

She knew that this was a request. Mr J.L.B. Matekoni was not one to ask for a favour directly. He was always willing to help other people, as Mma Potokwane, matron of the orphan farm, knew full well, but his diffidence usually prevented him from asking others to do things for him. There was sometimes a call for help, however, disguised as a comment about the pressures which were always threatening to overcome any owner of a garage; and this was one, to which Mma Ramotswe of course would respond.

She looked at her desk, which was largely clear of papers. There was a bill, still in its envelope but unmistakably a bill, and a half-drafted letter to a client. Both of these were things that she would happily avoid attending to, and so she smiled encouragingly at Mr J.L.B. Matekoni.

"If there is anything I can do?" she asked. "I can't fix cars for you, but maybe there's something else?"

Mr J.L.B. Matekoni tossed the greasy scrap of lint into the waste-paper basket. "Well, there is something, Mma," he said, "now that you ask. And although it has something to do with cars, it doesn't involve actually fixing anything. I know you are a detective, Mma Ramotswe, and not a mechanic."

"I would like to be able to fix cars," said Mma Ramotswe. "Maybe some day I will learn. There are many ladies now who can fix cars. There are many girls who are doing a mechanic's apprenticeship."

"I have seen them," said Mr J.L.B. Matekoni. "I wonder if they are very different from . . ." He did not finish the sentence, but tossed his head in the direction of the workshop behind him, where the two apprentices, Charlie and the younger one—whose name nobody ever used—were changing the oil in a truck.

"They are very different," said Mma Ramotswe. "Those boys spend all their time thinking about girls. You know what they're like."

"And girls don't spend any time thinking about boys?" asked Mr J.L.B. Matekoni.

Mma Ramotswe considered this for a few moments. She was not quite sure what the answer was. When she was a girl she had thought about boys from time to time, but only to reflect on how fortunate she was to be a girl rather than a boy. And when she became a bit older, and was susceptible to male charm, although she occasionally imagined what it would be like to spend time in the company of a particular boy, boys *as a breed* did not occupy her thoughts. Nor did she talk about boys in the way in which the apprentices talked about girls, although it was possible that modern girls were different. She had overheard some teenagers—girls of about seventeen—talking among themselves one day when she was looking for a book in Mr Kerrison's new book shop, and she had been shocked by what she had heard. Her shock had registered in her expression, and in the dropping of her jaw, and the girls had noticed this. "What's the trouble, Mma?" said one of the girls. "Don't you know about boys?" And she had struggled for words, searching for a reply which would tell these shameless girls that she knew all about boys—and had known about them for many years—while at the same time letting them know that she disapproved. But no words had come, and the girls had gone away giggling.

Mma Ramotswe was not a prude. She knew what went on between people, but she believed that there was a part of life that should be private. She believed that what one felt about another was largely a personal matter, and that one should not talk about the mysteries of the soul. One should just not do it, because that was not how the old Botswana morality worked. There was such a thing as shame, she thought, although there were many people who seemed to forget it. And where would we be in a world without the old Botswana morality? It would not work, in Mma Ramotswe's view, because it would mean that people could do as they wished without regard for what others thought. That would be a recipe for selfishness, a recipe as clear as if it were written out in a cookery book: *Take one country, with all that the country means, with its kind people, and their smiles, and their habit of helping one another; ignore all this; shake about; add modern ideas; bake until ruined.*

Mr J.L.B. Matekoni's question about whether girls thought about boys hung in the air, unanswered. He looked at her expectantly. "Well, Mma?" he asked. "Do girls not think about boys?"

"Sometimes," said Mma Ramotswe nonchalantly. "When

there is nothing better to think about, that is." She smiled at her husband. "But that is not what we were discussing," she continued. "What is this thing that you want me to do?"

Mr J.L.B. Matekoni explained to her about the errand he wished her to carry out. It would involve a trip to Mokolodi, which was half an hour away to the south.

"My friend who dealt with the cobra," he said. "Neil. He's the one. He has an old pickup down there, a bakkie, which he kept for years and years. And then . . ." Mr J.L.B. Matekoni paused. The death of a car diminished him, because he was involved with cars. "There was nothing much more I could do for it. It needed a complete engine re-bore, Mma Ramotswe. New pistons. New piston rings." He shook his head sadly, as a doctor might when faced with a hopeless prognosis.

Mma Ramotswe looked up at the ceiling. "Yes," she said. "It must have been very sad."

"But fortunately Neil did not get rid of it," he said. "Some people just throw cars away, Mma Ramotswe. They throw them away."

Mma Ramotswe reached for a piece of paper on her desk and began to fold it. Mr J.L.B. Matekoni often needed some time to get to the point, but she was used to waiting.

"I have a customer with a broken half-shaft," went on Mr J.L.B. Matekoni. "That is part of the rear axle. You know that, don't you? There's a shaft that comes down the middle until it gets to the gear mechanism in the middle of the rear axle. Then, on each side of that there's something called the half-shaft that goes to the wheel on either side."

The piece of paper in Mma Ramotswe's right hand had been folded in two and then folded again at an angle. As she held it up and looked past it, it seemed to her that it was now a bird, a stout bird with a large beak. She narrowed her eyes and squinted at it, so that the paper became blurred against the background of the office walls. She thought of the customer with a broken half-shaft—she understood exactly what Mr J.L.B. Matekoni meant, but she smiled at his way of expressing it. Mr J.L.B. Matekoni regarded cars and their owners as interchangeable, or as being virtually one and the same, with the result that he would talk of people who were losing oil or who were in need of bodywork. It had always amused Mma Ramotswe, and in her mind's eye she had seen people walking with a dribble of oil stretching out behind them or with dents in their bodies or limbs. So, too, did she picture this client with the broken half-shaft; poor man, perhaps limping, perhaps patched up in some way.

"So," said Mr J.L.B. Matekoni. "So, could you go and fetch this for me, Mma Ramotswe? You won't have to lift anything—he'll get one of his men to do that. All you have to do is to drive down there and drive back. That's all."

Mma Ramotswe rather liked the idea of a run down to Mokolodi. Although she lived in Gaborone, she was not a town person at heart—very few Batswana were—and she was never happier than when she was out in the bush, with the air of the country, dry and scented with the tang of acacia, in her lungs. On the drive to Mokolodi she would travel with the windows down, and the sun and air would flood the cabin of her tiny white van; and she would see, opening up before her, the vista of hills around Otse and beyond, green in the foreground and blue beyond. She would take the turning off to the right, and a few minutes later she would be at the stone gates of the camp and explaining to the attendant the nature of her business. Perhaps she would have a cup of tea on the verandah of the circular main building, with its thatch and its surrounding trees, and its outlook of hills. She tried to remember whether they served bush tea there; she thought they did, but just in case, she would take a sachet of her own tea which she could ask them to boil up for her.

Mr J.L.B. Matekoni looked at her anxiously. "That's all," he said. "That's all I'm asking you to do."

Mma Ramotswe shook her head. "No," she said. "That's fine. I was just thinking."

"What were you thinking?" asked Mr J.L.B. Matekoni.

"About the hills down there," said Mma Ramotswe. "And about tea. That sort of thing."

Mr J.L.B. Matekoni laughed. "You often think about tea, don't you? I don't. I think about cars and engines and things like that. Grease. Oil. Suspension. Those are my thoughts."

Mma Ramotswe put down the piece of paper she had been folding. "Is it not strange, Mr J.L.B. Matekoni?" she said. "Is it not strange that men and women think about such very different things? There you are thinking about mechanical matters, and I am sitting here thinking about tea."

"Yes," said Mr J.L.B. Matekoni. "It is strange." He paused. There was a car needing attention outside and he had to see to it. The owner wanted it back that afternoon or he would be obliged to walk home. "I must get on, Mma Ramotswe," he said. Nodding to Mma Makutsi, he left the office and returned to the garage.

Mma Ramotswe pushed her chair back and rose to her feet. "Would you care to come with me, Mma Makutsi?" she asked. "It's a nice day for a run."

Mma Makutsi looked up from her desk. "But who will look after the business?" she asked. "Who will answer the telephone?"

Mma Ramotswe looked at herself in the mirror on the wall behind the filing cabinet. The mirror was intended for the use of Mma Makutsi and herself, but was used most frequently by the apprentices, who liked to preen themselves in front of it. "Should

I braid my hair?" asked Mma Ramotswe. "What do you think, Mma Makutsi?"

"Your hair is very nice as it is, Mma," said her assistant, but added, "Of course, it would be even nicer if you were to braid it."

Mma Ramotswe looked round. "And you?" she asked. "Would you braid your hair too, if I had mine done?"

"I'm not sure," said Mma Makutsi. "Phuti Radiphuti is an old-fashioned man. I'm not sure what his views on braiding would be."

"An old-fashioned man?" asked Mma Ramotswe. "That's interesting. Does he know that you're a modern lady?"

Mma Makutsi considered the question for a moment. "I think he does," she said. "The other night he asked me if I was a feminist."

Mma Ramotswe stiffened. "He asked you that, did he? And what did you reply, Mma?"

"I said that most ladies were feminists these days," said Mma Makutsi. "So I told him, yes, I am."

Mma Ramotswe sighed. "Oh dear," she said. "I'm not sure that that's the best answer to give in such circumstances. Men are very frightened of feminists."

"But I cannot lie," protested Mma Makutsi. "Surely men don't expect us to lie? And anyway, Phuti is a kind man. He is not one of those men who are hostile to feminists because they are insecure underneath."

She's right about that, thought Mma Ramotswe. Men who put women down usually did so because they were afraid of women and wanted to build themselves up. But one had to be circumspect about these things. The term *feminist* could upset men needlessly because some feminists were so unpleasant to men. Neither she nor Mma Makutsi was that sort of person. They liked men, even if they knew that there were some types of men who bullied women. They would never stand for that, of course, but at the same time they would not wish to be seen as hostile to men like Mr J.L.B. Matekoni or Phuti Radiphuti—or Mr Polopetsi, for that matter; Mr Polopetsi, who was so mild and considerate and badly done by.

"I'm not saying that you should lie," said Mma Ramotswe quietly. "All I'm saying is that it's unwise to talk to men about feminism. It makes them run away. I have seen it many times before." She hoped that the engagement would not be threatened by this. Mma Makutsi deserved to find a good husband, especially as she had not had much luck before. Although Mma Makutsi never talked about it, Mma Ramotswe knew that there had been somebody else in Mma Makutsi's life—for a very brief time—and that she had actually married him. But he had died, very suddenly, and she had been left alone again.

Mma Makutsi swallowed hard. Phuti Radiphuti had seemed unnaturally quiet that evening after their conversation. If what Mma Ramotswe said was right, then her ill-considered remarks might prompt him to run away from her, to end their engagement. The thought brought a cold hand to her chest. She would never get another man; she would never find another fiancé like Phuti Radiphuti. She would be destined to spend the rest of her days as an assistant detective, scraping a living while other women found comfortably-off husbands to marry. She had been given a golden chance and she had squandered it through her own stupidity and thoughtlessness.

She looked down at her shoes—her green shoes with the sky-blue linings. And the shoes looked back up at her. *You've done it, Boss,* said the shoes. *Don't expect us to carry you all around town looking for another man. You had one and now you don't. Bad luck, Boss. Bad luck.*

Mma Makutsi stared at the shoes. It was typical of shoes to be so uncaring. They never made any constructive suggestions. They just censured you, crowed at you, rubbed it in; revenge, perhaps, for all the indignities to which they themselves were subjected. Dust. Neglect. Cracking leather. Oblivion.

THEY WERE SILENT as they left Gaborone, with the brooding shape of Kgale Hill to their right, and the road stretching out, undulating, to their front. Mma Ramotswe was silent because she was looking at the shape of the hills and remembering how, all those years ago, she had travelled this road on the way to stay with her cousin, who had been so good to her. And there had been unhappy journeys too, or journeys that had been happy and had become unhappy later on their being remembered. Those were the trips she had made, down this very road, with her former husband, Note Mokoti. Note used to play his trumpet in hotels down in Lobatse, and Mma Ramotswe had accompanied him on these engagements, her heart bursting with pride that she was the wife of this popular and talented man. She had accompanied him until she had realised that he did not want her to come with him. And the reason for that was that he had wanted to pick up women after the concerts, and he could not do that with his young wife there. She remembered this, and thought about it, and tried to put it from her mind; but the unhappy past has a way of asserting itself and sometimes it is best just to let such thoughts run their course. They will pass, she told herself; they will pass.

Beside her, in her own silence, Mma Makutsi was mulling over the brief exchange that she had had with Mma Ramotswe on the subject of feminism. Mma Ramotswe had been right—she was sure of that—and she had inadvertently frightened Phuti Radiphuti. It had been so foolish of her. Of course she believed in those things which the feminists stood up for—the right of women to have a good job and be paid the same amount as men doing the same work; the right of women to be free of bullying by their husbands. But that was all just good common sense, fairness really, and the fact that you supported these goals did not make you one of those feminists who said that men were finished. How could they say such a thing? We were all people—men and women—and you could never say that one group of people was less important than another. She would never say that, and yet Phuti Radiphuti now probably imagined that she would.

They passed a man asking for a ride, waving his hand up and down to stop a well-disposed vehicle. Other cars were driving past regardless, but Mma Ramotswe believed that this was not the old Botswana way and made an elaborate set of hand signals to indicate to him that they were shortly going to turn off. The tiny white van swerved as she did so, and for a moment it must have seemed to the man that they were intending to run him down, but he understood and acknowledged them with a friendly wave.

"People say that these days you should not stop for people like that," said Mma Ramotswe. "But how can they be so heartless? Do you remember when my van broke down and I had to get back to town in the darkness? Somebody stopped for me, didn't they? Otherwise I could still be out here at the side of the road, even now, getting thinner and thinner."

Mma Makutsi was glad to be distracted from her morbid thoughts of engagements broken on the grounds of undisclosed feminism. She laughed at Mma Ramotswe's comment. "That is one way to go on a diet," she said.

Mma Ramotswe threw her a sideways glance. "Do you think that I need to go on a diet, Mma?" she asked.

"No," said Mma Makutsi. "I do not think that you need to go on a diet." She paused, and then added, "Others may, of course."

"Hah!" said Mma Ramotswe. "You must be thinking of those people who hold that it is wrong to be a traditionally built lady. There are such people, you know."

"They should mind their own business," said Mma Makutsi. "I am traditionally built too, you know. Not as traditionally built as you, of course—by a long way. But I am not a very thin lady."

Mma Ramotswe said nothing. She was not enjoying this conversation, and she was glad that the turn-off to Mokolodi had now appeared. Slowing down, she steered the van off the main road and onto the secondary road that ran alongside for a short way until it headed off into the bush. As the van turned, an observer would have noticed that it listed markedly to one side, Mma Ramotswe's side, while Mma Makutsi's side was higher— an appearance that would have confirmed what had just been said by Mma Makutsi. But there was nobody to see this; only the grey lourie on the acacia branch, the go-away bird, which saw so much but confided in none.

CHAPTER SIX

HOW TO DEAL WITH
AN ANGRY OSTRICH

THE ARRIVAL OF Mma Ramotswe and Mma Makutsi at Mokolodi Game Reserve would normally be an occasion for the barking of dogs and for laughter and the shaking of hands. Mma Ramotswe was known here—her father's brother, her senior uncle, was also the uncle (by a second marriage) to the workshop supervisor. And if that were not enough, Mr J.L.B. Matekoni's cousin's daughter worked in the kitchen at the restaurant. So it was in Botswana, almost everywhere; ties of kinship, no matter how attenuated by distance or time, linked one person to another, weaving across the country a human blanket of love and community. And in the fibres of that blanket there were threads of obligation that meant that one could not ignore the claims of others. Nobody should starve; nobody should feel that they were outsiders; nobody should be alone in their sadness.

Now, though, there was nobody on duty at the gate, and they drove in quietly. They parked near an acacia tree. Several people had already had the same idea, as shade was always sought after, and cars competed with one another to find relief from the sun. The tiny white van, by virtue of its size, was able to nose into a space between two large vehicles, leaving just enough room for Mma Ramotswe to get out of her door and, by breathing in, to squeeze through the space between the van and the neighbouring vehicle. It was a tight squeeze, and it brought back to her the subject of her earlier conversation with Mma Makutsi. If she went on a diet, there would be fewer occasions like this where she would find that the passages and doorways of this world were uncomfortably narrow for a person of traditional build. For a moment she was stuck, and Mma Makutsi was poised to render help, but then with a final push she was free.

"People should think a bit more of others when they park their cars," said Mma Ramotswe. "There is enough room in Botswana for everybody's car. There is no need for all this crushing."

Mma Makutsi was about to say something, but did not. Mma Ramotswe had chosen that spot to park, and the owners of the two other cars might well take the view that she, not they, was the cause of the crush. She did not say this, though, but smiled in a way that could have signalled agreement or merely polite tolerance. Mma Ramotswe's views were, in general, very balanced, and Mma Makutsi found no difficulty in agreeing with them. But she had discovered that when it came to any matter connected with the tiny white van, then her otherwise equable employer could become quite touchy. As she stood and watched Mma Ramotswe squeezing herself through the gap between the vehicles, she remembered how a few weeks ago she had asked Mma Ramotswe how two large scratches and a dent had appeared on the side of her van. She had been surprised by the vigour with which Mma Ramotswe denied the evidence.

"There is nothing wrong with my van," she said. "There is nothing wrong."

"But there is a big scratch here," said Mma Makutsi. "And

another one here. And a dent. Look. There it is. I am putting my finger on it. Look."

Mma Ramotswe glanced in a cursory way at the side of the van and shook her head. "That is nothing," she said dismissively. "That is just a bang that happened."

Mma Makutsi had shown her surprise. "A bang?"

"Yes," said Mma Ramotswe. "A bang. It is not a big thing. I was parking the van in town and there was a post. It had no business being there. Somebody had put this post in the wrong place and it hit the side of the van. There was a little bang. That is all."

Mma Makutsi bit her lip. Posts did not move; vans moved. But a warning glance from Mma Ramotswe told her that it would be unwise to pursue the matter further, and she had not. Now at Mokolodi, as then, she thought that it would be best not to say anything on the subject of parking or vans in general, and so they walked together in silence towards the office. A woman came out to greet them, a woman who appeared to recognise Mma Ramotswe.

"He is expecting you, Mma," said the woman. "Your fiancé telephoned to tell us that you were coming."

"He is my husband now," said Mma Ramotswe, smiling.

"Oh!" exclaimed the woman. "That is very good. You must be very happy, Mma. He is a good man, Mr L.J.B. Matekoni."

"J.L.B.," corrected Mma Ramotswe. "He is Mr J.L.B. Matekoni, and thank you, Mma. He is a very good man."

"I would like to find a man like that," said the woman. "I have a husband down in Lobatse. He never comes to see me. And when I go down there, he is never in."

Mma Ramotswe made a clucking sound of sympathy, and disapproval—sympathy for the woman in her plight, and disapproval of what she thought was only-too-common masculine behaviour. There were many good men in Botswana, but there were some who seemed to think that their women were only there to flatter them and give them a good time when they felt in need. These men did not think of what women themselves needed, which was comfort and support, and a bit of help in the hundred and one tasks which women had to perform if homes were to be kept going. Who did the cooking? Who kept the yard tidy? Who washed and fed the children and put them to bed at night? Who weeded the fields? Women did all these things, and it would be nice, thought Mma Ramotswe, if men could occasionally lend a hand.

It was particularly hard for women now, when there were so many children left without parents because of this cruel sickness. These children had to be looked after by somebody, and this task usually fell to the grandmothers. But in many cases the grandmothers were finding it difficult to cope because there were simply so many children coming to them. Mma Ramotswe had met one woman who had been looking after twelve grandchildren, all orphaned. And there this woman was at seventy-five, at a time when a person should be allowed to sit in the sun and look up at the sky, cooking and washing and scraping around for food for the hungry mouths of all those children. And if that grandmother should become late, she thought, what then?

The woman led them back towards the office, a round building, made of stone, with a thatched roof that came down in low eaves. A man stepped from the door, looked momentarily surprised when he saw Mma Ramotswe and Mma Makutsi, and then gave a broad grin.

"Dumela, Mma Ramotswe," he said, raising a hand in greeting. "And Mma . . ."

"This is Mma Makutsi, Neil," said Mma Ramotswe.

"Of course," said Neil. "This is the lady who keeps cobras under her desk!"

Mma Makutsi laughed. "I do not wish to think about cobras, Rra," she said. "I am only glad that you came when you did. I do not like snakes."

"Those apprentices were not going about it the right way," said Neil, smiling at the recollection. "You don't throw spanners at snakes. It doesn't help."

He gestured for the two women to follow him to the terrace in front of the verandah. Several chairs were set under the shade of a tree, and they sat on these and looked out over the tops of the trees to the hills in the distance. A cicada was screeching somewhere in the grass nearby, a shrill, persistent sound, a call for another cicada, a warning, a protest against some injustice down in the insect world. The sky above was clear, a great echoing bowl of blue, drenched in light. There could be nothing wrong.

"It is very beautiful here," said Mma Ramotswe. "If I worked here I would do no work, I think. I would sit and look at the hills."

"You are welcome to come and look at these hills any time, Mma," said Neil. He paused before continuing. "Are you here on business?"

Mma Ramotswe nodded. "Yes, we are."

Neil signalled to a young woman to bring them tea. "One of our people is in trouble? Is that it?" He frowned as he spoke.

For a moment Mma Ramotswe looked confused. Then she realised. "No, not my business—Mr J.L.B. Matekoni's business. Garage business."

The misunderstanding cleared up, they sat and waited for the tea. Their conversation wandered. Mma Makutsi seemed to be thinking of something else, and Mma Ramotswe found herself expressing a view on something she knew nothing about—a plan to build some houses nearby. Then the subject of ostriches came up. This was more interesting to Mma Ramotswe, although when she came to think of it, what did she know about ostriches? Very little.

"We've got a number of ostriches over there," said Neil, pointing in the direction of a small hillock in the mid-distance.

Mma Ramotswe followed his gaze. The expanse of bush was wide, the acacia trees like small umbrellas dotted thickly over the land. A patch of high grass on the edge of the clearing in which the camp sat moved slightly in the wind. There was nothing wrong; or was there? Why, thought Mma Ramotswe, do I feel that sensation, not fear, but something like it? Dread, perhaps; the sort of dread that can be felt in broad daylight, like this, with the sun all about and the shadows short and the presence of people— a man whistling as he attended to a task outside the office building, a woman leaning against her broom, chatting with somebody through a window.

"The thing about ostriches," said Neil, "is that they are not very intelligent. In fact, ostriches are very stupid, Mma Ramotswe."

"They are a bit like chickens, then," said Mma Ramotswe. "I have never thought that chickens were very clever."

Neil laughed. "That's a good way of putting it! Yes. Big chickens."

Mma Ramotswe remembered her meeting with Mr Molefelo, who had told her of how he had seen a man kicked by an ostrich and become late, immediately. "Chickens are not so dangerous," she said. "I am not frightened of chickens."

Neil raised an admonitory finger. "Stay away from ostriches, Mma Ramotswe. But, if you find yourself face-to-face with an angry ostrich, do you know what to do? No? I'll tell you. You put your hat on the top of a stick and raise it well above your head. The ostrich will think that you are much taller than he is, and he will back off. It works every time—every time!"

Mma Makutsi's eyes opened wide. What if she had no hat? Could she put something else on a stick and hold it up instead— one of her shoes, one of the green shoes with sky-blue linings perhaps? Or would the ostriches just laugh at that? There was no telling, but it was still an extraordinary piece of information, and she made a mental note to pass it on to Phuti Radiphuti the next time she saw him. She stopped herself; she had forgotten. She was not sure whether there would be a next time . . .

Neil reached for the tea-pot and poured tea for his guests. "You know, Mma Ramotswe, there's something I want to talk to you about. I wasn't going to mention it to you, but since you're here, you might be just the person to deal with something. I know that you're a . . . what do you call yourself, a detective?"

"Yes, Rra," said Mma Ramotswe. "I call myself a detective. And other people call me that too."

Neil cleared his throat. "Yes, of course," he said. "Well, a detective is maybe what we need around here."

Mma Ramotswe raised her cup to her lips. She had been right—there was something wrong. She had picked it up and, rather than doubting it, she should have trusted her instincts. There were usually ways of telling what was happening; there were signs, if one was ready to see them; there were sounds, if one was ready to hear them.

She looked at Neil across the rim of her cup. He was a very straightforward man, and although he was not a Motswana he was a man who had been born in Africa and lived all his life there. Such people may be white people, but they knew, they under-stood as well as anybody else. If he was worried about something, then there would be reason to worry.

"I felt that there was something wrong, Rra," she said quietly. "I could tell—I could just tell that there was something wrong." As she spoke, she felt it again—that feeling of dread. She half-turned in her seat and looked behind her, back into the darkened interior of the building behind them, where the kitchen was. A woman was standing in the doorway, just standing, doing nothing. Mma Ramotswe could not quite make out her face, and the woman withdrew, back into the shadows.

Neil had replaced his cup on the table and was rubbing the rim of it gently, as if to coax out a sound. Mma Ramotswe noticed that one of his fingers had been scratched: a small line of dried blood ran across the skin, which was weathered, cracked, the skin of a man who worked with stone and machinery and the branches of thorn trees. She waited for him to speak.

"This is generally a pretty happy place," he began. "You know what it's like, don't you?"

Mma Ramotswe did. She remembered when Mokolodi had first been set up, the dream of Ian Kirby, who had been a friend of Seretse Khama and his family. He had created the game park and had given it over to a trust for the nation so that people could come out from Gaborone, which was so close, and see animals in the wild. It was an idealistic place, and it attracted people who loved the bush and wanted to preserve it. These were not people to argue or fight with one another. Nor was it the sort of place where a dishonest or difficult person would wish to work. And yet there was something wrong. What was it? What was it? She closed her eyes, but opened them again quickly. It was fear; it was unmistakable.

"I know what this place is like normally," she said. "It is happy. I have a cousin here, you know. She has always liked working here."

"Well, it's not like that now," said Neil. "There's something very odd going on, and I don't seem able to find out what the trouble is. I've asked people and they just clam up. They look away. You know how people do that when they don't want to talk. They look away."

Mma Ramotswe understood that. People did not always talk about the things that were worrying them. Sometimes this was because they thought it rude to burden others with their troubles; sometimes it was because they did not know how to say what had to be said; there were many reasons. But fear was always a possible explanation: you did not talk about things that you were worried might happen. If you did, then the very things you worried about could come to pass.

"Tell me, Rra," she asked, "how do you know that there is something? How can you tell?"

Neil picked up a dried leaf which had blown onto the table and crushed it slowly between his fingers. "How do I know? Well, I'll give you an example. Last Saturday I wanted to drive round the reserve at night. I do that from time to time—we've had a bit of trouble with poachers, and I like to go out at odd times, without lights, so that if there's anybody thinking of getting up to anything they will know that we're in the habit of coming round the corner at any time, night or day. I usually take two or three of the men when I do this.

"Normally there's no difficulty in getting some men to come with me. They take it in turns, and pitch up of their own accord. Well, last Saturday it seemed to be a very different situation. Nobody was willing to volunteer, and when I went down to the houses to see what was going on, everybody's door was firmly shut."

Mma Ramotswe raised an eyebrow. "They were scared?"

"That's the only explanation," said Neil.

"Scared of poachers?"

Neil shrugged his shoulders. "It's difficult to say. I would have thought that was unlikely. The sort of poachers we get round here will usually run a mile rather than come up against any of us. They're not a very impressive breed of poacher, I'm afraid."

"So?" pressed Mma Ramotswe. "Was there anything else?"

Neil thought for a moment. "There have been other odd things. One of the women who works in the kitchen ran out screaming her head off the other day. She was hysterical. She said that she had seen something in the storeroom."

"And?" encouraged Mma Ramotswe.

"I called one of the other women to calm her down," said Neil. "Then I went and had a look in the storeroom. Of course, there was nothing. But when I tried to get the women to come in with me so that I could show them that there was nothing there, they both refused. Both of them. The woman who was trying to calm her friend down was just as bad."

Mma Ramotswe listened carefully. This was beginning to sound familiar to her. Although it happened relatively infrequently, it still happened. Witchcraft. Somebody was practising witchcraft, and the moment that happened, then all reason, all sound ideas and rationality, could be abandoned. Just below the surface, there were deep wells of fear and superstition that could suddenly be revealed by something like this. It was less common than it used to be, but it was there.

She looked at her watch. Mr J.L.B. Matekoni needed that axle, and she and Mma Makutsi did not have the time to sit and talk much longer, pleasant though it was to sit under that tree.

"I will come back sometime soon," said Mma Ramotswe. "And when I come back, I shall look into these things for you. In the meantime, we must get that axle for Mr J.L.B. Matekoni. That is what we need to do first. The other thing can wait."

Mma Ramotswe went back to her van and drove it down to the workshop area, while Neil and Mma Makutsi walked together down the track to meet her there. It took no more than a few minutes for the half-axle to be found among a pile of greasy spare parts. Then it was loaded into the back of the tiny white van, where it rested on some spread-out newspapers. Mma Ramotswe noticed that the two men who picked up the axle and manoeuvred it into the van said nothing beyond a mumbled greeting, completing their task in silence and then turning away, melting back into the workshop.

"You won't forget to come out soon?" Neil said as Mma Ramotswe prepared to leave.

"I won't," said Mma Ramotswe. "Don't worry. I'll come out and have a word with a few people."

"If they'll talk," said Neil gloomily. "It's as if somebody has stuck their lips together with tape."

"Somebody probably has," said Mma Ramotswe quietly. "It's just that we can't see the tape."

She drove back up the Mokolodi road to join the main road back to Gaborone. Mma Makutsi was still silent, sitting next to her, morosely looking out of her window. Mma Ramotswe glanced at her companion and was on the point of saying something, but did not. It seemed to her as if she was surrounded by silence—those silent men at the workshop, the silent woman beside her, the silent sky.

She looked again at Mma Makutsi. She had been about to say: "You know, Mma, I might just as well have come out here by myself, for all the fun you're being." But she did not. If I said anything like that, she told herself, I rather think Mma Makutsi would burst into tears. She wanted to reach across and lay a hand on Mma Makutsi's arm, to comfort her, but could not. They were coming to a bend in the road, and they would end up in a ditch if she took her hands off the wheel. That would not help, thought Mma Ramotswe.

CHAPTER SEVEN

MR POLOPETSI, AND THE
COMPLICATIONS IN HIS LIFE

MR J.L.B. MATEKONI was very pleased with the half-axle that he had obtained from Mokolodi. Fitting it, though, was a major job, requiring the assistance of the two apprentices—who needed to be instructed on this matter anyway. So the next morning, while the three of them conferred under the raised vehicle, Mr Polopetsi, who was the most recent addition to the staff of Tlokweng Road Speedy Motors, was left in charge of the routine work of the garage. He had been recruited after Mma Ramotswe's van had knocked him off his bicycle and she had arranged for it to be fixed by Mr J.L.B. Matekoni. It was after this that he had revealed what had happened to him, how he had been sent to prison for negligence after the wrong drug had been dispensed from the hospital pharmacy in which he worked. It had not been his fault, but lies had been told by another, and the magistrate had felt that a conviction and prison sentence were necessary to satisfy the outrage of the patient's family. Mma Ramotswe had been moved by the story and by his plight, and had arranged work for him in the garage. It had been a good choice: Mr Polopetsi was a methodical worker who had rapidly learned how to service a car and carry out the more mundane repairs. He was an intelli-

gent man, and discreet too, and Mma Ramotswe foresaw the
day when he would be useful in the No. 1 Ladies' Detective
Agency. He could never be a partner in the agency, as a ladies'
detective agency could not allow that, but he could certainly perform some of the tasks for which a man would be useful. It would
be handy, for instance, to have a man who could go and observe
what was going on in a particular bar, if that should be necessary
in a case. A lady detective could not very well do that, as she
would spend half her time fending off the men who pestered
ladies in bars.

One of the pleasures of having Mr Polopetsi in the garage
was that he would often come through to the office to have his
tea break with Mma Ramotswe and Mma Makutsi. Mr J.L.B.
Matekoni was frequently too busy to take a tea break, and the
apprentices liked to have their tea sitting on upturned oil drums
and watching girls walk past along the road outside. But Mr
Polopetsi would come through with his mug and ask Mma
Makutsi if there might be enough tea for him. He would always
receive the answer that there certainly would be and that he
should take a seat on the client's chair and they would fill his mug
for him. And Mr Polopetsi would always say the same thing in
reply, as if it were a mantra: "You are very kind, Mma Makutsi.
There are not many ladies as kind as you and Mma Ramotswe.
That's the truth." He did not seem to notice that he said the same
thing every time, and the ladies never pointed out to him that
they had heard the remark before. "We say the same things all the
time, you know," Mma Ramotswe had once observed to Mma
Makutsi, and Mma Makutsi had replied, "You're right about that,
Mma Ramotswe"—which is something that she always said.

Mr Polopetsi came into the office that morning wiping his
brow from the heat. "I think that it's tea-time," he said, placing
his mug on the top of the metal filing cabinet. "It's very hot

through there. Do you know why drinking a hot liquid like tea can cool you down, Mma Ramotswe?"

Mma Ramotswe had, in fact, thought about this but had reached no conclusion. All she knew was that a cup of bush tea always refreshed her in a way in which a glass of cold water would not. "You tell me, Rra," she said. "And Mma Makutsi will turn on the kettle at the same time."

"It's because hot liquids make you sweat," explained Mr Polopetsi. "Then as the sweat dries off the skin it gives a feeling of coolness. That is how it works."

Mma Makutsi flicked the switch of the kettle. "Very unlikely," she said curtly.

Mr Polopetsi turned to her indignantly. "But it's true," he said. "I learned that on my pharmacy course at the hospital. Dr Moffat gave us lectures on how the body works."

This did not impress Mma Makutsi. "I don't sweat when I drink tea," she said. "But it still cools me off."

"Well, you don't have to believe me if you don't want to," he said. "I just thought that I would tell you—that's all."

"I believe you, Rra," said Mma Ramotswe soothingly. "I'm sure that you're right." She glanced at Mma Makutsi. There was definitely something worrying her assistant; it was unlike her to snap at Mr Polopetsi, whom she liked. She had decided that it was something to do with that conversation which she had had with Phuti Radiphuti—the conversation in which she had confessed to feminism. Had he taken that to heart? She very much hoped he had not; Mma Ramotswe was appalled at the thought of something going wrong with Mma Makutsi's engagement. After all those years of waiting and hoping, Mma Makutsi had eventually found a man, only to ruin everything by frightening him off. Oh, careless, careless Mma Makutsi! thought Mma Ramotswe. And foolish, foolish man to take a casual remark so seriously!

Mma Ramotswe smiled at Mr Polopetsi. "I know Dr Moffat's wife," she said. "I can go and ask her myself. She can speak to the doctor. We can settle this matter quite easily."

"It is already settled," said Mr Polopetsi. "There is no doubt in my mind, at least."

"Well, then," said Mma Ramotswe. "You need not worry about it any more."

"I wasn't worried," said Mr Polopetsi, as he sat down in the client's chair. "I have bigger things to worry about. Unlike some people." The last few words were said softly, but Mma Ramotswe heard them. Mma Makutsi, for whom they were half-intended, did not. She was standing by the kettle, waiting for it to boil, looking up at the tiny white gecko suspended by its minute suction pads on the ceiling.

Mma Ramotswe saw this as an opportunity to change the subject. When Mma Makutsi was in that sort of mood, then she had found that the best tactic was to steer away from controversy. "Oh?" she said. "Bigger worries? What are they, Rra?"

Mr Polopetsi glanced over his shoulder at Mma Makutsi. Mma Ramotswe noticed this, and made a discreet signal with her hand. It was a "don't you worry about her" signal, and he understood immediately.

"I am very tired, Mma," he said. "That is my problem. It is all this bicycle-riding in this heat. It is not easy."

Mma Ramotswe looked out of the window. The sun that day was relentless; you felt it on the top of your head, pressing down. Even in the early mornings, shortly after breakfast, a time when one might choose to walk about the yard and inspect the trees— even then, it was hot and uncomfortable. And it would stay like this, she knew—or get even worse until the rains came, cooling and refreshing, like a cup of tea for the land itself, she found herself thinking.

She looked back at Mr Polopetsi. Yes, he looked exhausted, poor man, sitting there in the client's chair, crumpled, hot.

"Couldn't you come in by minibus?" she said. "Most other people do."

Mr Polopetsi seemed to crumple even more. "You have been to my house, Mma Ramotswe. You know where it is. It is no good for minibuses. There is a long walk to the nearest place that a minibus stops. Then they are often late."

Mma Ramotswe nodded sympathetically. It was not easy for people who lived out of town. The cost of housing in Gaborone itself was going up and up, and for most people a house in town would be an impossible dream. That left places like Tlokweng, or even further afield, and a long journey into work. It was all right, she supposed, if one were young and robust, but Mr Polopetsi, although he was only somewhere in his forties, did not look strong: he was a slight man, and with that crumpled look of his . . . If a powerful gust of wind should come sweeping in from the Kalahari, he could easily be lifted up and blown away. In her mind's eye, she saw Mr Polopetsi in his khaki trousers and khaki shirt, arms flailing, being picked up by the wind and cartwheeled through the sky, off towards Namibia somewhere, and dropped down suddenly on the ground, confused, in another land. And then she saw Herero horsemen galloping towards him and shouting and Mr Polopetsi, dusting himself off, trying hard to explain, pointing to the sky and gesturing.

"Why are you smiling, Mma Ramotswe?" asked Mr Polopetsi.

She corrected herself quickly. "I'm sorry," she said. "I was thinking of something else."

Mr Polopetsi shifted in his chair. "It must have been funny," he muttered.

Mma Ramotswe looked away. "Funny things come to mind," she said. "You can be thinking of something serious, and then something very funny comes to mind. But look, Rra, what about a car? Would it not be possible now to buy a car—now that you're earning here; and your wife has a job, doesn't she? Could you not afford a cheap car, an old one, which is still going? Mr J.L.B. Matekoni would be able to find something for you."

Mr Polopetsi shook his head vehemently. "I cannot afford a car," he said. "I would love one, and it would solve all my troubles. I could give people a ride in with me and pay for the petrol that way. My neighbour works not far away—he could come in with me, and he has a friend too. They would love to come by car. My brother has a car. He is lucky."

The tea was now ready, and Mma Makutsi brought over Mr Polopetsi's mug and placed it on the edge of Mma Ramotswe's desk in front of him.

"You are very kind, Mma Makutsi," said Mr Polopetsi. "There are not many ladies as kind as you and Mma Ramotswe. That's the truth."

Mma Ramotswe lowered her head briefly to acknowledge the compliment. "This brother of yours, Mr Polopetsi," she said. "Is he a wealthy man?"

Mr Polopetsi took a sip of his tea. "No," he answered. "He is not a rich man. He has a good job, though. He works in a bank. But that is not how he managed to get the car. He was given a loan by my uncle. It was one of those loans that you can pay off in such small installments that you never notice the cost. My uncle is a generous man. He has a lot of money in the bank."

"A rich uncle?" said Mma Ramotswe. "Could this rich uncle not lend you money too? Why should he prefer your brother? Surely an uncle . . ." She tailed off. It occurred to her that there was a very obvious reason why this uncle would prefer one brother to another, and she saw, from the embarrassment in his demeanour, that she was right.

"He has not forgiven me," said Mr Polopetsi simply. "He has not forgiven me for . . . for being sent to prison. He said that it brought shame on the whole family when I was sent to that place."

Mma Makutsi, who had poured her own tea now and had taken it to her desk, looked up indignantly. "He should not think that," she expostulated. "What happened was not your fault. It was an accident."

"I tried to tell him that," said Mr Polopetsi, turning to address Mma Makutsi, "but he would not listen to me. He refused. He just shouted." He hesitated. "He is an old man, you know. Old men sometimes do not want to listen."

There was silence as Mma Ramotswe and Mma Makutsi digested this information. Mma Ramotswe understood. There were some older people in Botswana—men in particular—who had very strong ideas of what was what and who were notoriously stubborn in their attitudes. Her father, the late Obed Ramotswe, had not been like that at all—he had always had an open mind—but she remembered some of his friends being very difficult to persuade. He had even spoken of one of them who had been hostile to independence, who had wanted the Protectorate to continue. This man had said that it would be better to have somebody to protect the country against the Boers, and had continued to say this even when Obed had asked him: "Where are these troops you say will protect us? Where are they?" And, of course, there were none. He could understand, though, loyalty to Queen Elizabeth. She was a friend of Africa, Obed said; she had always been, for she understood all about loyalty and duty, and about how, during the war, there had been many men from the Protectorate who had gone to fight. They had been brave men, who had seen terrible things in Italy and North Africa, and now most people had forgotten about them. We should not forget these things, he had said; we should not forget.

"I understand," she said to Mr Polopetsi. "Sometimes when somebody makes up his mind, it is difficult to shift him. The elders are sometimes like that." She paused. "What is the name of this uncle of yours, Mr Polopetsi? Where does he live?"

Mr Polopetsi told her. He drained the rest of the tea from his mug and rose to his feet; he did not see Mma Ramotswe reaching for a pencil and writing a note on a scrap of paper. And then this scrap of paper she tucked in her bodice, the safest place to keep anything. She never forgot to do anything filed in that particular place, and so she would not forget the details on that piece of paper: Mr Kagiso Polopetsi, Plot 2487, Limpopo Drive. After which she had scrawled—*mean old uncle*.

MMA MAKUTSI WENT BACK to the house early that afternoon. She had told Mma Ramotswe that she would be cooking a meal for Phuti Radiphuti that evening and wanted to make it a special one. Mma Ramotswe had told her that this was a very good idea and that it would also be a good idea to talk to him about feminism.

"Set his mind at rest," she said. "Tell him that you are not going to be one of those women who will give him no peace. Tell him that you are really quite traditional at heart."

"I will do that," agreed Mma Makutsi. "I will show him that he need not fear that I will always be criticising him." She stopped and looked at Mma Ramotswe. There was misery in her expression, and Mma Ramotswe felt an immediate rush of sympathy for her. It was different for her. She was married to Mr J.L.B. Matekoni and felt quite secure; if Mma Makutsi lost Phuti Radiphuti she would have nothing—just the prospect of hard work for the rest of her life, making do with the small salary she earned and the little extra she made from the Kalahari Typing

School for Men. The typing school was a valuable source of extra funds, but she had to work so hard keeping that going that she had very little time to herself.

Back at her house, Mma Makutsi made the evening meal with care. She boiled a large pot of potatoes and simmered a thick beef stew into which she had put carrots and onions. The stew smelled rich and delicious, and she dipped a finger into the pot to taste it. It needed a little bit more salt, but after that it was perfect. She sat down to wait for Phuti Radiphuti, who normally arrived at seven o'clock. It was now six thirty, and she flicked through a magazine, only half-concentrating, for the remaining half hour.

At seven thirty she looked out of the window, and at eight o'clock she went out to stand at her gate and peer down the road to see if he was coming. It was a warm evening and the air was heavy with the smell of cooking and dust. From her neighbour's house she heard the sound of a radio, and laughter. Somebody coughed; she felt the brush of insect wings against her leg.

She walked back up the path to her front door and into her house. She sat down on her sofa and stared up at the ceiling. I am a girl from Bobonong, she said to herself. I am a girl from Bobonong, with glasses. There was a man who was going to marry me, a kind man, but I frightened him away through my foolish talk. Now I am alone again. That is the story of my life; that is the story of Grace Makutsi.

CHAPTER EIGHT

A MEETING IN THE TINY WHITE VAN

THE FOLLOWING DAY, Mma Ramotswe went to see Mma Tsau, the cook for whom Poppy worked, the wife of the man who had grown prosperous-looking on government food. It was an auspicious day—a Friday at the end of the month. For most people, that was pay day, and for many it was the end of the period of want that always seemed to occur over the last few days of the month, no matter how careful one was with money for the other twenty-five days or so. The apprentices were a good example of this. When they had first started to work at Tlokweng Road Speedy Motors, Mr J.L.B. Matekoni had warned them that they should husband their resources carefully. It was tempting, he pointed out, to view money as something to be spent the moment it came into one's hands. "That is very dangerous," he said. "There are many people whose bellies are full for the first fifteen days of the month who then have hungry stomachs for the last two weeks."

Charlie, the older apprentice, exchanged a knowing glance with his younger colleague. "That makes twenty-nine days," he said. "What about the other two days, Boss?"

Mr J.L.B. Matekoni sighed. "That is not the point," he said, his tone level. It would be easy to lose his temper with these boys, he realised, but that was not what he intended to do. He was their apprentice-master, and that meant that he should be patient. One got nowhere if one shouted at young people. Shouting at a young person was like shouting at a wild animal—both would run away in their confusion.

"What you should do," said Mr J.L.B. Matekoni, "is work out how much money you need for each week. Then put all your money in the post office or somewhere safe like that and draw it out weekly."

Charlie smiled. "There is always credit," he said. "You can buy things on credit. It is cheaper that way."

Mr J.L.B. Matekoni looked at the young man. Where does one start? he thought. How does one make up for all the things that young people do not know? There was so much ignorance in the world—great swathes of ignorance like areas of darkness on a map. That was the job of teachers, to put this ignorance to flight, and that was why teachers were respected in Botswana—or used to be. He had noticed how people these days, even young people, treated teachers as if they were the same as anybody else. But how would people learn if they did not respect a teacher? Respect meant that they would be prepared to listen, and to learn. Young men like Charlie, thought Mr J.L.B. Matekoni, imagined that they knew everything already. Well, he would simply have to try to teach them in spite of their arrogance.

Grace Makutsi and Mma Ramotswe knew all about the end of the month. Mma Ramotswe's financial position had always been considerably easier than most people's, thanks to the late Obed Ramotswe's talent for the spotting of good cattle, but she was well aware of the enforced penny-pinching that was the daily lot of those about her. Rose, the woman who cleaned her house in Zebra Drive, was an example. She had a number of children—Mma Ramotswe had never been sure just how many—and these children had all known what it was to go to bed hungry, in spite of their mother's best efforts. And one of the children, a small boy, had difficulties with his breathing and needed inhalers, which were expensive to buy, even with the help of the government clinic. And then there was Mma Makutsi herself, who had supported herself at the Botswana Secretarial College by doing cleaning work in a hotel in the early mornings before she went to her classes at the college. That could not have been easy, getting up at four in the morning, even in the winter, when the skies were sharp-empty (as Mma Makutsi put it) with cold and the ground hard below the feet. But she had been careful, husbanding every spare thebe, and now, at long last, had achieved some measure of comfort with her new house (or half house, to be precise), her new green shoes with sky-blue linings, and, of course, her new fiancé . . .

The end of the month, pay day; and now Mma Ramotswe parked her tiny white van near the kitchen building of the college and waited. She looked at her watch. It was three o'clock, and she imagined that Mma Tsau would have finished supervising the clean-up after lunch. She was not sure where the cook had her office, but it was likely to be in the same building as the kitchens, and there was no doubt which building that was; one only had to wind down the window and sniff the air to know where the kitchens were. What a lovely smell it was, the smell of food. That was one of the great pleasures of life, in Mma Ramotswe's view—the smell of cooking drifting on the wind; the smell of maize cobs roasting on the open fire, of beef sizzling in its fat, of large chunks of pumpkin boiling in the pot. All these smells were good smells, part of the smells of Botswana, of home, that warmed the heart and made the mouth water in anticipation.

She looked towards the kitchen building. There was an open

door at one end and a large window, through which she could just make out the shape of a cupboard and an overhead fan turning slowly. There were people in it too; a head moved, a hand appeared at the window, briefly, and was withdrawn. That was the office, she thought, and she could always just go up to it, knock on the door, and ask for Mma Tsau. Mma Ramotswe had always believed in the direct approach, no matter what advice Clovis Andersen gave in *The Principles of Private Detection*. Clovis Andersen seemed to endorse circumspection and the finding out of information by indirect means. But in Mma Ramotswe's view, the best way of getting an answer to any question was to ask somebody face-to-face. Experience had shown her that if one suspected that there was a secret, the best thing to do was to find out who knew the secret and then ask that person to tell it to you. It nearly always worked. The whole point about secrets was that they demanded to be told, they were insistent, they burned a hole in your tongue if you kept them for too long. That was the way it worked for most people.

For her part, Mma Ramotswe knew how to keep a secret, if the secret was one which needed to be kept. She did not divulge her clients' affairs, even if she felt that she was bursting to tell somebody, and even Mr J.L.B. Matekoni would not be told of something if it really had to be kept confidential. Only very occasionally, when she felt that the burden of some bit of knowledge was too great for one person to shoulder, would she share with Mr J.L.B. Matekoni some hidden fact which she had uncovered or which had been imparted to her. This had happened when she had heard from one client that he was planning to defraud the Botswana Eagle Insurance Company by making a false claim. He had told her this in a matter-of-fact way, as if she should not be surprised; after all, was this not the way in which practically everybody treated insurance companies? She had gone to Mr J.L.B. Matekoni to discuss this with him, and he had advised her to bring her professional relationship with that client to an end, which she did, and was crudely threatened for her pains. That had resulted in a trip to the Botswana Eagle Insurance Company, which had been most grateful for the information Mma Ramotswe had provided, and had taken steps to protect its interests.

But the direct approach would not work now. If she went to the office, there was every chance that she would see Poppy, and that would lead to difficulties. She had not warned Poppy that she was coming to speak to Mma Tsau, and she would not want the cook to suspect that Poppy had consulted her. No, she would have to make sure that she spoke to Mma Tsau by herself.

A small group of students emerged from a building beside the kitchen. It was the end of a class, and they stood in groups of two or three outside the classroom, talking among themselves, laughing at shared jokes. It was the end of the month for them too, Mma Ramotswe assumed, and they would have their allowances in their pockets and thoughts of the weekend's socialising ahead of them. What was it like, she wondered, to be one of them? Mma Ramotswe herself had gone from girlhood to the world of work without anything in between and had never known the student life. Did they know, she wondered, just how fortunate they were?

One of the students detached herself from a group and started to walk across the patch of ground that separated the van from the kitchen building. When she drew level with the van, she glanced in Mma Ramotswe's direction.

"Excuse me, Mma," shouted Mma Ramotswe through the open window of her van. "Excuse me, Mma!"

The young woman stopped and looked across at Mma Ramotswe, who was now getting out of the van.

"Yes, Mma," said the student. "Are you calling me?"

Mma Ramotswe made her way over to stand before the young woman. "Yes, Mma," she said. "Do you know the lady who works in the kitchen? Mma Tsau? Do you know that lady?"

The student smiled. "She is the cook," she said. "Yes, I know her."

"I need to speak to her," said Mma Ramotswe. "I need to speak to her out here, in my van. I do not want to speak to her when there are other people about."

The student looked blank. "So?" she said.

"So I wonder if you would go and tell her, Mma," said Mma Ramotswe. "Could you go and tell her that there is somebody out here who needs to speak to her?"

The young woman frowned. "Could you not go yourself, Mma? Why do you need me to do this for you?"

Mma Ramotswe looked searchingly into the face of the young woman before her. What bond was there between them? Were they strangers, people who would have no reason to do anything for one another? Or was this still a place where one might go and speak to another, even a complete stranger, and make a request for help, as had been possible in the past?

"I am asking you," said Mma Ramotswe quietly. "I am asking you . . ." And then she hesitated, but only for a moment, before she continued, "I am asking you, my sister."

For a moment the young woman said nothing, but then she moved her head slightly; she nodded. "I will do that," she said. "I will go."

MMA TSAU, a squat, rather round woman, appeared from the door of the kitchen office, paused, and looked out over the grounds of the college. Her gaze fell upon the tiny white van and she hesitated for a moment. Within the van, Mma Ramotswe raised a hand, which Mma Tsau did not see, but she saw the van, and the young woman had said, "There is a woman who needs to see you urgently, Mma. She is outside in a small white van. She is too big for that van, if you ask me, but she wants to see you there."

The cook made her way across the ground to the van. She had a curious gait, Mma Ramotswe observed; a slight limp perhaps, or feet that pointed out to the side rather than forwards. Mma Makutsi was slightly inclined to do that, Mma Ramotswe had noticed, and although she had never said anything about it, one day she would pluck up the courage to suggest that she should think about the way she walked. One had to be careful, though: Mma Makutsi was sensitive about her appearance and might be demoralised by such a remark, even if it was meant helpfully.

Mma Tsau peered into the van. "You are looking for me, Mma?" The voice was a loud one, surprisingly loud for one of such small stature; it was the voice of one who was used to shouting at people. Professional cooks had a reputation for shouting, Mma Ramotswe recalled. They shouted at the people who worked for them in their kitchen, and some of them—the really famous ones—threw things too. There was no excuse for that, of course. Mma Ramotswe had been shocked when she had read in a magazine about a famous chef somewhere overseas who threw cold soup over the heads of his junior staff if they did not measure up to his expectations. He swore at them too, which was almost as bad. To use strong language, she thought, was a sign of bad temper and lack of concern for others. Such people were not clever or bold simply because they used such language; each time they opened their mouths they proclaimed *I am a person who is poor in words*. Was Mma Tsau one of those chefs, she wondered; this round little person with the blue spotted scarf tied round her head like a doek? It seemed unlikely that she would throw cold soup over somebody's head.

"Yes, Mma," said Mma Ramotswe, trying to put to the back of her mind the sudden mental picture which had come to her of Mma Tsau tipping a pot of soup over . . . Charlie. What a picture! And it was replaced immediately by an image of Mr J.L.B. Matekoni, frustrated by some piece of sloppy work, doing a similar thing to the apprentice; and Mma Makutsi pouring soup over . . . She stopped herself. "I would like to talk to you, please."

Mma Tsau wiped her brow. "I am listening," she said. "I can hear you."

"This is private," said Mma Ramotswe. "We could talk in my van, if you don't mind."

Mma Tsau frowned. "What is this private business?" she asked. "Are you trying to sell something, Mma?"

Mma Ramotswe looked about her, as one might do if about to impart a confidence. "It is about your husband," she said.

The words had their desired effect. When her husband was mentioned, Mma Tsau gave a start, as if somebody had poured . . . She moved her head back and squinted at Mma Ramotswe through narrowed eyes.

"My husband?"

"Yes, Mma, your husband." Mma Ramotswe nodded in the direction of the passenger door. "Why don't you get into the van, Mma? We can talk in here."

For a moment it seemed as if Mma Tsau was going to turn around and go back to her office. There was a moment of hesitation; the eyes moved; she continued to stare at Mma Ramotswe. Then she started to walk round the front of the van, slowly, her eyes still on Mma Ramotswe.

"You can wind down that window, Mma," said Mma Ramotswe as the other woman lowered herself into the seat beside her. "It will be cooler that way. It is very hot today, isn't it?"

Mma Tsau had folded her hands on her lap and was staring down at them. She did not respond to Mma Ramotswe's remark. In the confines of the van, her breathing was audibly laboured. Mma Ramotswe said nothing for a moment, allowing her to get her breath back. But there was no change in Mma Tsau's breathing, which sounded as if the air was working its way through a small thicket of leaves, a rustling sound, the sound of a tree in the wind. She turned and looked at her visitor. She had been prepared to dislike this woman who had been stealing food from the college; this woman who had so unfairly threatened the inoffensive Poppy with dismissal. But now, in the flesh, with her laboured breathing and her odd walk, it was difficult not to feel sympathy. And of course it was always difficult for Mma Ramotswe not to feel sympathy for another, however objectionable his conduct might be, however flawed his character, simply because she understood, at the most intuitive, profound level what it was to be a human being, which is not easy. Everybody, she felt, could do evil, so easily; could be weak, so easily; could be selfish, so easily. This meant that she could understand—and did—which was not the same thing as condoning—which she did not—or taking the view—which she did not—that one should not judge others. Of course one could judge others, and Mma Ramotswe used the standards of the old Botswana morality to make these judgements. But there was nothing in the old Botswana morality which said that one could not forgive those who were weak; indeed, there was much in the old Botswana morality that was very specifically about forgiveness. One should not hold a grudge against another, it said, because to harbour grudges was to disturb the social peace, the bond between people.

She felt sorry, then, for Mma Tsau, and instinctively, without giving it any thought, she reached out and touched the other woman gently on the forearm, and left her hand there. Mma Tsau tensed, and the breath caught in her throat, but then she turned her head and looked at Mma Ramotswe, and her eyes were moist with tears.

"You are the mother of one of those girls," Mma Tsau said quietly. It was not a question; it was a statement. Her earlier confidence was drained from her, and she seemed even smaller now, hunched in her seat.

Mma Ramotswe did not understand, and was about to say so. But then she thought, and it came to her what this other woman meant. It was a familiar story, after all, and nobody should be surprised. The husband, the father, the respectable citizen; such a man might still carry on with other women in spite of everything, in spite of his wife's pain, and many did. And some of these men went further, and picked up girls who were far younger than themselves, some still at high school. They felt proud of themselves, these men, with their youthful girlfriends, whose heads they turned because they had money to throw around, or a fast car, or power perhaps.

"I hear what you say, Mma," Mma Ramotswe began. "Your husband. I did not mean . . ."

"It has been going on for many years," Mma Tsau interrupted her. "Just after we were married—even then, he started this thing. I told him how stupid he looked, running after these young girls, but he ignored me. I told him that I would leave him, but he just laughed and said that I should do that. But I could not, Mma. I could not . . ."

This was a familiar story to Mma Ramotswe. She had come across so many women who could not leave unworthy men because they loved them. This was quite different from those cases where women could not leave because they were frightened of the man, or because they had no place to go; some women could not leave simply because, in spite of everything that had been done to them, in spite of all the heartbreak, they stubbornly loved the man. This, she suspected, was what was happening here. Mma Tsau loved Rra Tsau, and would do so to the end.

"You love him, Mma?" she probed gently. "Is that it?"

Mma Tsau looked down at her hands. Mma Ramotswe noticed that one of them had a light dusting of flour on it; the hand of a cook.

"Eee," said Mma Tsau, under her breath, using the familiar, long-drawn-out Setswana word of assent. "Eee, Mma. I love that man. That is true. I am a weak woman, I know. But I love him."

Mma Ramotswe sighed. There was no cure for such love. That was the most basic thing one found out about human affairs, and one did not have to be a private detective to know that simple fact. Such love, the tenacious love of a parent or a devoted spouse, could fade—and did—but it took a long time to do so and often persisted in the face of all the evidence that it was squandered on an unworthy choice.

"I was going to say that I hadn't come about that," said Mma Ramotswe. "I do not know your husband."

It took Mma Tsau a few moments to take in what Mma Ramotswe had told her. When she did, she turned to look at her. She was still defeated.

"What have you come about?" she asked. There was no real curiosity in her voice now. It was as if Mma Ramotswe had come about the supply of eggs, or potatoes perhaps.

"I have come because I have heard that you have threatened to dismiss one of your staff," she said. She did not want to suggest that Poppy had complained, and so she said, quite truthfully—in the strictest sense—that nobody had asked her to come. That was not a lie. It was more what Clovis Andersen called *an indirect statement;* and there was a distinction.

Mma Tsau shrugged. "I am the head cook," she said. "I am called the catering manager. That is who I am. I take on some staff—and push some staff out. Some people are not good workers." She dusted her hands lightly, and for a moment Mma Ramotswe saw the tiny grains of flour, like specks of dust, caught in a slant of sunlight.

The sympathy that Mma Ramotswe had felt for her earlier was now being replaced by irritation. She did not really like this woman, she decided, although she admired her, perhaps, for her loyalty to her philandering husband. "People get dismissed for other reasons," she said. "Somebody who was stealing food, for example—that person would be dismissed if it were found out that government food was being given to her husband."

Mma Tsau was quite still. She reached her hand out and touched the hem of her skirt, tugging at it gently, as if testing the strength of the seam. She took a breath, and there was the rattling sound of phlegm.

"Maybe it was you who wrote that letter," she said. "Maybe . . ."

"I did not," said Mma Ramotswe. "And nor did that girl."

Mma Tsau shook her head. "Then who did?"

"I have no idea," said Mma Ramotswe. "But it had nothing to do with that girl. There is somebody else who is blackmailing you. That is what this is, you know. This is blackmail. It is normally a matter for the police."

Mma Tsau laughed. "You think I should go to the police? You think that I should say to them: *I have been giving government food to my husband. Now somebody is threatening me?* I'm not stupid, Mma."

Mma Ramotswe's voice was even. "I know that you're not stupid, Mma Tsau. I know that." She paused. She doubted that Mma Tsau intended now to do anything more about Poppy, and that meant that she could regard the matter as closed. But it left the issue of the blackmail unresolved. It was a despicable act, she thought, and she was offended that somebody might do such a thing and get away with it. She might look into it, perhaps, if she had the time, and there were always slack periods when she and Mma Makutsi had nothing to do. Perhaps she could even put Mma Makutsi on the case and see what she made of it. No blackmailer would be a match for Mma Makutsi, assistant detective at the No. 1 Ladies' Detective Agency and graduate of distinction of the Botswana Secretarial College—Mma Ninety-Seven Per Cent, as Mma Ramotswe sometimes irreverently thought of her. She could imagine a confrontation between the blackmailer and Mma Makutsi, with the latter's large round glasses flashing with the fire of indignation and the blackmailer, a wretched, furtive man cowering in the face of female wrath.

"What are you smiling at?" asked Mma Tsau. "I do not think this is funny."

"No," said Mma Ramotswe, bringing herself back to reality. "It is not funny. But tell me, Mma—do you still have that letter? Could you show it to me? Perhaps I can find out who this person is who is trying to blackmail you."

Mma Tsau thought for a moment. "And you won't do anything about . . . about my husband?"

"No," said Mma Ramotswe. "I am not interested in your husband." And that was true, of course. She could just imagine Mma Tsau's husband, a lazy womaniser, being fed by his devoted wife and getting fatter and fatter until he could no longer see the lower part of his body, so large had his stomach become. That would serve him right, thought Mma Ramotswe. Being a traditionally built lady was one thing; being a traditionally built man was quite another. And it was certainly not so good.

The thought made her smile again, but Mma Tsau did not see the smile, as she was struggling with the door handle, preparing to go off and retrieve the letter which she had in her office, in one of the secret places she had there.

CHAPTER NINE

FILING CABINETS, LOCKS, CHAINS

MMA RAMOTSWE looked into her tea cup. The red bush tea, freshly poured, was still very hot, too hot to drink, but good to look at in its amber darkness, and very good to smell. It was a pity, she thought, that she had become accustomed to the use of tea-bags, as this meant that there were no leaves to be seen swirling around the surface or clinging to the side of the cup. She had given in on the issue of tea-bags, out of weakness, she admitted; tea-bags were so overwhelmingly more convenient than leaf tea, with its tendency to clog drains and the spouts of tea-pots too if one was not careful. She had never worried about getting the occasional tea leaf in her mouth, indeed she had rather enjoyed this, but that never happened now, with these neatly packed tea-bags and their very precise, enmeshed doses of chopped leaves.

It was the first cup of the morning, as Mma Ramotswe did not count the two cups that she took at home before she came to work. One of these was consumed as she took her early stroll around the yard, with the sun just up, pausing to stand under the large acacia tree and peer up into the thorny branches above her, drawing the morning air into her lungs and savouring its freshness. That morning she had seen a chameleon on a branch of the tree and had watched the strange creature fix its riveting eye upon her, its tiny prehensile feet poised in mid-movement. It was a great advantage, she thought, to have a chameleon's eyes, which could look backwards and forwards independently. That would be a fine gift for a detective.

Now at her desk, she raised the cup to her lips and took a sip of the bush tea. She looked at her watch. Mma Makutsi was usually very punctual, but today she was late for some reason. This would be the fault of the minibuses, thought Mma Ramotswe. There would be enough of them coming into town from Tlokweng at that hour of the morning, but not enough going in the opposite direction. Mma Makutsi could walk, of course—her new house was not all that far away—but people did not like to walk in the heat, understandably enough.

She had a report to write, and she busied herself with this. It was not an easy one, as she had to detail the weaknesses she had found in the hiring department of a company which provided security guards. They imagined that they screened out applicants with a criminal record when they sought jobs with the company; Mma Ramotswe had discovered that it was simplicity itself to lie about one's past on the application form and that the forms were usually not even scrutinised by the official in charge of the personnel department. This man, who had got the job through lying about his qualifications and experience, rubber-stamped the applications of virtually anybody, but particularly of applications submitted by any of his relatives. Mma Ramotswe's report would not make comfortable reading for the company, and she knew to expect some anger over the results. This was inevitable—people did not like to be told uncomfortable truths, even if they had asked for them. Uncomfortable truths meant that one had to go back and invent a whole new set of procedures, and that was not always welcome when there were so many other things to do.

As she listed the defects in the firm's arrangements, Mma Ramotswe thought of how difficult it was to have a completely secure system for anything. The No. 1 Ladies' Detective Agency was a case in point. They kept all their records in two old filing cabinets, and neither of these, she realised, had a lock, or at least a lock that worked. There was a lock on the office door, naturally enough, but during the day they rarely bothered to use that if both of them went out on some errand. There were always people around the garage, of course—either Mr J.L.B. Matekoni or the apprentices, and surely intruders would be deterred by their presence . . . No, she thought, perhaps not. Mr J.L.B. Matekoni was often so absorbed in tinkering with an engine that he would not notice it if the President himself drew up in his large official car. And as for the apprentices, they were completely unobservant and missed the most glaring features of what went on round about them. Indeed, she had given up on asking them for descriptions of clients who might have called while she was out and spoken to one of them. "There was a man," they would say. "He came to see you. Now he is gone." And in response to questioning for some clue as to the caller's identity, they would say, "He was not a very tall man, I think. Or maybe he was a bit tall. I could not tell."

Her pen stopped in mid-sentence. Who was she to criticise when it would be possible for virtually anybody to walk into the office of the No. 1 Ladies' Detective Agency at an unguarded moment and rifle through the secrets of their clients? Are you interested in who is suspected by his wife of adultery? Please, help yourself: there are plenty of reports about that in an old filing cabinet on the Tlokweng Road—just help yourself! And why was that man dismissed from that hotel last month, with no reason given? Well, the report on that—freely available from the No. 1 Ladies' Detective Agency, and signed by Mma Grace Makutsi, Dip. Sec. (Botswana Secretarial College) (97%)—may be obtained by the simple expedient of looking in the top drawer of the second desk of an unlocked office beside Tlokweng Road Speedy Motors.

Mma Ramotswe rose to her feet and made her way over to the filing cabinet nearest her. Bending forward, she peered at the lock which was built into the top of the cabinet. It was a small, oval silver-coloured plate with an incised key-hole. At the top of the plate the maker's sign, a small rampant lion, was stamped into the metal. The lion looked back at Mma Ramotswe, and she shook her head. There was rust in the key-hole, and the edges of the hole were dented. Even if they could locate the key, it would be impossible to insert it. She looked at the lion, a symbol of the pride which somebody must once have felt, somewhere, in the construction of the cabinet. And perhaps this pride was not entirely misplaced—the cabinet must have been made decades ago, perhaps even forty or fifty years previously, and it still worked. How many modern cabinets, with their plastic trimmings and their bright colours, would still be holding files in fifty years' time? And it was the same with people, she thought. Bright, modern people were all very well, but did they last the course? Traditionally minded (and traditionally built) people might not seem so fashionable, but they would always be there, doing what they always did. A traditional mechanic, for example—somebody like Mr J.L.B. Matekoni—would be able to keep your car going when a modern mechanic—somebody like Charlie—would shrug his shoulders and say that everything needed to be renewed.

She reached out and gave the filing cabinet an affectionate pat. Then, on impulse, she bent down and kissed its scratched and dented metal surface. The metal felt cool to her lips and smelled acrid, as metal can—a smell of rust and sharpness.

"Dumela, Mma," said Mma Makutsi from the doorway.

Mma Ramotswe straightened up.

"Don't worry about me," said Mma Makutsi. "Just carry on doing whatever it was that you were doing . . ." She glanced at the filing cabinet and then at her employer.

Mma Ramotswe returned to her desk. "I was thinking about that filing cabinet," she said. "And suddenly I felt very grateful to it. I know that it must have looked very strange to you, Mma."

"Not at all," said Mma Makutsi. "I am grateful to it too. It keeps all our records safe."

Mma Ramotswe frowned. "Well, I'm not sure if they're completely safe," she said. "In fact, I was just wondering whether we should do something about locking them. Confidentiality is very important. You know that, Mma."

Mma Makutsi looked thoughtfully at the filing cabinets. "That is true," she said. "But I do not think we would ever find a key for those old locks." She paused. "Maybe we could put a chain around them, with a padlock?"

Mma Ramotswe did not think that this would be a good idea. It would look absurd to have chained filing cabinets, and would give quite the wrong impression to clients. It was bad enough having an office inside a garage, but it would be worse to have something quite so odd-looking as a chain around a cabinet. It would be better to buy a couple of new filing cabinets, even if they would not be as sturdy and substantial as these old ones. There was probably enough money in the office account to do this, and they had not spent very much on equipment recently. In fact, they had spent nothing, apart from three pula for a new teaspoon, which had been required after one of the apprentices had used their existing teaspoon to fix a gearbox and had broken it. The thought of furniture reminded her. Mma Makutsi was about to marry, was she not? And was she not about to marry into the furniture trade?

"Phuti Radiphuti!" Mma Ramotswe exclaimed.

Mma Makutsi looked up sharply. "Phuti?"

"Your fiancé, Mma," went on Mma Ramotswe. "Does he do office furniture as well as house furniture?"

Mma Makutsi looked down at her shoes. *Fiancé?* she imagined hearing the shoes say. *We used to be engaged to a pair of men's shoes but we haven't seen them for some time! Is it still on, Boss?*

Mma Ramotswe smiled across her desk. "I wouldn't expect a new filing cabinet for nothing," she said. "But he could give us a trade price, could he not? Or he would know where we could get it cheaply." She noticed Mma Makutsi's expression, and tailed off. "If he could . . ."

Mma Makutsi seemed reluctant to speak. She looked up at the ceiling for a moment, and then out of the door. "He did not come to my place last night," she said. "I had cooked for him. But he did not come."

Mma Ramotswe caught her breath. She had feared that something like this would happen. Ever since Mma Makutsi had become engaged, she had been concerned that something would go wrong. That had nothing to do with Phuti Radiphuti himself, who seemed a good candidate for marriage, but it had everything to do with the bad luck that seemed to dog Mma Makutsi. There were some people who were badly treated by life, no matter how hard they worked and no matter what efforts they made to better their circumstances. Mma Makutsi had done her very best, but perhaps she would never get any further than she had already got, and would remain an assistant detective, a woman from Bobonong, with large round glasses, and a house that, although comfortable, had no hot water supply. Phuti Radiphuti could have changed everything, but now would not. He would be just another missed opportunity, another reminder of what might have been had everything been different.

"I think that he must have been working late," said Mma Ramotswe. "You should call him on the telephone and find out. Yes, just use the office phone. That is fine. Call Phuti."

Mma Makutsi shook her head. "No, I cannot do that. I cannot chase him."

"You're not chasing him," said Mma Ramotswe. "It is not chasing a man just to speak to him on the telephone and ask him why he did not come to your house. Men cannot let women cook for them and not eat the food. Everybody understands that."

This remark did not seem to help, and in the face of Mma Makutsi's sudden and taciturn gloominess, Mma Ramotswe herself became silent.

"That is why I'm late this morning," Mma Makutsi said suddenly. "I could not sleep at all last night."

"There are many mosquitoes," said Mma Ramotswe. "They do not make it easy."

"It had nothing to do with mosquitoes," Mma Makutsi mumbled. "They were sleeping last night. It was because I was thinking. I think it is all over, Mma."

"Nonsense," said Mma Ramotswe. "It is not over. Men are very strange—that is all. Sometimes they forget to come to see ladies. Sometimes they forget to get married. Look at Mr J.L.B. Matekoni. Look at how long it took him to get round to marrying me."

"I cannot wait that long," said Mma Makutsi. "I was thinking of being engaged for six months at the most." She reached for a piece of paper on her desk and stared at it. "Now I shall be doing this filing for the rest of my life."

Mma Ramotswe realised that she could not allow this self-pity to continue. That would only make it worse, in her view. So she explained to Mma Makutsi that she would have to seek out Phuti Radiphuti and reassure him. If she did not wish to do that, then she herself, Mma Ramotswe, could do it for her. Her offer was not taken up, but she repeated it, and it was reflected upon. Then the working day began. It was the day on which bills were due to be sent out, and that was always an enjoyable experience. If only there were a day on which bills were all returned, fully paid, that would be even more enjoyable. But the working world was not like that, and there were always more that went out than came in, or so it seemed. And in this sense, Mma Ramotswe mused, the working world reflected life; which was an adage worthy of Aunty Emang herself, even if she was not quite sure whether it was true or not.

THE BILLS ALL TYPED UP and sealed in their neat white envelopes, Mma Ramotswe remembered that she had something that she wanted to show to Mma Makutsi. Reaching into the old leather bag that she used for carrying papers and lists and the one hundred and one other accoutrements of her daily life, she extracted the letter which Mma Tsau had handed over to her the previous day. She crossed the room and handed it to Mma Makutsi.

"What do you make of this?" she said.

Mma Makutsi unfolded the letter and laid it on the desk before her. The paper, she noted, was crumpled, which meant that somebody could have crunched it up and tossed it away. This was not a cherished letter. This was a letter which had brought only anger and fear.

"So, Mma Tsau," Mma Makutsi read out. "So there you are in that good job of yours. It is a good job, isn't it? You have lots of people working for you. You get your cheque at the end of the month. Everything is fine for you, isn't it? And for that husband of yours too. He is very happy that you have this good job, as he can go and eat for nothing, can't he? It must be very nice to eat for nothing in this life. There are very few people who can do that, but he is one.

"But, you see, I know that you are stealing food for him. I saw him getting fatter and fatter, and I thought: that's a man who is eating for nothing! I could tell that. Of course you wouldn't want other people to know that, and so, you listen to me, listen carefully please: I will be getting in touch with you about how you can keep me from telling anybody about this. Don't worry—you'll hear from me."

When she had finished reading out the letter, Mma Makutsi looked up. Her earlier expression of defeat, brought on by Phuti Radiphuti's non-appearance and by her contemplation of her future, had been replaced by one of anger. "That's blackmail," she said. "That's . . . that's . . ." Her outrage had got the better of her; there were no words strong enough to describe what she felt.

"That's simple wickedness," supplied Mma Ramotswe. "Even if Mma Tsau is a thief, the writer of that letter is much worse."

Mma Makutsi was in strong agreement with this. "Yes. Wickedness. But how are we going to find out who wrote it? It's anonymous."

"Such letters always are," said Mma Ramotswe.

"Have you got any ideas?"

Mma Ramotswe had to confess that she had none. "But that doesn't mean that we shall not find out," she said. "I have a feeling that we are very close to that person. I don't know why I feel that, but I am sure that we know that lady."

"A lady?" asked Mma Makutsi. "How do we know it's a lady?"

"I just feel it," said Mma Ramotswe. "That's a woman's voice."

"Are you sure that that's not just because I was reading it?" said Mma Makutsi.

Mma Ramotswe replied with care. No, it was not just that. The voice—the voice inside the letter—was the voice of a woman. And, as she explained to Mma Makutsi, she had the feeling, vague and elusive though it might be, that she *knew* this woman.

CHAPTER TEN

YOU ARE FRIGHTENED

OF SOMETHING

THAT AFTERNOON Mma Ramotswe made one of her lists. She liked to do this when life seemed to be becoming complicated, which it was now, as the mere fact of listing helped to get everything into perspective. And there was more to it than that; often the listing of a problem produced a solution, as if the act of writing down the issues gave the unconscious mind a nudge. She had heard that sleep could have the same effect. "Go to sleep on a problem," Mr J.L.B. Matekoni had once advised her, "and in the morning you will have your answer. It always works." He had then proceeded to describe how he had gone to sleep wondering why a rather complicated diesel engine would not fire and had dreamed that night of loose connections in the solenoid. "And when I got to the garage that morning," he said, "there it was—a very bad connection, which I replaced. The engine fired straightaway."

So that was what he dreamed about, thought Mma Ramotswe. Diesel engines. Solenoids. Fuel pipes. Her dreams were quite different. She often dreamed of her father, the late Obed Ramotswe, who had been such a kind man, and a loving one; a man whom everybody respected because he was such a fine judge of cattle, but also because he showed in all his actions the dignity which had been the hallmark of the Motswana of the old school. Such men knew their worth, but did not flaunt it. Such men could look anybody in the eye without flinching; even a poor man, a man with nothing, could stand upright in the presence of those who had wealth or power. People did not know, Mma Ramotswe felt, just how much we had in those days—those days when we seemed to have so little, we had so much.

She thought of her father, the Daddy as she called him, every day. And when she had those dreams at night, he was there, as if he had never died, although she knew, even in the dream, that he had. One day she would join him, she knew, whatever people said about how we came to an end when we took our last breath. Some people mocked you if you said that you joined others when your time came. Well, they could laugh, those clever people, but we surely had to hope, and a life without hope of any sort was no life: it was a sky without stars, a landscape of sorrow and emptiness. If she thought that she would never again see Obed Ramotswe, then it would make her shiver with loneliness. As it was, the thought that he was watching gave a texture and continuity to her life. And there was somebody else she would see one day, she hoped—her baby who had died, that small child with its fingers that had grasped so tightly around hers, whose breathing was so quiet, like the sound of the breeze in the acacia trees on an almost-still day, a tiny sound. She knew that her baby was with the late children in whatever place it was that the late children went, somewhere over there, beyond the Kalahari, where the gentle white cattle allowed the children to ride upon their backs. And when the late mothers came, the children would flock to them and they would call to them and take them in their arms. That was what she hoped, and it was a hope worth having, she felt.

But this was a time for making lists, not for dreaming, and

she sat at her desk and wrote down on a piece of paper, in order of their priority, the various matters which concerned her. At the top of the list she simply wrote *blackmail*, and under that she left a blank space. This was where ideas might be noted, and a few words were immediately scribbled in: *Who could know?* Then below that there was *Mr Polopetsi*. Mr Polopetsi himself was not a problem, but Mma Ramotswe had been moved by his description of his wealthy uncle and his cutting out of his nephew. That was an injustice, in her view, and Mma Ramotswe found it hard to ignore injustice. Under Mr Polopetsi's name she wrote: *Mean uncle—speak to him?* Then there was *Mokolodi*, under which was written: *something very odd going on.* And then, finally, almost as an afterthought, she wrote: *Phuti Radiphuti: Could I say something to him about Mma Makutsi?* Her pencil poised at the end of the last question, she then added: *Mind own business?* And finally, she wrote: *Find new shoes.* That was simple, or at least it sounded simple; in reality the question of shoes could be a complicated one. She had been meaning for some time to buy herself a pair of shoes to replace the ones which she always wore to the office and which were becoming a bit down-at-heel. Traditionally built people could be hard on shoes, and Mma Ramotswe sometimes found it difficult to get shoes which were sufficiently well constructed. She had never gone in for fashionable shoes—unlike Mma Makutsi, with her green shoes with the sky-blue linings—but she wondered now whether she should not follow her assistant's lead and choose shoes which were perhaps just slightly more elegant. It was a difficult decision to make, and it would require some thought, but Mma Makutsi might help her, and this would at least take her mind off her problems with Phuti Radiphuti.

She looked at her list, sighed, and let the slip of paper fall from her hand. These were difficult issues, indeed, and not one

of them, as far as she could see, involved a fee. The trickiest one
was undoubtedly the blackmail problem, and now that she had
established that Poppy was unlikely to lose her job—for which
she could hardly charge very much, if anything—there was no
financial reason to become further involved. There was a moral
reason, of course, and that would inevitably prevail, but the set-
ting of wrong to right often brought no financial reward. She had
sighed, but it was not a sigh of desperation; she knew that there
would be other cases, lucrative ones in which bills could be sent
to firms that could well afford to pay. And had they not just
posted a whole raft of such bills, each of which would bring in a
comfortable cheque? And was there not an awful lot of banging
and clattering going on in the garage next door, all of which
meant money in the till and food on several tables? So she could
afford to spend the time, if she wanted to, on these unremunera-
tive matters, and she need not feel bad about it.

She picked up the list again and looked at it. Blackmail was
too difficult. She would come back to it, she knew, but for now
she felt like dealing with something which was more manageable.
The word *Mokolodi* stood out on the page. She looked at her
watch. It was three o'clock. She had nothing to do (ignoring, for
the moment, everything else on the list), and it would be pleasant
to drive down to Mokolodi and talk to her cousin perhaps and see
whether she could find out what was happening down there. She
could take Mma Makutsi with her for company; but no, that
would not be much fun, with Mma Makutsi in her current
mood. She could go by herself or, and here another possibility
came to mind, she could take Mr Polopetsi. She was keen to
train him to do the occasional piece of work for the agency, as
well as the work that he did for the garage. He was always interesting company and would keep her entertained on the short
drive south.

"I HAVE NEVER BEEN to this place," said Mr Polopetsi. "I have heard of it, but I have never been here."

They were no more than a few minutes away from the main gate of Mokolodi, with Mma Ramotswe at the wheel of the van and Mr Polopetsi in the passenger seat, his arm resting on the sill of the open window as he looked with interest at the passing landscape.

"I do not like wild animals very much," he continued. "I am happy for them to be there, out in the bush, but I do not like them to be too close."

Mma Ramotswe laughed. "Most people would agree with you," she said. "There are some wild animals that I would prefer not to come across."

"Lions," said Mr Polopetsi. "I don't like to think that there are things which would like to have me for breakfast." He shuddered. "Lions. Of course, they would probably go for you first, Mma Ramotswe, rather than me." He made the remark without thinking, almost as a joke, and then he realised that it was not in very good taste. He glanced quickly at Mma Ramotswe, wondering whether she had missed what he had said. She had not.

"Oh?" she said. "And why would a lion prefer to eat me rather than you, Rra? Why would that be?"

Mr Polopetsi looked up at the sky. "I'm sure that I'm wrong," he said. "I thought that they might eat you first because . . ." He was about to say that it was because he would be able to run faster than Mma Ramotswe, but he realised that the reason that he would be able to run faster was because she was too large to run fast, and that she would think that he was commenting on her size, which was the real reason for his original remark. Of course any lion would prefer Mma Ramotswe, in the same way as any customer in a butcher's shop would prefer a tasty rump steak to a scrap of lean meat. But he could not say that either, and so he was silent.

"Because I'm traditionally built?" prompted Mma Ramotswe.

Mr Polopetsi raised his hands in a defensive gesture. "I did not say that, Mma," he protested. "I did not."

Mma Ramotswe smiled at him reassuringly. "I know you didn't, Rra," she said. "Don't worry. I don't mind. I've been thinking, you know, and I've decided that I might go on a diet."

They had now arrived at the Mokolodi gate, where stone-built rondavels guarded the entrance to the camp. This gave Mr Polopetsi the respite he needed: there need be no further talk of lions or diets now that they had people to talk to. But he would not put to the back of his mind the extraordinary news which Mma Ramotswe had so casually imparted to him and which he would breathlessly pass on to Mma Makutsi the moment he saw her. It was news of the very greatest import: if Mma Ramotswe, stern and articulate defender of the rights of the fuller-figured as she was, could contemplate going on a diet, then what would happen to the ranks of the traditionally built? They would be thinned, he decided.

MMA RAMOTSWE HAD TOLD Mr Polopetsi that there was something brewing at Mokolodi. She could not be more specific than that, as that was all she knew, and she wondered whether, as a man, he would understand. It seemed to her that men were often unaware of an atmosphere and could assume that all was well when it very clearly was not. This was not the case with all men; there were some who were extremely intuitive in their approach, but many men, alas, were not. Men were interested in hard facts, and sometimes hard facts were simply not available and one had to make do with feelings.

Mr Polopetsi looked puzzled. "So what do you want me to do?" he asked. "Why are we here?"

Mma Ramotswe was patient. "Private detection is all about soaking things up," she said. "You speak to people. You walk around with your eyes wide open. You get a feel for what's happening. And then you draw your conclusions."

"But I don't know what I'm meant to be reaching conclusions about," protested Mr Polopetsi.

"Just see what you feel," said Mma Ramotswe. "I'm going to talk to a relative of mine. You just . . . just walk about the place as if you're a visitor. Have a cup of tea. Look at the animals. See if you *feel* anything."

Mr Polopetsi still looked doubtful, but he was beginning to be intrigued by the assignment. It was rather like being a spy, he thought, and that was something of a challenge. When he was a boy he had played at being a spy and had positioned himself beneath a neighbour's window and listened to the conversation within. He had noted down what was said (the conversation had mostly been about a wedding which was going to take place the following week), and he was in the middle of writing when a woman came out of the house and shouted at him. Then she had hit him with a broom, and he had run away and hidden in a small cluster of paw-paw trees. How strange it was, he thought, that here he was now doing what he had done as a boy, although he could not see himself crouching beneath a window. If Mma Ramotswe expected him to do that, then she would have to think again; she could crouch under windows herself, but he would certainly not do that, even for her.

MMA RAMOTSWE'S RELATIVE, the nephew (by a second marriage) of her senior uncle, was the supervisor of the workshop.

Leaving Mr Polopetsi in the parking place, where he stood, rather awkwardly, wondering what to do, she made her way down the track that led to the workshops. This track took her past a small number of staff houses, shady buildings finished in warm earth, with comfortable windows of the traditional type—eyes for the building, thought Mma Ramotswe; eyes that made the buildings look human, which is how buildings should look. And then, at the bottom of the track, close to the stables, was the workshop, a rambling set of buildings around a courtyard. With its grease and its working litter—an old tractor, engine parts, the metal bars of an animal cage awaiting welding—it had some of the feel of Tlokweng Road Speedy Motors, the sort of place in which one might expect the wife of a mechanic to feel at home. And Mma Ramotswe did. Had Mr J.L.B. Matekoni himself strolled out of a doorway, wiping his hands on a piece of lint, she would not have been surprised; instead of him, though, it was her relative, looking at her in surprise, and breaking into a broad grin.

They exchanged family news, standing there in the courtyard. Was his father well? No, but he was still cheerful, and spent a lot of his time talking about the old days. He had talked about Obed Ramotswe recently, and still missed his advice on cattle. Mma Ramotswe lowered her eyes; there was nobody who knew more about cattle than her late father, and it touched her that this knowledge should still be talked about; wise men are remembered, they always are.

And what was she doing? Was it true that she had a detective agency, of all things? And that husband of hers? He was a good man, as everybody knew. There was a local man whose car had broken down in Gaborone and who had been helped by Mr J.L.B. Matekoni, who had seen this man standing in despair beside that car and who had stopped and towed him back to the garage, where he had fixed the car—for nothing. That had been talked about.

So the conversation continued, until Mma Ramotswe, hot under the slanting afternoon sun, had mopped her brow and had been invited inside for a mug of tea. It was the wrong sort of tea, of course, but it was still welcome, even if it did cause a slight fluttering of the heart, which ordinary tea or coffee always did to her.

"Why have you come out here?" the relative asked. "I heard that you were here the other day. I was in town. I did not see you."

"I was collecting a part for Mr J.L.B. Matekoni," she explained. "Neil had found it for him. But I didn't manage to speak to anybody. So I thought I would come back and say hallo."

The relative nodded. "You are always welcome," he said. "We like to see people out here."

There was a silence. Mma Ramotswe picked up the mug of tea he had prepared and took a sip. "Is everything going well here?" she asked. It was an innocent-seeming question, but one which was asked with an ulterior motive, and it did not sound innocent to her.

The relative looked at her. "Going well? I suppose so."

Mma Ramotswe waited for him to say something else, but he did not. She saw, though, that he was frowning. People did not normally frown when they said that something was going well.

"You look unhappy," she said.

This remark seemed to take the relative by surprise. "You noticed?" he said.

Mma Ramotswe tapped the table with a finger. "That is what I am paid to do," she said. "I am paid to notice things. Even when I am off duty, I notice things. And I can tell that there's something uncomfortable going on here. I can tell."

"What can you tell, Mma Ramotswe?" said the relative.

Mma Ramotswe patiently explained to him about atmospheres, and about how one could always tell when people were frightened. It showed in their eyes, she said. Fear always showed in the eyes.

The relative listened. He looked away as she spoke, as people will do when they did not wish their eyes to be seen. This confirmed her impression.

"You yourself are frightened of something," she coaxed, her voice low. "I can tell."

The relative glanced back at her. His look was a pleading one. He rose to his feet and closed the door. There was only one small window in the room, a small rectangle of sky, and they were immediately enveloped in gloom. It was slightly cold too, as the floor of the room was of uncovered concrete and the warming sunlight which had slanted in through the door was now excluded. In the background, against one of the walls, a tap that ran into a dirty basin dripped water.

Mma Ramotswe had suspected it, but had put the thought to the back of her mind. Now, to her dismay, the possibility returned, and it chilled her. She could cope with anything. She understood very well what people were capable of, how cruel they could be, how perverse in their selfishness, how ruthless; she could cope with all that, and with all the general misfortunes of life. She was not afraid of human wickedness, which was usually tawdry and banal, something to be pitied, but there was one thing, one dark thing, which frightened her no matter how much she saw it for what it was. That thing, she now felt, might be present here, and it might explain why people were frightened.

She reached out and took her relative's hand. And at that moment she knew that she had been right. His hand was shaking.

"You must tell me, Rra," she whispered. "You must tell me

what it is that is frightening you. Who has done it? Who has put a curse on this place?"

His eyes were wide. "There is no curse," he said, his voice low. "There is no curse . . . yet."

"Yet?"

"No. Not yet."

Mma Ramotswe digested this information in silence. She was convinced that behind this there would be some scruffy witch doctor somewhere, a traditional healer, perhaps, who had found the profits of healing too small and had taken to the selling of charms and potions. It was a bit like a lion turning man-eater: an old lion, or an injured one, would discover that he could no longer run down his usual prey and turned to those slower two-legged creatures for easier pickings. It was easy for a healer to be tempted. *Here's something to make you strong; here's something to deal with your enemies.*

Of course, there was much less of that sort of thing than there used to be, but it still existed, and its effects could be potent. If you heard that somebody had put a curse on you, then however much you might claim not to believe in all that mumbo-jumbo, you would still feel uneasy. This was because there was always a part of the human mind that was prepared to entertain such no-tions, particularly at night, in the world of shadows, when there were sounds that one could not understand and when each one of us was in some sense alone. Some people found this intoler-able, and succumbed, as if life itself simply gave out in the face of such evil; and when this happened, it served only to strengthen the belief of some that such things worked.

She looked at the relative, and saw his terror. She put her arms around him and whispered something. He looked at her, hesitated, and then whispered something in return.

Mma Ramotswe listened. On the roof, a small creature, a lizard perhaps, scuttled across the tin, making a tiny tapping sound. Rats did that, thought Mma Ramotswe; made such a sound at night in the rafters, which could wake up a light sleeper and leave her tossing and turning in the small hours of the morning.

The relative finished, and Mma Ramotswe moved her arms. She nodded, and placed a finger against his lips in a gesture of conspiracy.

"We don't want him to know," he said. "Some of us are ashamed of this."

Mma Ramotswe shook her head. No, she thought, one need not be ashamed about such a thing. Superstitions persist. Anybody—even the most rational people—can be a little worried about things like that. She had read that there are people who throw salt over their shoulder if they spilled some, or who would not walk under ladders, or sit in any seat numbered thirteen. No culture was immune to that sort of thing, and there was no reason for African people to be ashamed of such beliefs, just because they did not sound modern.

"You need not feel ashamed," she said. "And I shall think of some way of dealing with this. I shall think of some tactful way."

"You are very kind, Mma Ramotswe," he said. "Your late father would have been proud of you. He was a kind man too."

It was the most generous remark that anybody could possibly have made, and for a moment Mma Ramotswe was unable to respond. So she closed her eyes and there came to her, unbidden, the image of Obed Ramotswe, standing before her, holding his hat in his hands, and smiling. He was there for a moment, and then the image faded and was gone, leaving her alone, but not alone.

THAT WAS NOT the only encounter Mma Ramotswe had at
Mokolodi that day. From the workshop she walked up the path to
the restaurant next to the office. A few visitors, clad in khaki with
field guides stuffed into pockets, sat at tables set out on the plat-
form in front of the restaurant. At one table, a woman smiled at
Mma Ramotswe and waved, and she returned the greeting
warmly. It pleased her to see these visitors, who came to her country and seemed to fall head over heels in love with it. And why
should they not do this? The world was a sad enough place and it
needed a few points of light, a few places in which people could
find comfort, and if Botswana was one of these, then she was
proud of that. *If only more people knew*, thought Mma Ramotswe.
*If only more people knew that there was more to Africa than all the
problems they saw. They could love us too, as we love them.*

The woman stood up. "Excuse me, Mma," she said. "Would
you mind?"

She pointed to her friend, a thin woman with a camera
around her neck. Such thin arms, thought Mma Ramotswe, with
pity; like the arms of a praying mantis, like sticks.

Mma Ramotswe did not mind, and gestured to the woman
to stand beside her while the other woman took her camera from
its case.

"You can stand here with me, Mma," she said to the woman.

The woman joined her, standing close to her. Mma Ramotswe
felt her arm against hers, flesh against flesh, warm and dry as the
touch of human flesh so often and so surprisingly is. She had
sometimes thought that this is what snakes said about people:
*And, do you know, when you actually touch these creatures they
aren't slimy and slippery, but warm and dry?*

She moved, so that they were now standing arm in arm: two ladies, she thought, a brown lady from Botswana and a white lady from somewhere far away, America perhaps, somewhere like that, some place of neatly cut lawns and air conditioning and shining buildings, some place where people wanted to love others if only given the chance.

The photograph was taken, and the thin woman with the camera asked if she might hand over the camera and in turn stand beside Mma Ramotswe, to which Mma Ramotswe readily agreed. And so they stood together, and Mma Ramotswe took her arm too, but was afraid that she might break it, so fragile it seemed. This woman was wearing a heavy scent, which Mma Ramotswe found pleasant, and she wondered whether she might one day be able to wear such a perfume and leave a trail of exotic flowers behind her, as this thin woman must.

They said goodbye to one another. Mma Ramotswe noticed that the first woman was fumbling with the camera as she gave it back to her friend. But she managed to get it back into its case, and as Mma Ramotswe walked away, this woman followed her and took her aside.

"That was very kind of you, Mma," she said. "We are from America, you see. We have come to your country to see it, to see animals. It is a very beautiful country."

"Thank you," said Mma Ramotswe. "I am glad that . . ."

The foreign woman reached out and took her hand. Again there was this feeling of dryness. "My friend is very ill," she said, her voice lowered. "You may not have noticed it, but she is not well."

Mma Ramotswe cast a glance in the direction of the thin woman, who was busying herself with the pouring of orange juice from a jug on their table. She noticed that even the lifting of the jug seemed an effort.

"You see," went on the other woman, "this trip is a sort of farewell. We used to go everywhere together. We went to many places. This will be our last trip. So thank you for being so kind and having your photograph taken with us. Thank you, Mma."

For a moment Mma Ramotswe stood quite still. Then she turned and walked back to the table, to stand beside the woman, who looked up at her in surprise. Mma Ramotswe went down on her haunches, squatting beside the thin woman, and slipped an arm around her shoulder. It was bony beneath the thin blouse, and she was gentle, but she hugged her, carefully, as one might hug a child. The woman reached for her hand, and clasped it briefly in her own and pressed it, and Mma Ramotswe whispered very quietly, but loudly enough for the woman to hear, *The Lord will look after you, my sister*, and then she stood up and said goodbye, in Setswana, because that is the language that her heart spoke, and walked off, her face turned away now, so that they should not see her tears.

CHAPTER ELEVEN

YOU WILL BE VERY HAPPY
IN THAT CHAIR

MMA MAKUTSI LOOKED at her watch. Mma Ramotswe and Mr Polopetsi were away on their trip to Mokolodi—she had felt slightly irritated that Mma Ramotswe should have chosen him to accompany her rather than herself; but she should not begrudge him the experience, she reminded herself, particularly if he was in due course to become her own assistant, an assistant–assistant detective. With the two of them gone for the rest of the afternoon and everything in the office, filing and typing, up-to-date, there was no real reason for her to stay at her desk now that it was four o'clock. In the garage itself, Mr J.L.B. Matekoni had finished the work he had been doing on a customer's persnickety French car and had sent the apprentices home. He would probably stay for an hour or so and clear up; if the telephone went, then he could answer it and take a message. It was unlikely to ring, though, as clients very rarely got in touch in the late afternoon. The morning was the time of important telephone calls, as it was at the start of the day that people plucked up the courage to contact a private detective; for an act of courage was what it often was, an admission of a troubling possibility, something suppressed and not thought about, something fretted over and dreaded. The morning brought the strength to tackle such matters; the dying hours of the day were hours of defeat and resignation.

Yet here was Mma Makutsi, in the late afternoon, reaching a decision which required considerable courage. She had been putting off doing anything about Phuti Radiphuti, but now she felt that she should seek him out and see what he had to say about his failure to appear for dinner the previous night. It had suddenly occurred to her that there might be a perfectly reasonable explanation for his absence. People got days mixed up; she herself had spent an entire Tuesday last week under the impression that it was a Wednesday, and if she could do that—she who was so organised in her personal life, thanks to that early, invaluable training at the Botswana Secretarial College—then how easy it would be for a man who had a whole business to run to get the days mixed up. If that had happened, then Phuti might have gone to eat at his father's house, and his father would not have found anything amiss, even if it was the wrong day for his meal with him, as most of the time these days the old man seemed to be unaware of what day of the week it was. His memory of the distant past, of old friends, of much-loved cattle; all those memories which such people carried of the early days, of the days of the Protectorate, of Seretse Khama's father, of times even earlier than that; that was all still there. But now the recent past, the crowded, hurried present, seemed to pass him by. She had seen this before, in others; he would not have pointed out to Phuti that this was not his day for coming to eat.

The thought that Phuti might merely have mistaken the day cheered her, but only briefly. Phuti went to eat at his father's house on a Sunday, and it was unlikely that he would have mistaken a

Sunday for any other day, as he did not go to work on a Sunday. If, then, he had mixed the days up and gone to eat elsewhere, it could only have been because he had gone to either his sister's or his aunt's house, as those were the only other houses where he went to eat. Neither the aunt nor the sister would have failed to point out to him that he had come to them on the wrong day. Both were very well aware of what day of the week it was, especially the aunt. That aunt, who had played an important role in the building up of the family furniture business, was noted for the acuity of her mind. Phuti himself had told Mma Makutsi how his aunt had an uncanny ability for remembering the details of what everything cost, and this applied not only to present-day prices, but to prices going back to the days before independence. She knew, for example, what the traders in the local store used to ask for paraffin in those silver-coloured jerry cans, and how much a large tin of Lyons golden syrup or a can of Fray Bentos bully beef cost in the late nineteen-fifties; or Lion matches, for that matter, or a Supersonic Radio imported from the radio factory in Bulawayo. Such an aunt would have informed Phuti that he was in the wrong house on the wrong day, had he come to her door unexpectedly.

No, she realised that this was clutching at straws; Phuti Radiphuti had not come to dinner because he had gone cool on her after her feminist disclosure. He had been frightened off, he had been discouraged by the thought that he would have to live with a feminist who would nag and bully him. Whatever the rights and wrongs of it were, some men, and he must be one of them, wanted women who did not make them feel guilty for wanting the things that they wanted. And she should have sensed that, she told herself. Phuti Radiphuti so obviously had a confidence problem, with his speech impediment and his hesitant ways, and of course such a man would not want to marry a woman who would be too forceful. He would want a woman who looked up to him, just a little, and who made him feel manly. She should have understood that, she realised, and she should have built him up rather than made him feel threatened.

She looked at her watch again, and then she looked down at her shoes. *Don't look at us*, they seemed to be saying. *Don't look at us, Miss Feminist!* There was clearly no help from that quarter; there never was. She would have to sort her troubles out by herself, and that meant that she would have to go right now, without any further delay, to the Double Comfort Furniture Shop and speak to Phuti before he left work. She would ask Mr J.L.B. Matekoni to drive her there; he was a kind man, and never turned down a request for a favour. And then an idea occurred. Mma Ramotswe had spoken about the need to get Mr J.L.B. Matekoni a new chair. She could go with him to the store on the pretext of helping him to choose this chair. And in that way she could speak to Phuti without giving him the impression that she had come specially to see him.

She left her desk and made her way into the garage, where she found Mr J.L.B. Matekoni standing at the entrance, staring out on to the Tlokweng Road. He was wiping his hands on an old cloth, almost absent-mindedly, as if he was thinking about something much more important than the problem of oil on the skin.

"I am glad to see that you have nothing to do, Rra," she said, as she came up behind him. "I have had an idea."

Mr J.L.B. Matekoni turned round and looked at her vacantly. "I was very far away," he said. "I was thinking."

"I have been thinking too," said Mma Makutsi. "I was thinking about that new chair which Mma Ramotswe said that she wanted to buy you."

Mr J.L.B. Matekoni tucked the piece of cloth into his pocket. "It would be good to be able to sit comfortably again," he said. "I cannot find a comfortable position in any of the chairs in Zebra Drive. I don't know what has happened to them. They are full of lumps and springs."

Mma Makutsi knew very well what had happened to the furniture in Zebra Drive, but did not want to say as much. She had always suspected that Mma Ramotswe was hard on anything with springs—look at the way in which the tiny white van listed to one side (the driver's side)—and then there was her office chair, which, although it had no springs, also had a marked inclination to the right, where one of the legs had buckled slightly under Mma Ramotswe's traditional form.

"You will be very comfortable in a new chair," she said. "And I think we should go off to the store right now to take a look. Not to buy anything, of course—that can wait until Mma Ramotswe has the time to get out there. But at least we could go and take a look and put your name on something comfortable."

Mr J.L.B. Matekoni glanced at his watch. "It would mean closing the garage early."

"Why not?" said Mma Makutsi. "The apprentices have gone home. Mma Ramotswe and Mr Polopetsi are out at Mokolodi. There is nothing for us to do here."

Mr J.L.B. Matekoni hesitated, but only briefly. "Very well," he said. "We can go out there and then I can drop you at your place afterwards. That will save you a walk."

Mma Makutsi thanked him and went to fetch her things from the office. It would be easy to find a suitable chair for Mr J.L.B. Matekoni, she thought, but how easy would it be to talk to Phuti Radiphuti now that she had frightened him off? And what would he say to her? Would he simply say that he was sorry, but it was now time to end their engagement? Would he find the words to do that, or would he simply stare at her, as he used to do, while his tongue tried desperately to find the words that simply would not come?

AT THE DOUBLE COMFORT FURNITURE SHOP Phuti Radiphuti was standing at the window of his office, looking out over the barn-like showroom. The lay-out had been designed with just that in mind: from where he stood the manager could look down and signal to the staff below. If customers brought children who bounced on the chairs, or if people came to try out the beds and showed signs of lying too long on the comfortable mattresses—which they sometimes did, even those who had no intention at all of buying a bed but who merely wanted a few minutes of comfort before continuing with their shopping tasks elsewhere—he could draw the attention of his assistants to the problem and tell them what to do with a quick hand signal. A finger pointed in the direction of the door meant *out;* the clenching of a fist meant *tell them to keep their children under control;* and the shaking of a finger directed at a member of staff meant *there are customers waiting to be served and you are sitting there talking to your friends.*

He saw Mma Makutsi come in with Mr J.L.B. Matekoni and for a moment he did nothing. He swallowed hard. He had meant to telephone Mma Makutsi and apologise for his failure to turn up last night, but it had been a frantic day, with the visit to the hospital to see his aunt and the list of things that she had given him to do. She had been admitted to the Princess Marina Hospital the previous morning, her face drawn with pain, and they had removed the bloated appendix barely an hour later. It had been close to bursting, they explained, and that would have been perilous. As it was, she had been sitting up in bed that morning, ready to give him instructions, and he had spent much of the rest of the day performing the chores that she had set him. There had been no time to telephone Mma Makutsi, and now here she was in search of an explanation, with Mr J.L.B. Matekoni in support, and he would have to explain everything to her. As he watched her enter the showroom, he felt that familiar knot of anxiety in his stomach—the knot that he had always felt in the past when he had been faced with the need to talk and which always seemed so effectively to paralyse his tongue and vocal cords.

He turned away from the window and went down into the showroom. Mma Makutsi had not spotted him yet, although he had seen her glancing around as if to look for him. Now she was standing before a large armchair covered in black leather and was pointing it out to Mr J.L.B. Matekoni, who was bending down to examine the label attached to the chair. Oddly, Phuti found himself trying to remember the price. It was not expensive, that chair, covered as it was in soft leather, but it was certainly not a bargain. He wondered whether Mr J.L.B. Matekoni was the sort of man to spend a lot of money on a chair. He remembered, of course, that Mma Makutsi had said that Mma Ramotswe had a comfortable house in Zebra Drive and so there was some money there. And perhaps that garage of his on the Tlokweng Road did well, although on the few occasions that he had been there he had not seen signs of great activity.

He made his way past a display of dining-room tables, noting with irritation that somebody had placed a sticky hand print on one of them, the finest in the room, with its highly polished black surface. It would be somebody's child, he thought; a child had reached out and touched the furniture with a hand that had been used to push sweets into his mouth. And the same hand would have been placed on the light red velvet of the sofas on the other side of the table, and they would have to get some of that cleaning fluid . . . He sighed. There was no point getting exercised over this; the country was full of dust and children with sticky hands, and termites that liked nothing better than to eat people's furniture; that was just how it was, and if one worried about it, then it simply made one stammer all the more and feel hot at the back of the neck. Mma Makutsi had told him that he should stop worrying, and he had made a real effort to do so, with the result that he stammered less and felt less hot. He was a fortunate man, he thought, to be engaged to a woman like that. Many women made life worse for their husbands with their nagging and hectoring; one saw such men in the store, defeated men, men with all the cares of the world on their shoulders, looking at the furniture as if it was just one more thing to worry about in lives already full of anxieties.

"That is a very g . . . goo . . . ," said Phuti Radiphuti as he approached Mma Makutsi and Mr J.L.B. Matekoni.

He closed his eyes. There was that sensation of heat at the back of his neck and the familiar, cramping feeling in the muscles of the tongue. He saw the word *good* written down on an imaginary piece of paper; he had only to read it out, as she had told him to do, but he could not. She had read a book about this problem and she had helped him, but now he could not say that this chair was good.

"A ve . . ." He tried again, but it would not come. He should have telephoned her, and told her, and now she would be angry with him and might be having second thoughts about their marriage.

"It looks very comfortable," said Mr J.L.B. Matekoni, reaching out to touch the leather on one of the armrests. "This leather . . ."

"So soft," said Mma Makutsi quietly. "Some of these leather chairs you see are very hard. They are from old, old cows."

"Chairs like that are called cowches," said Mr J.L.B. Matekoni, and laughed.

Mma Makutsi looked at him. Mr J.L.B. Matekoni was a good man, and much admired, but he was not noted for his witty remarks. Now it was possible that he had said something very amusing, and she found herself so taken by surprise that she did not laugh.

Phuti Radiphuti fiddled nervously with a shirt button. Making a conscious effort to relax, he opened his mouth again and made a statement. This time the words came more easily.

"A couch usually has two or three seats," he said. "It is also called a sofa. That chair over there—the big one—is a couch. This one is just a chair."

Mma Makutsi nodded. She had been taken aback by his sudden appearance and now she was uncertain what to do. She had imagined that she would start their conversation by asking after his health, as was polite, but now he had launched into a technical discussion of couches, and so she explained that Mr J.L.B. Matekoni was looking for a new chair and they wondered whether something like this would be suitable.

Phuti Radiphuti listened attentively. Then he turned to Mr J.L.B. Matekoni. "Do you like this chair, Rra?" he asked. "Why don't you sit down in it and see how you feel? It is always best to sit in a chair before you make up your mind."

"I was just looking around," said Mr J.L.B. Matekoni hurriedly. "I saw this chair, but there are many other chairs . . ." He had seen the price on the ticket and had realised that the chair was not cheap. One could get an engine re-bore for the price of that chair.

"Just sit in it, Rra," said Phuti Radiphuti, smiling at Mma Makutsi. "Then you will know for sure if it is a good chair."

He sat down, and Phuti Radiphuti looked at him enquiringly.

"Well, Rra?" said Phuti. "It is very comfortable, isn't it? That chair is made in Johannesburg, in a big chair factory there. There are many chairs like that in Johannesburg."

"It is very comfortable," said Mr J.L.B. Matekoni. "Yes, it is very comfortable. But I must look at some other chairs. I think that there will be many other good chairs in your store."

"Oh, there are," said Phuti. "But when you find a chair that is right, then it is a good idea to choose that one."

Mr J.L.B. Matekoni glanced at Mma Makutsi. He wanted her help now, but she seemed to be having thoughts of her own. She was watching Phuti Radiphuti, staring at him in a way which Mr J.L.B. Matekoni found rather disconcerting. It was as if she was expecting him to say something which he was not saying; some private business between them, he thought, which they should go away and discuss rather than exchanging glances like this. Women always had private business to raise with men, he reflected. There was always something going on in the background—some plotting or mulling over some slight or lack of attention, quite unintended, of course, but noted and filed away for subsequent scrutiny. And much of the time men would be unaware of it, until it all came out in a torrent of recrimination and tears. Fortunately, Mma Ramotswe was not like that, he thought. She was cheerful and direct; but this Mma Makutsi, with her big round glasses, might be different when it came to men, and this poor man, this Phuti Radiphuti, could be in for a difficult time. He would not like to be engaged to Mma Makutsi. Certainly not. He would be terrified of her, with her ninety-seven per cent, or whatever it was, and her determined ways. Poor Phuti Radiphuti.

Mma Makutsi had not said anything since the arrival of Phuti Radiphuti, but now she spoke. "It is very important for a man to have a good chair," she announced. "Men have so many important decisions to make, they need to have good chairs in which to sit and think about these things. I have always thought that."

When she had finished making this observation, she stole a glance at Phuti Radiphuti and then looked down at her shoes. It was almost as if she expected the shoes to contradict her, to reproach her for this sudden departure from the view that she had always held that women made the really important decisions for men, subtly and without letting the men know that they were doing it, but doing it nonetheless. She had enjoyed countless conversations with Mma Ramotswe along those lines, and the two women had always agreed on that point. And now here she was cravenly suggesting that it was men, seated in their comfortable chairs, who did all the deciding. She stared at her shoes for a moment, but they were silent, stunned into speechlessness, perhaps, by the suddenness of the volte-face.

Phuti Radiphuti looked at Mma Makutsi. He was smiling, as a man might when he makes a new and pleasant discovery. "That is true," he said. "But everyone deserves a good chair. Women too. They have important things to think about."

Mma Makutsi was quick to nod her assent. "Yes, they do, but, and you can call me old-fashioned maybe, but I have always thought that men are particularly important. That is just the way I have been brought up, you see."

This remark seemed to make Phuti Radiphuti smile even more. "I hope that you are not too traditional in your views," he said. "Modern men do not like that. They like wives who have their own views."

"Oh, I have those all right," said Mma Makutsi quickly. "I do not let anybody else do my thinking for me."

"That is g . . . g . . . good," said Phuti Radiphuti. He had realised that he had been speaking smoothly and without a stutter, and the realisation made him stumble slightly, but he felt relieved that his omitting to tell Mma Makutsi why he had not arrived for dinner seemed not to have upset her. And now the words came tumbling out, as he explained about his aunt's illness and about his trip to the hospital. She reassured him that although she had noticed his absence, she had realised that he must have a good reason and that she had not been worried.

You're such a liar, Boss, her shoes suddenly said to her. But Mma Makutsi, listening to the man who, once again, was to be her husband, had no time for the grumbling of shoes and did not hear them.

"Now, then," said Phuti Radiphuti. "Shall we look at other chairs, or is that the one you like?"

Mr J.L.B. Matekoni stroked the leather stretched across the arms of the chair. It had a soft feel, and he could imagine himself in the sitting room at Zebra Drive, ensconced in the chair, stroking the leather on the arms and staring up at the ceiling in contemplation. In the background, in the kitchen, Mma Ramotswe would be preparing the evening meal and the tantalising smell of one of her rich stews would come wafting down the corridor. It was a vision of perfection, a glimpse of what heaven might be like, if one ever got there. Was there anything wrong with men sitting in such chairs and thinking such thoughts? he asked himself. Not really, although there did seem to be rather a lot of people about these days who wanted to make men feel guilty about that. He had heard one on the radio recently, and she had said that men were fundamentally lazy and just wanted to be waited on hand and foot by women. What a thing to say! He, for one, was not in the slightest bit lazy. He worked hard all day at Tlokweng Road Speedy Motors, he never let his customers down, and he handed over all the money he earned to Mma Ramotswe for their joint expenses. And if he wanted to sit in a chair from time to time and rest his weary bones, then was there anything wrong with that? Mma Ramotswe liked cooking, and if he went into the kitchen to try to help her, she would chase him out with very little ceremony. No, such people were very unfair about men, and very wrong too. But then he thought of the apprentices, and suddenly he realised that perhaps there was some truth in what had been said. They were the ones who gave men a bad name, with their slipshod ways and their arrogant attitudes towards women. They were the ones.

"So that's the chair you like?" Phuti Radiphuti's question brought Mr J.L.B. Matekoni back to the Double Comfort Furniture Shop and to the realisation that he was sitting in a chair that he would be unlikely to be able to afford.

"I like it," he said. "But I think that perhaps we should look at something that is not quite so costly. I do not think that Mma Ramotswe . . ."

Phuti Radiphuti raised his hands to stop him. "But that chair has just gone on sale," he said. "It is fifty per cent off. Right now. Specially for you."

"Fifty per cent!" exclaimed Mma Makutsi. "That is very good. You must buy that chair, Mr J.L.B. Matekoni. It is a very big bargain."

"But what will Mma Ramotswe . . ."

"She will thank you for it," said Mma Makutsi firmly. "Mma Ramotswe likes a bargain as much as any other woman. She will be very pleased."

Mr J.L.B. Matekoni hesitated. He longed for a comfortable chair. His life had been full of axles and engine parts and grease. It had been a battle, all of it; a battle to keep engines going in spite of the dust and the bumps in the road that were such enemies of machinery; a battle to keep the apprentices from ruining any engine they touched. It had all been a struggle. At the end of the day a chair like this could make up for a lot. It was irresistible.

He looked at Phuti Radiphuti. "Can you deliver it to Zebra Drive?"

"Of course," said Phuti Radiphuti. He reached out and patted the back of the chair. "You will be very happy in that chair, Rra. Very happy."

BLOOD PRESSURE

I F ONE PRESSED Mma Ramotswe on the point, really pressed, she would admit that very little happened in the No. 1 Ladies' Detective Agency. Very little in general, that was; certainly there were spikes of activity, in which suddenly there would be several problems to be looked into at once. These, though, were the exception; normally the issues with which the agency was required to deal were very small ones, which were readily solved by Mma Ramotswe's simple expedient of asking somebody a direct question and getting a direct answer. It was all very well for Clovis Andersen to go on about the complexity of many investigations, and indeed the danger in at least some of them, but that was not really what life in the No. 1 Ladies' Detective Agency was like.

But there were times, thought Mma Ramotswe, when even Clovis Andersen would be impressed by the number of major issues with which she and Mma Makutsi had to deal, and over the days that followed the trip out to Mokolodi, it seemed to her that this was rapidly becoming one such period.

On the morning after she and Mr Polopetsi had paid their

visit, one of those glorious mornings in which the sun is not too
fierce, when the air is clear, and when even the doves in their
leafy kingdoms seem to be more alert and alive than usual; on
that morning Mma Makutsi announced that she could see a
woman standing outside the door of the agency, hesitant about
knocking.

"There is a lady wanting to come in," she said to Mma
Ramotswe. "I think that she is one of the ones who are embarrassed to come to us."

Mma Ramotswe craned her neck to see. "Go and invite her
in," she said. "Poor woman."

Mma Makutsi rose from her desk. Adjusting her glasses,
those big, round glasses that she wore, she made her way to
where she had seen the woman standing.

She greeted their caller politely. Then she asked, "Are you
wanting to come in, Mma? Or are you just standing?"

"I'm looking for Mma Ramotswe," said the young woman.
"Are you that lady?"

Mma Makutsi shook her head. "I am a different lady," she
said. "I am Mma Makutsi. I am the assistant detective."

The young woman glanced at her, and then looked away.
Mma Makutsi noticed that she was fiddling with a handkerchief
that she was holding in her hands, twisting it in her anxiety. I
used to do the same thing, she thought. I used to do exactly the
same thing with my handkerchief when I was anxious. I twisted
it at interviews; I twisted it in examinations. And the thought
made her feel a rush of sympathy for this woman, whoever she was,
and for the problem that had brought her to their doorstep. It
would be a man problem, of course; it so often was. She would
have been treated badly by some man, perhaps by a man to whom
she had lent money. Perhaps she had taken the money from her

employer and then lent it to some worthless man. That happened
so often that it was hardly a matter of remark. And now here was
another case.

Mma Makutsi reached out and touched the young woman
lightly on the arm. "If you come with me, my sister," she said, "I will
take you to Mma Ramotswe. She is sitting inside."

"I do not want to trouble her," said the woman. "She is very
busy."

"She is not busy right now," said Mma Makutsi. "She will be
happy to see you."

"How much does . . ."

Mma Makutsi put a finger to her lips. "We do not need to talk
about that just yet," she said. "It is not as expensive as you think.
And we charge according to how much people can afford to pay.
We do not charge very much."

The reassuring words had their effect, and as she entered the
office with Mma Makutsi, the young woman was visibly more
relaxed. And seeing Mma Ramotswe sitting behind her desk,
beaming at her encouragingly, seemed to allay her fears even more.

"Mma Makutsi will make us some tea," said Mma Ramotswe.
"And I believe we have some doughnuts too! Are there doughnuts
this morning, Mma Makutsi?"

"There are doughnuts," said Mma Makutsi. "I bought three,
just in case." She had bought the third one for herself, to eat on the
way home, but she would happily give it to this young woman who
was now settling into the chair in front of Mma Ramotswe's desk.

"Well," said Mma Ramotswe. "What is it, Mma? What can the
No. 1 Ladies' Detective Agency do for you?"

"I am a nurse," began the young woman.

Mma Ramotswe nodded. This did not surprise her. There was
something about nurses that she could always pick up—a neat-
ness, a clinical carefulness. She could always tell.

"It is a good job," said Mma Ramotswe. "But you have not told me your name yet."

The young woman stared down at her hands, which she had folded across her lap. "Do I have to tell you who I am? Do I have to?"

Mma Ramotswe and Mma Makutsi exchanged glances across the room.

"It would be better if you did," said Mma Ramotswe gently. "We do not speak to other people about what we hear in this room, do we, Mma Makutsi?"

Mma Makutsi confirmed that they did not. But there was still some hesitation from the young woman.

"Look, Mma," said Mma Ramotswe. "We have heard everything that there is to be heard. There is no need to be ashamed."

The young woman gave a start. "But I am not ashamed, Mma," she protested. "I have done nothing wrong. I am not ashamed."

"Good," said Mma Ramotswe.

"You see, I am frightened," said the young woman. "I am not ashamed; I am frightened."

For a few moments, the young woman's words hung in the air. Mma Ramotswe sat at her desk, her elbows resting comfortably on its surface, her shoes slipped off, allowing the cool of the polished concrete floor to chill the soles of her feet. She thought: *This is the second time in two days in which I have heard these words.* First there was her cousin at Mokolodi, and now there was this woman. Fear might be talked about in the clear light of day, when people were going about their business, and when the sun was strong in the sky, and yet it was nonetheless chilling for that. She looked at the woman before her, this nurse who worked in a world of white walls and disinfectant, and who was, in spite of that, preyed upon by something dark and dangerous. Fear was like that; it worked from the inside and was indifferent to what was going on outside.

Mma Ramotswe signalled to Mma Makutsi. The kettle needed to be switched on and tea made. Whatever was troubling this young woman, the making and drinking of tea would help to take her mind off her fears. Tea was like that. It just worked.

"You need not be frightened here," said Mma Ramotswe gently. "We are your friends here. You need not be frightened."

The young woman looked at her for a moment and then she spoke. "My name is Boitelo," she said. "I am Boitelo Mampodi."

Mma Ramotswe nodded encouragingly. "I am glad that you have told me," she said. "Now, Mma, we can have some tea together and you can tell me what is frightening you. You can take your time. Nobody is in a hurry in this place. You can take as long as you like to tell me what this trouble is. Do you understand?"

Boitelo nodded. "I'm sorry, Mma," she said. "I hope that you did not think that I distrusted you."

"I did not think that," said Mma Ramotswe.

"It's just that you are the first person I have talked to about . . . about this thing."

"It is not easy," said Mma Ramotswe. "It is not easy to talk about things that are worrying you. Sometimes we cannot even talk to our friends about these things."

From the back of the room there came the hissing sound of the kettle as it began to bring the water to the boil. Outside, in the branches of the acacia tree that shaded the back wall of the building, a grey dove cooed to its mate. *They mate for life*, thought Mma Ramotswe inconsequentially. *Those doves. For life.*

"Do you mind if I start from the beginning?" asked Boitelo.

This was more than most people did, thought Mma Ramotswe. Most people started at the end, or somewhere around the middle. Very few people put events in order and explained clearly to others what happened. But Boitelo, of course, was a nurse, and nurses knew how to take a history from people, separating unrelated facts from each other and getting to the bottom of a matter that way. She gestured to Boitelo to begin, while Mma Makutsi spooned red bush tea into one tea-pot and black tea into another (for herself). It is important to give the client a choice, thought Mma Makutsi. Mma Ramotswe, by contrast, imagined that everybody would like bush tea, and not everybody did. She, for one, preferred ordinary tea, and so did Phuti Radiphuti. Phuti Radiphuti! Just the thought of him made her feel warm and contented. My man, she thought; I have a man. I have a fiancé. And soon I shall have a husband. Which is more, I suspect, than this poor Boitelo has.

"I AM FROM A SMALL VILLAGE," began Boitelo. "Over that way. Near Molepolole. You will not have heard of it, I think, because it is very small. I trained at the hospital in Molepolole—you know the one? The one they used to call the Scottish Livingstone Hospital. The one where Dr Merriweather worked."

"He was a very good man," said Mma Ramotswe.

Boitelo's reply came quickly. "Some doctors are good men," she said.

There was a note in her voice which alerted Mma Ramotswe. And then she thought: *Yes, that is it!* That is the oldest problem that nurses have. Doctors who make advances to them. This young woman has had a doctor pestering her. That is why she is frightened. It's simple. There is very little new in the affairs of people. The same things happen again and again.

But then Boitelo continued. "Do you think that a doctor can be a criminal, Mma?" she asked.

Mma Ramotswe remembered the doctors she had met all those years ago—those two doctors, twins, involved in a profitable fraud in which they shared only one medical qualification between them. Yes, doctors could be criminals. Those had been criminal doctors; they had shown no concern for the safety of their patients, just like those doctors one read about who deliberately killed their patients as if out of sheer bravado. Those stories were shocking because they represented the most extreme breach of trust imaginable, but it appeared that they were true. And for a moment Mma Ramotswe considered the terrible possibility that Boitelo had found herself working for one of those homicidal doctors, right here in Gaborone. That would be a powerful cause for fear; indeed, just to think of it made her flesh come up in goose bumps.

"Yes," she answered. "I do think that. There have been some very wicked doctors who have even killed their patients." She paused, hardly daring to ask the question. "You haven't stumbled across something like that, Mma?"

She had hoped that Boitelo's answer would be a swift denial, but it was not. For a moment the young woman seemed to dwell on the question, and then at last she answered. "Not quite," she said.

Behind her, Mma Makutsi let out a little gasp. Mma Ramotswe had been to the doctor only a few days earlier and had been given a bottle of small white pills which she had been taking religiously. It would be so easy for a doctor to substitute something fatal, should he wish to do so, in the knowledge that his trusting patient would pop the poison into her mouth. But why would any doctor want to do that? What drove a doctor to kill the very person he was meant to save? Was it a madness of some sort; an urge that people have from time to time to do something utterly bizarre and out of character? She herself had felt that once or twice when she had been suddenly tempted to throw a tea-pot at Mr J.L.B. Matekoni. She had been astonished that such an outrageous thought had even entered her mind, but it had, and she had sat there wondering what would happen if she picked up the tea-pot from the table and threw it across the room at poor Mr J.L.B. Matekoni as he sat drinking his afternoon tea, his head full of thoughts of gearboxes and brakes, or whatever it was that Mr J.L.B. Matekoni's head was full of. Of course she had not done it, and never would, but the thought had been there, an unwelcome visitor to her otherwise quite rational mind. Perhaps it was the same with those strange cases of the doctors who deliberately killed their patients. Perhaps . . .

"Not quite?" asked Mma Ramotswe. "Do you mean . . ."

Boitelo shook her head. "I mean I don't think that the doctor I'm talking about would go up to a patient and inject too much morphine. No, I don't mean that. But I still think that what he is doing is wicked." She paused. "But I was going to start at the beginning, Mma. Would you like me to do that?"

"Yes," said Mma Ramotswe. "And I won't interrupt you again. You just start. But first, Mma Makutsi will give you a cup of tea. It's red bush tea, Mma. Do you mind?"

"This tea is very good for you," said Boitelo, taking the cup which Mma Makutsi was handing her. "My aunt, who is late, used to drink it."

Mma Ramotswe could not help smiling. It seemed strange to say that something was good for one and in the same breath say that one who used it is now late. There need be no connection, of course, but it seemed strange nonetheless. She imagined an advertisement: *Red Bush Tea: much appreciated by people who are late.* That would not be a good recommendation, she felt, whatever the intention behind it.

Boitelo took a sip of the bush tea and put her cup down on the table in front of her.

"After I qualified, Mma," Boitelo went on, "I came to work in the Princess Marina. I became a theatre nurse there, and I think that I was good at the job. But then, after a while, I became tired of standing behind the doctors all the time and passing them things. I also didn't like the bright lights, which I think gave me headaches. And I don't think that they are good for your eyes, those lights. When I came out of the theatre and closed my eyes I could still see bright circles, as if the lights were still there. So I decided to do something different, and I saw an advertisement for a nurse to work in a general practitioner's clinic. I was interested in this. The surgery was not too far from where I lived, and I would even be able to walk there in the cooler weather. So I went for an interview.

"My interview was on a Monday afternoon, after the doctor had finished seeing his patients. I was due to work that day, but I was able to change my duties around so that I was free to go. I went along and there was Dr . . ." She had been on the point of giving the name, but she checked herself.

"You don't have to tell me," said Mma Ramotswe, remembering that Boitelo had confessed to feeling frightened.

Boitelo looked relieved. "The doctor was there. He was very kind to me and said that he was very pleased to see that I had been a theatre nurse, as he thought that such people were hard workers, and that I would be a good person to have in his clinic. Then he spoke about what the job would involve. He asked me if I understood about confidentiality and about not talking to people about things that I might see or hear while I was working in the clinic. I said I did.

"Then he said to me, 'I have a friend who has just had an operation in the Princess Marina. Maybe you can tell me how he is doing.'

"He gave me the name of his friend, who is a well-known person because he plays football very well and is very handsome. I had been on duty for that operation and I was about to say that I thought that it had gone very well. But then I realised that this was a trick and that I should say nothing. So I said, 'I cannot speak about these things. I'm sorry.'

"He looked at me, and for a little while I thought that he was very cross and would shout at me for not answering his question. But then he smiled and he said, 'You are very good at keeping confidences. Most people are not. I think that you will be a very good nurse for this clinic.'"

Boitelo took a further sip of her tea. "I had to work out a month's notice at the Princess Marina, but that was simple enough. Then I started and I found that the work was very enjoyable. I did not have to stand about as I had to do in the theatre, and I was also permitted to do things that nurses sometimes are not allowed to do. He let me do little surgical procedures on people—dealing with an in-growing toe-nail, for example, or freezing off a wart. I liked freezing off warts, as the dry ice made my fingers tingle with the cold.

"I was happy in my work, and I thought that I must have been one of the luckiest nurses in the country, to work for this doctor and to be allowed to do all these things. But then something happened which made me wonder. I was puzzled by something, and I decided to check up on it. And that was when I learned something which made me very worried. I have been worrying about this thing so much that I decided to come and speak to you, Mma Ramotswe, because people say that you are a good woman and that you are very kind to those who come to you with their troubles. That is why I am here."

Mma Ramotswe, listening intently, had allowed her bush tea to become cooler than she liked it. She preferred to drink bush tea when it was fresh from the pot, piping hot, and this cup, now, was lukewarm. Boitelo's story was a familiar one, at least in that it followed a pattern which she had come across so often. Things started well for somebody and then, and then . . . well, then a path was crossed with a person who would change everything. That had happened to her, with her former husband, Note Mokoti, the jazz player and ladies' man who had, for a brief period, transformed her world from one of happiness and optimism to one of suffering and fear. Such people—men like Note—went through life spreading unhappiness about them like weedkiller, killing the flowers, the things that grew in the lives of others, wilting them with their scorn and spite.

As a young woman she had been too naïve to see evil in others. The young, Mma Ramotswe thought, believe the best of people, or don't imagine that people they know, people of their own age, can be cruel or worthless. And then they find out, and they see what people can do, how selfish they can be, how ruthless in their deal-ings. The discovery can be a painful one, as it was for her, but it is one that has to be made. Of course it did not mean that one had to retreat into cynicism; of course it did not mean that. Mma Ramotswe had learned to be realistic about people, but this did not mean that one could not see some good in most people, however much that might be obscured by the bad. If one persisted, if one gave people a chance to show their better nature, and—and this was important—if one was prepared to forgive, then people could show a remarkable ability to change their ways. Except for Note Mokoti, of course. He would never change, even though she had forgiven him, that final time, when he had come to see her and asked her for money and had shown that his heart, in spite of everything, was as hard as ever.

Boitelo was looking at her. Mma Ramotswe thought that the nurse must be wondering what she was thinking. She would have no idea that the woman before her, the traditionally built detective with her cup of rapidly cooling bush tea before her, was dreaming about human nature and forgiveness and matters of that sort.

"I'm sorry, Mma," said Mma Ramotswe. "Sometimes my mind wanders. Something you said made my mind wander. Now it is back. Now it is listening to you again."

"One of the things that I didn't do," continued Boitelo, "was to take the blood pressure of patients. All nurses can do that. There is an instrument which you wind round the patient's arm and then you pump a bulb. You will have had your blood pressure taken, Mma? You will know what I am talking about."

Mma Ramotswe did. Her blood pressure had been taken and had caused her doctor to say something to her about trying to keep her weight down. She had tried for a short time, and somehow had failed. It was difficult. Sometimes doctors did not know how difficult it was. Traditionally built doctors did, of course, but not those young thin doctors, who had no feeling for tradition.

"My blood pressure was a bit high," said Mma Ramotswe.

"Then you should lose weight," said Boitelo. "You should go on a diet, Mma Ramotswe. That is what I have to say to many of the ladies who come to the clinic. Many of them are . . . are the same shape as you. Go on a diet and reduce your salt intake. No biltong or other things with lots of salt in them."

Mma Ramotswe thought that she heard Mma Makutsi snigger at this, but she did not look in her assistant's direction. She had never been told before by a client to go on a diet, and she wondered what Clovis Andersen would make of such a situation. He was always stressing the need to be courteous to the client—indeed, there was a whole chapter on the subject in *The Principles of Private Detection*—but it said nothing, she thought, on the subject of clients who told one to go on a diet.

"I will think about that, Mma," she said politely. "Thank you for the advice. But let us get back to this thing that you found out. What has it got to do with blood pressure?"

"Well," said Boitelo, "I was rather surprised that I was never asked to take the patients' blood pressure. The doctor always did that, and he kept the sphygmomanometer in his room, in a desk drawer. I saw him using it if I came into the room to give him something, but he never let me use it. I thought that maybe it was because he liked pumping up the instrument—you know how men are sometimes a bit like boys in that way—and I did not think too much about it after that. But then one day I used the instrument myself, and that was when I had a big surprise.

"It was a Friday, I think, not that that matters, Mma. But it was because it was a Friday that the doctor was not in the clinic at the time. On Fridays he likes to meet some of his friends for lunch at the President Hotel, and sometimes he is not back until after three o'clock. There are some other Ugandan doctors who work here, and he likes to meet with them. Their lunch sometimes goes on a bit long.

"I never make an appointment for a patient between two and three on a Friday afternoon, to give him time to get back from the hotel. Well, on that Friday the patient for the three o'clock appointment arrived early. It was a man from the Ministry of Water Affairs, a nice man who goes to the church round the corner from my place. I have seen him on Sundays, walking with his wife and their young son to church. Their dog follows them and sits outside the church until the service is over. It is a very faithful dog, that one.

"This man had half an hour to wait, and he started talking to me. He told me that he was worried about his blood pressure and that he had been trying hard to get it down, but the doctor said that it was still too high. The doctor's door was open while this man was saying this, and I saw the sphyg on his desk. So I thought that there would be no harm in my taking his blood pressure, just out of interest, and just to keep up my skills. So I said to the patient that I would do this, and he rolled up the sleeve on his right arm.

"I inflated the band around the arm and looked at the mercury. The pressure was normal in every respect. So I did it again, and I was about to say to the patient that everything was fine. But I stopped and thought, and I realised that if I did this, then he would say to the doctor that I had taken the reading and that it was now normal. I was worried that this would make the doctor cross with me for doing something to a patient without his permission. So I muttered something about not being able to understand these figures and I replaced the instrument before the doctor came back.

"Now, Mma, that was not a busy afternoon and I was able to catch up on the filing of the patient records. Every so often I go through the files just to check up that all the records are in the right order. The doctor gets very cross if he cannot have the records on his desk when a patient comes in to see him. Well, I was sorting out the records and I came across the record of the man who had come for the three o'clock appointment. And I noticed that the latest entry was about the consultation that this man had just had."

Boitelo paused. Mma Ramotswe was sitting quite still, as was Mma Makutsi. The nurse had a simple, direct way of talking, and the two women had been caught up in her narrative.

"I see," said Mma Ramotswe. "The record. Yes. Please go on, Mma. This is a very interesting story."

Boitelo looked down at her hands. "The doctor had taken his blood pressure and had entered the reading. It was very high."

Mma Ramotswe frowned. "Does blood pressure go up and down?"

The nurse shrugged. "It can do. If you are very excited your blood pressure can go right up, but it doesn't seem very likely, does it?"

Mma Makutsi now intervened. "Perhaps there was something wrong with the instrument. Things go wrong, you know, with these complicated machines."

Boitelo half-turned to stare at Mma Makutsi. "These instruments are very simple," she said quietly. "They are not complicated machines."

"Then it must have been a mistake," said Mma Ramotswe. "Does the doctor drink over lunch?"

"He never drinks," said Boitelo. "He says that he does not like the taste of alcohol, and he also says that it is far too expensive. Water is cheaper, he says."

There was a brief silence as Mma Ramotswe and Mma Makutsi contemplated the possibilities. Neither was sure about the significance of the misreading—if that was what it was. It sounded important, but what did it mean? Doctors made mistakes all the time—as everybody did—and why should this make the nurse so anxious? It seemed that an important part of the story was yet to come, and this was what Boitelo now provided.

"I was puzzled by this," she said. "As you said, it could have been a mistake, but now there was something that was making me wonder if something strange was going on. It seemed odd that the doctor should be so determined that I should not take blood pressure and then that he himself should go and make such a mistake. So I decided to carry out a little investigation myself. I have a friend who is a nurse too. She works in another clinic, and she had once told me that there was some old equipment lying about in a cupboard there. I asked her if there was a sphyg, and she said that she would look and see. When she reported back that there was one, I asked her if I could borrow it for a few weeks. She was a bit surprised, but she agreed.

"I hid the sphyg in my drawer at work. And then I waited for my chance, which eventually arrived. I had been paying attention to the medical records now, and each time I got them out for the doctor I looked to see whether it was a high blood pressure case. There were many of them, I noticed, and I began to wonder about them. All of them were on the same drug, which is quite an expensive one. We give them supplies of it from the clinic."

Mma Ramotswe sat up, almost upsetting her cup of cold tea as she did so. "Now, Mma," she exclaimed, "I think that I can already see what is happening here. The doctor is giving false blood pressure readings. He tells patients that they have high blood pressure when they really do not. Then he makes them take the expensive drug, which he provides for them. It must be a very good business for him."

Boitelo stared at her. "No, Mma," she said flatly. "That is not what is happening."

"Then why did he enter the false reading? Why did he do that?"

"It must have been a genuine mistake," said Boitelo.

Mma Ramotswe sighed. "But you said that you yourself were suspicious of it. You didn't think it was a mistake."

Boitelo nodded. "I didn't," she said. "You are right, Mma. I did not. But now I do. You see, I did two further tests. In each case it was while the doctor was busy with somebody else and there was one of these blood pressure patients in the waiting room. I took their blood pressure and then I compared the results I got with the results that the doctor later noted on their records."

"And?"

"And they were the same."

Mma Ramotswe thought for a moment. She was no statistician, but she had read Clovis Andersen on the subject of unusual occurrences. *The fact that something happens once,* the author of *The Principles of Private Detection* had written, *does not mean that it will happen again. And remember that some events are pure one-offs. They are freaks. They are coincidences. Don't base a whole theory on them.* Clovis Andersen was probably right in general, and if he was also right in this particular case, then there was nothing untoward occurring. But if that were so, then why had Boitelo come to see her?

"You are probably wondering what happened," said Boitelo.

"I am, Mma," said Mma Ramotswe. "I am not very sure where this is going. I thought I did, but now . . ."

"Well, I will tell you. I shall tell you what happened. One of our patients had a stroke. It was not a serious stroke, and he recovered very well. But he had a stroke. And he was one of the ones with high blood pressure."

Mma Ramotswe nodded. "I have heard that this is a danger from high blood pressure." She shifted in her chair. That was why that doctor had told her to lose some weight. He had talked about heart problems and strokes, and it had all made her feel most uncomfortable. What use, she wondered, was a doctor who made people feel uncomfortable? Doctors were meant to provide reassurance, which of course made people feel better. Everybody knew that.

"Yes," Boitelo went on. "High blood pressure can lead to strokes. And this patient ended up in hospital for a few days. I don't think that there was any real danger, but the doctor became quite agitated about it. He asked me to get out the patient's records and he kept them with him for a while. Then he gave them back to me for filing."

"And you looked?" asked Mma Makutsi.

Boitelo smiled. "Yes, Mma. I was nosy. I looked."

"And did you see anything unusual?" prompted Mma Ramotswe.

Boitelo spoke slowly, seemingly aware of the dramatic effect that her words were having. "I found that the figures for a blood pressure reading had been changed."

A large fly landed on the table in front of Mma Ramotswe and she watched it as it took a few steps towards the edge. It hesitated and then launched itself into the air again, its tiny buzz just audible. Boitelo had been watching it too, and she swatted ineffectively at it.

"Rubbed out?" asked Mma Ramotswe. "Were there marks on the page?"

"No," answered Boitelo. "There was no sign of that. It must have been done very skilfully."

"Then how could you tell?" challenged Mma Makutsi. "How did you know?"

Boitelo smiled. "Because the patient was the first one whose blood pressure I had taken in the waiting room while the doctor was busy. It was the same person. And I had written down my reading on a scrap of paper which I had put away in my drawer. I remember comparing those figures with the ones which the doctor put on the card that day. They were the same. But now, that very same figure had been changed. A high reading had been changed to a low one."

Boitelo sat back in her chair and looked at Mma Ramotswe. "I think, Mma," she said, "I think that this doctor is doing something very wrong. I went to see somebody in the Ministry of Health and I told him about it. But he said that I had no proof. And I don't think that he believed me anyway. He said that from time to time they had complaints from nurses who did not like the doctor they worked for. He said that they had to be very careful, and until I could come up with something more concrete I should be careful what I said."

She looked at Mma Ramotswe defensively, as if she, too, would pour scorn on her story. But Mma Ramotswe did not do this. She was noting something down on a piece of paper, and she did not react in any way when Boitelo went on to explain that she had brought this matter to the attention of the No. 1 Ladies' Detective Agency out of a sense of public duty and she hoped that in the circumstances there would be no fee, which she would be unable to pay anyway.

CHAPTER THIRTEEN

BLUE SHOES

MMA RAMOTSWE KNEW that she should not have left the office that afternoon. She now had rather more to do than she wanted, and none of the problems which had landed on her desk appeared to have any answer. There was a series of issues, each of them demanding to be resolved but each curiously resistant to solution. There was Mokolodi, which she should do something about sooner or later; there was Mma Tsau and the blackmailing letter; and then there was the question of Mr Polopetsi's mean uncle and his favouritism towards Mr Polopetsi's brother, for whom he had bought a car. She thought about that. No, there was nothing that she could do—just now—about that. The world was imperfect, and there were just too many claims. One day, perhaps, but not now. So that came off the list, which left one remaining item, the most difficult of course: the doctor. She admired Boitelo for coming to see her; many people would just have given up in the face of a wrong which they could not right, but she had brought the issue to her. And Boitelo had been correct, Mma Ramotswe thought, about civic duty. It was her duty not to stand by in the face of evidence of medical wrongdoing; and it was Mma Ramotswe's civic duty to do something now that the issue had been brought to her attention. But it was difficult to think what to do, and, as she often did in such circumstances, Mma Ramotswe decided that the best thing to do would be to go shopping. She often found that ideas came to her when shopping, halfway down the vegetable aisle in the supermarket, or when trying on a skirt—which would inevitably be just a little bit too tight—she would have an idea and what had previously been a log-jam would gradually begin to shift.

"We shall go shopping, Mma Makutsi," she announced after Boitelo had taken her leave. "We shall go downtown."

Mma Makutsi looked up from her desk. She was working on a rather complex matter at the moment, the pursuit of a debtor on behalf of a firm of lawyers. The debtor, a Mr Cedric Disani, had established a hotel which had gone spectacularly bankrupt. It was thought that he had extensive holdings in land, and they now had a list of properties from the land register and were trying to work out which were owned by companies in which he had an interest. It was one of the most testing cases Mma Makutsi had ever been allocated, but at least it had a fee attached to it—a generous one—and this would make up for all the public-spirited work which Mma Ramotswe seemed to be taking on.

"Yes, yes," urged Mma Ramotswe. "You can leave those lists for a while. It will do us both good to get downtown and do some shopping. And maybe we'll have some ideas while we're about it. I always find that shopping clears the head, don't you agree, Mma?"

"And it clears the bank account," joked Mma Makutsi as she closed the file in front of her. "This Mr Cedric Disani must have done a bit of shopping—you should see how much he owes."

"I knew a lady of that name once," said Mma Ramotswe. "She was a very fashionable lady. You used to see her in very expensive clothes. She was a very fancy lady."

"That will be his wife," said Mma Makutsi. "The lawyers told me about her. They said that Mr Disani put a lot of things in her name so that his creditors cannot touch them. They said that she still drives around in a Mercedes-Benz and wears very grand clothing."

Mma Ramotswe made a clucking sound of disapproval. "Those Mercedes-Benzes, Mma—have you noticed how whenever we come across them in our line of work they are driven by the same sort of people? Have you noticed that, Mma?"

Mma Makutsi replied that she had. "I would never get a Mercedes-Benz," she said. "Even if I had the money. They are very fine cars, but people would talk."

Mma Ramotswe, halfway to the door, paused and looked at Mma Makutsi. "You said *Even if I had the money*, Mma. Do you realise that?"

Mma Makutsi looked blank. "Yes," she said. "That is what I said."

"But, Mma," said Mma Ramotswe. "Don't you realise that now you could have a Mercedes-Benz if you wanted one? Remember who you're going to marry. Phuti Radiphuti is very well off with that Double Comfort Furniture Shop of his. Yes, he is well off—not that I really like the furniture that he sells in that shop, Mma. Sorry to say that, but it's not really to my taste."

Mma Makutsi looked at Mma Ramotswe for a moment, and swallowed hard. It had not occurred to her that Mr J.L.B. Matekoni might fail to inform her of his purchase of the new chair, but now it struck her that this was precisely what had happened. And when he eventually came to explain that he had bought a chair, he would reveal, no doubt, that she had taken him there and had encouraged him to make the purchase. She was uncertain as to whether she should tell Mma Ramotswe herself; whether she should make a clean breast of it, or whether she should let matters take their natural course.

"So you would never buy a chair there?" she asked innocently. "Not even if it was on sale? Say, fifty per cent off?"

Mma Ramotswe smiled. "Not even ninety-seven per cent off, Mma. No. I'm sure that the furniture is very good, it's just that it's not for me."

Nor for Mr J.L.B. Matekoni, thought Mma Makutsi ruefully. But what was this about a Mercedes-Benz? Why did Mma Ramotswe think that she might buy a Mercedes-Benz? It was an impossible thought . . . and yet, it was true that Phuti was quite a rich man; perhaps she should get used to being the wife of a man who even if not very wealthy was nonetheless comfortably off by any standards. It was a strange thought. Phuti Radiphuti was so modest and unassuming, and yet he undoubtedly had the resources to live a showier life if he chose to do so.

"When Phuti and I get married," said Mma Makutsi, "we will not act like rich people. We will be just the same as we always have been. That is the way we are."

"And that is very good," said Mma Ramotswe. It was not the Botswana way to be showy. Here it was quietness and discretion that people admired. A great person was a quiet person. Mr J.L.B. Matekoni, for instance; he was a quiet man and a great man too, like many mechanics and men who worked well with their hands. And there were many such men in Africa—men whose lives had been ones of hardship and suffering, but who were great men nonetheless.

MMA RAMOTSWE locked the door of the office behind them and said goodbye to Mr J.L.B. Matekoni. He was bent over the engine of a car, explaining something to the apprentices, who stood up and stared at the two women.

"We are going shopping," said Mma Makutsi, taunting the

young men. "That is what women like to do, you know. They much prefer shopping to going out with men. That is very well known."

The younger apprentice let out a howl of protest. "That is a lie!" he shouted. "Boss, listen to how that woman lies! You cannot have a detective who lies, Mma Ramotswe. You need to fire that woman. Big glasses and all. Fire her."

"Hush!" said Mr J.L.B. Matekoni. "We have plenty of work to do. Let the ladies go shopping if it makes them feel better."

"Yes," said Mma Ramotswe, as she let herself into the tiny white van. "It certainly makes us feel better."

They drove down the Tlokweng Road to the busy round-about. There were hawkers at the side of the road selling rough-hewn stools and chairs, and a woman with a smoking brazier on which maize cobs were being grilled. The smell of the maize, the sharp-sweet smell that she knew so well and which spoke so much of the African roadside, wafted through the window of the tiny white van, and for a moment she was back in Mochudi, a child again, at the fireside, waiting for a cob to be passed over to her. And she saw herself all those years ago, standing away from the fire, but with the wood-smoke in her nostrils; and she was biting into the succulent maize, and thinking that this was the most perfect food that the earth had to offer. And she still thought that, all these years later, and her heart could still fill with love for that Africa that she once knew, our mother, she thought, our mother who is always with us, to provide for us, to nourish us, and then to take us, at the end, into her bosom.

They passed the roundabout and drove on to the busy set of shops that had sprung up near Kgale Hill. She did not like these shops, which were ugly and noisy, but the fact of the matter was that there were many different stores there and their selection of merchandise was better than any other collection of shops in the country. So they would put up with the crowds and the noise and see what the shops had to offer. And it would not be all window-shopping. Mma Ramotswe had long promised herself a pressure cooker, and Mr J.L.B. Matekoni had urged her to buy one. They could look for a pressure cooker, and even if they did not buy it today it would be interesting to see what was on offer.

The two women spent an enjoyable half hour browsing in a shop that sold kitchen equipment. There was a bewildering array of cooking utensils—knives and chopping boards and instruments with which to slice onions into all sorts of shapes.

"I have never needed anything like that to cut up onions," Mma Ramotswe observed. "I have found that a knife is usually enough."

Mma Makutsi agreed with her on this, but made a secret mental note of the name of the implement. When Phuti Radiphuti gave her the money to restock her kitchen—as he had promised to do—then she would undoubtedly buy one of those onion-slicers, even if Mma Ramotswe said that they were unnecessary. Mma Ramotswe was certainly a good cook, but she was not an expert on onions, and if somebody had invented an onion-slicer, then it must have been because there was a need for one.

They left the shop having identified and priced a pressure cooker. "We shall find another shop that sells those cookers," said Mma Ramotswe, "and then we shall compare their prices. It is not good to waste money. Seretse Khama himself said that, you know. He said that we should not waste money."

Mma Makutsi was non-committal. Mma Ramotswe had a habit of quoting Seretse Khama on a wide range of subjects, and she was not at all sure whether her employer was always strictly accurate in this. She had once asked Mma Ramotswe to supply chapter and verse for a particular quotation and had been fobbed off with a challenge. "Do you think I invent his words?"

Mma Ramotswe had asked indignantly. "Just because people are beginning to forget what he said, that doesn't mean that I've forgotten."

Mma Makutsi had left it at that, and now said very little when the late President was quoted. It was a harmless enough habit, she thought, and if it helped to keep alive the memory of that great man, then it was, all in all, a good thing. But she wished that Mma Ramotswe would be a little bit more *historically* accurate; just a bit. The problem was that she had not been to the Botswana Secretarial College, where the motto, proudly displayed above the front entrance to the college, was *Be Accurate*. Unfortunately, there was a spelling mistake, and the motto read *Be Acurate*. Mma Makutsi had spotted this and had pointed it out to the college, but nothing had been done about it so far.

They walked together in the direction of another shop that Mma Ramotswe had identified as a possible stockist of pressure cookers. All about them there were well-dressed crowds, people with money in their pockets, people buying for homes that were slowly beginning to reflect Botswana's prosperity. It had all been earned, every single pula of it, in a world in which it is hard enough to make something of one's country, in a world of selfish and distant people who took one's crops at rock-bottom prices and wrote the rules to suit themselves. There were plenty of fine words, of course—and lots of these came from Africa itself—but at the end of the day the poor, the people who lived in Africa, so often had nothing to show for their labours, nothing. And that was not because they did not work hard—they did, they did—but because of something that was wrong which made it so hard for them to get anywhere, no matter how hard they tried. Botswana was fortunate, because it had diamonds and good government, and Mma Ramotswe was well aware of that, but her pride did not allow her to forget the suffering of others, which was there, not far away, a suffering which made mothers see their children fade away before their eyes, their little bodies thin and rickety. One could not forget that in the middle of all this plenty. One could not forget.

But now Mma Makutsi stopped, and took Mma Ramotswe by the arm, pointing to a shop window. A woman was peering into the window, a woman in a striped blue dress, and for a moment Mma Ramotswe thought that it was this woman who had attracted Mma Makutsi's attention. Was she a client, perhaps, or somebody else who had come to the attention of the No. 1 Ladies' Detective Agency, one of those adulterous wives that men sometimes asked them to follow and report upon? But Mma Makutsi was not pointing at the woman, who now moved away from the window, but to the contents of the window display itself.

"Look, Mma Ramotswe," she said. "Look over there!"

Mma Ramotswe looked into the window. There was a sale of some sort on, with large reductions, the window claimed. Indeed, shouted a sign within, the sale amounted to madness on the part of the shoe shop.

"Bargains," said Mma Ramotswe. "There always seem to be so many bargains."

But it was not the bargain shoes that had made Mma Makutsi stop and look—it was the full-price offerings, all neatly arrayed along a shelf and labelled *Exclusive models, as worn in London and New York*.

"You see that pair over there?" said Mma Makutsi, pointing into the window. "You see that pair? The blue pair?"

Mma Ramotswe's gaze followed the direction in which Mma Makutsi was pointing. There, set aside from the other exclusive models, but still in the category of the exclusive, was a pair of fashionable blue shoes, with delicate high heels and toes which came to a point, like the nose of a supersonic aircraft. It was difficult to see the linings from where they were, but by standing on her tip-toes and craning her neck Mma Makutsi was able to report on their colour.

"Red linings," she said with emotion. "Red linings, Mma Ramotswe!"

Mma Ramotswe stared at the shoes. They were certainly very smart, as objects, that is, but she doubted whether they were much use as shoes. She had not been to London or New York, and it was possible that people wore very fashionable shoes in those places, but she could not believe that many people there would be able to fit into such shoes, let alone walk any distance in them.

She glanced at Mma Makutsi, who was staring at the shoes in what seemed to be a state of near-rapture. She was aware of the fact that Mma Makutsi had an interest in shoes, and she had witnessed the pleasure that she had derived from her new pair of green shoes with sky-blue linings. She had entertained her doubts about the suitability of those particular shoes, but now, beside this pair that she was staring at in the window, those green shoes seemed practicality itself. She drew a breath. Mma Makutsi was a grown woman and could look after herself, but she felt, as her employer and as the person who had inducted her into the profession of private detection, that she had at least some degree of responsibility to ensure that Mma Makutsi did not make too many demonstrably bad decisions. And any decision to buy these shoes would be unambiguously bad—the sort of decision that one would not want a friend to make.

"They are very pretty shoes," Mma Ramotswe said cautiously. "They are a very fine colour, that is certainly true, and . . ."

"And the toes!" interrupted Mma Makutsi. "Look at how pointed those toes are. Look at them." And, as she herself looked, she let out a whistle of admiration.

"But nobody is that shape," said Mma Ramotswe. "I have never met anybody with pointed feet. If your feet were pointed like that, then you would have only one toe." She paused, uncertain as to how her comments were being received; it was difficult to tell. "Perhaps those are shoes for one-toed people. Perhaps they are specialist shoes."

She laughed at her own comment, but Mma Makutsi did not.

"They are not for one-toed people, Mma," she said disapprovingly. "They are very fine shoes."

Mma Ramotswe was apologetic. "I'm sorry, Mma. I know that you do not like to joke about shoes." She looked at her watch. "I think that we should move on now. There is much to do."

Mma Makutsi was still gazing intently at the shoes. "I did not think we had all that much to do," she said. "There is plenty of time to look at pots and pans."

It seemed to Mma Ramotswe that looking at pots and pans, as Mma Makutsi put it, was a rather more useful activity than looking at blue shoes in shop windows, but she did not say this. If Mma Makutsi wished to admire shoes in a window, then she would not spoil her fun. It was an innocent enough activity, after all; like looking at the sky, perhaps, when the sun was going down and had made the clouds copper-red, or looking at a herd of fine cattle moving slowly over the land when rains had brought on the sweet green grass. These were pleasures which the soul needed from time to time, and she would wait for Mma Makutsi until she had examined the shoes from all angles. But a word of caution, perhaps, would not go amiss, and so Mma Ramotswe cleared her throat and said, "Of course, Mma, we must remember that if we have traditionally shaped feet, then we should stick to traditionally shaped shoes."

For a moment, in spite of all the hustle and bustle about the shops, there was a cold silence. Mma Makutsi glanced down at

Mma Ramotswe's feet. She saw the wide-fitting flat shoes, with their sensible buckles, rather like the shoes which Mma Poto-kwane wore to walk around the orphan farm (though perhaps not quite so bad). Then she glanced at her own feet. No, there was no comparison, and at that moment she decided that she must have those blue shoes. She simply had to have them.

They went inside, with Mma Makutsi in the lead and Mma Ramotswe following passively. Mma Ramotswe remained silent during the resulting transaction. She watched as Mma Makutsi pointed to the window. She watched as the assistant reached for a box from a shelf and took out a pair of the blue shoes. She said nothing as Mma Makutsi, seated on a stool, squeezed her foot into one of the shoes, to the encouragement of the assistant who pushed and poked at her foot with vigour. And she remained silent as Mma Makutsi, reaching into her purse, paid the deposit that would have the shoes set aside for her; the precious, hard-earned Bank of Botswana notes being placed down on the counter; those notes with the pictures of cattle, which in their heart of hearts the people of Botswana thought were the real foundation of the country's wealth.

As they left the shop, Mma Ramotswe made amends and told Mma Makutsi that she really thought the blue shoes very beauti-ful. There was no point in disapproving of a purchase once the deed had been done. She remembered learning this lesson from her father, the late Obed Ramotswe, about whom she thought every day, yes, every day, and who had been, she believed, one of the finest men in Botswana. He had been asked for his view of a bull which a man in Mochudi had bought, and although he had already confided in Precious that the bull would not be good for the herd—too lazy, he had said; a bull who would often say to the cows that he was too tired—although that was his view, he had not said that to the new owner.

"That is a bull who will give you no trouble," he had said.

And that, she thought, had been just the right thing to say about that particular bull. But could she say the same thing about Mma Makutsi's new shoes? She thought not. For those shoes would most certainly give Mma Makutsi trouble—the moment she tried to walk anywhere in them. That, thought Mma Ramotswe, was glaringly obvious.

CHAPTER FOURTEEN

AT DINNER

THAT EVENING, Mr Polopetsi had his dinner early, almost immediately after he had returned from Tlokweng Road Speedy Motors. It had been a hard afternoon for him, as he had been replacing tyres on a large cattle truck owned by a loyal friend of Mr J.L.B. Matekoni. This client, who had a fleet of such trucks, could have taken his vehicles to one of the large garages which specialised in looking after such concerns, but chose instead to stick with his old friend. With the growth of the cattle transport firm, their business had become increasingly valuable, and now accounted for almost one eighth of the income of Tlokweng Road Speedy Motors.

Changing the tyres on such large trucks was very physical work, and Mr Polopetsi, who was a relatively slight man, found that it sorely taxed his strength. But it was not physical tiredness that caused him to ask for an early dinner; there was quite another reason. "I have work to do tonight," he announced to his wife, slightly mysteriously. "Work for the agency."

Mma Polopetsi raised an eyebrow. "Does Mma Ramotswe ask you to do overtime? Will she pay you?"

"No," he said. "She does not know that I am doing this work. I am doing it quietly."

Mma Polopetsi stirred the pot of maize meal. "I see," she said. "It's nothing illegal, is it?" She remembered her husband's imprisonment—how could one forget that spell of loneliness and shame?—and she had not been very enthusiastic about the thought that he would engage in detective work, which could so easily go wrong. And yet everything she had heard about Mma Ramotswe had inspired confidence, and she shared her husband's gratitude to one whom she regarded as the family's saviour.

Mr Polopetsi hesitated for a moment, but then shook his head. "It is not illegal," he said. "And the only reason I have not told Mma Ramotswe is that it is a problem which is worrying her. I have found out what is happening and I can fix it. I want it to be a nice surprise for her."

The surprise, as he called it, had required some planning, and the co-operation of his friend and neighbour David, who had a battered old taxi which he used to ferry office-workers home from a parking place under a tree near the central mall. David owed Mr Polopetsi a favour, going back to an argument which had flared up with other neighbours over the ownership of a goat. Mr Polopetsi had sided with him and helped his side of the case to prevail, and this had cemented the friendship between the two men. So when Mr Polopetsi had asked him to drive him down to Mokolodi and to help him with something that needed doing down there, he readily agreed.

They set off shortly after seven. In town, this was still a busy time, with the traffic quite heavy, but by the time they reached the last lights of Gaborone and the dark shape of Kgale Hill could be made out to their side, it was difficult to imagine that there were people about, not far behind them. There was the occasional car on the Lobatse Road, but nothing very much, and on either side of the road there were just the dark shapes of the acacia trees, caught briefly in their headlights and then lost to the night. Mr Polopetsi had not told David about the precise nature of the errand, but now he did so.

"You don't have to come with me," he said. "You just park the car nearby. I'll do the rest."

David stared at the road ahead. "I'm not happy about this," he said. "You didn't tell me."

"It is quite safe," said Mr Polopetsi. "You aren't superstitious, are you?"

It was a challenge that had to be met. "I am not scared of these things," said David.

They reached the turn-off to Mokolodi, and David nosed the taxi down the road which led in the direction of the game park. There were several houses in the bush to one side, and lights shone out from one or two of these, but for the rest they were in darkness. After a while, Mr Polopetsi tapped his friend on the shoulder and told him to extinguish the headlights.

"We can go very slowly from here," he said. "Then you can park under a tree and wait until I come back. Nobody will see you."

They stopped, and the car's engine was turned off. Now Mr Polopetsi got out of the car and closed the door quietly behind him. It was utterly still, apart from the sound of insects, the persistent chirruping sound that seems to come from nowhere and from everywhere. It was a curious sound, which some people said was the sound of the stars calling their hunting dogs. He looked up. There was no moon that night, and the sky was filled with stars, so high, so white, that they were like an undulating blanket above him. He turned round to find south, and there it was, low down in the sky, as if suspended by something that he could not see, the Southern Cross. He had seen that constellation at night from the window of the prison, from the board and blankets that was his bed, and it had, in a strange way, sustained him. He was unjustly imprisoned; what had happened had not been his fault, and the sight of the stars had reminded him of the smallness of the world of men and their injustices.

Now he made his way to a point in the fence below the main gate. He pulled the strands of wire apart and slipped through. To his right there were the lights of the staff houses, squares of yellow in the black. He paused, waiting to see if there was anybody about; people might sit outside their houses on a warm night like this, but tonight there was nobody. Mr Polopetsi moved on. He knew exactly what he had to do, and he hoped that there would be no noise. If there was, then he would have to run off into the bush and crouch down until it had subsided. But with the bag that he had in his hand, there was no reason why it should not be quiet, and quick. And in the morning they would find out what had happened and there would be talk, but the fear, the dread that he had sensed, would be over. They would be pleased—all of them—although they would never be able to thank him because he would have acted in complete secrecy. Mma Ramotswe would thank him for it; he was sure of that.

AS IT HAPPENED, at the precise moment that Mr Polopetsi was creeping through the darkness, imagining the gratitude of his employer, Mma Ramotswe was sitting with Mr J.L.B. Matekoni at their dining table, having just completed a short conversation on the subject of Mr Polopetsi and his good work in the garage. The two foster children, Motholeli and Puso, were sitting at their places, eyes fixed on the pot of stew which she was about to

serve. At a signal from Mr J.L.B. Matekoni, the children folded
their hands together and closed their eyes.

"We are grateful for this food which has been cooked for us,"
he said. "Amen."

The grace completed, the children opened their eyes again
and watched as Mma Ramotswe ladled their helpings onto their
plates.

"I have not seen this uncle," said Motholeli. "Who is he?"

"He is working at the garage," said Mma Ramotswe. "He is a
very good mechanic, just like you, Motholeli."

"He is not a mechanic," Mr J.L.B. Matekoni corrected her. "A
mechanic is somebody who has had the proper training. You are
not a mechanic until you have completed an apprenticeship."
The mention of apprenticeships seemed to make him sombre,
and he stared grimly at his plate for a few moments. He had
reminded himself of his two apprentices, and as a general rule he
did not like to think too much about them. He was not sure when
they would finish their apprenticeships, as both of them had
failed to complete one of the courses they had been sent off on,
and would have to repeat it. They had said that they had failed
only because of a mix-up in the papers and an ambiguity in one
of the questions about diesel systems. He had looked at them
with pity; did they really expect him to swallow such a story? No,
it was best not to think too much about those two when he was
away from the garage.

"What I mean is that he is good with cars," said Mma
Ramotswe. "And he is a good detective too."

"But is he really a detective?" Mr J.L.B. Matekoni asked,
loading his fork with a piece of meat. "You cannot call just anybody a detective. There must be some training . . ." He tailed off.
Mma Ramotswe had had no training, of course, although she

had at least read *The Principles of Private Detection* by Clovis Andersen. He doubted whether Mr Polopetsi had read even that.

"Being a private detective is different from being a mechanic," said Mma Ramotswe. "You can be a detective without formal qualifications. There is no detective school, as far as I know. I do not think that Mr Sherlock Holmes went to a detective school."

"Who is this Rra Holmes?" asked Motholeli.

"He was a very famous detective," said Mma Ramotswe. "He smoked a pipe and was very clever."

Mr J.L.B. Matekoni stroked his chin. "I do not know if he really existed," he said. "I think that he was just in a book."

Motholeli looked to Mma Ramotswe for clarification. "Maybe," said Mma Ramotswe. "Perhaps."

"He is from a book," said Puso suddenly. "My teacher told us about him. She said that he went to a waterfall and fell over the edge. She said that is what sometimes happens to detectives."

Mma Ramotswe looked thoughtful. "I have never been to the Victoria Falls," she said.

"If you fell over the Victoria Falls," said Mr J.L.B. Matekoni cheerfully, "I do not think that you would drown. You are too traditionally built for that. You would float over and bounce up at the bottom like a big rubber ball. You would not be hurt."

The children laughed, and Mma Ramotswe smiled, at least for a moment. Then her smile faded. She normally paid no attention to any references to her traditional build—indeed, she was proud of it and would mention it herself. But now, it seemed to her, rather too many people were drawing attention to it. There had been that remark from Mr Polopetsi, an ill-considered, casual remark it is true, but still a suggestion that lions would like to eat her because she was large and juicy. And then the nurse had said that she should watch her blood pressure and that one way to do this was to go on a diet. And now here was Mr

J.L.B. Matekoni himself suggesting that she looked like a round rubber ball and the children laughing at the idea (and presumably agreeing).

Mma Ramotswe looked down at her plate. She did not think that she ate too much—if one excluded cake and doughnuts and pumpkin, and perhaps a few other things—and the fact that she was traditionally built was just the way she was. And yet there was no doubt but that she could afford to shed a few pounds, even if only to avoid the embarrassment which had arisen the other day when she had stooped to sit down on her office chair and the seams of her skirt had given way. Mma Makutsi had been tactful about this, and had pretended not to hear anything, but she had noticed and her eyes had widened slightly. There were many arguments in favour of being traditionally built, but it had to be said that it would be pleasant if these digs from other people could be headed off. Perhaps there was an argument for going on a diet after all and showing everybody that she could lose weight if she wanted to. And of course what they said about diets was that you had to start straightaway—the moment the idea crossed your mind. If you put it off, and said that your diet would start the following day, or the following week, then you would never do it. There would always be some reason why it was impossible or inconvenient. So she should start right now, right at this very moment, while the tempting plate of stew lay before her.

"Motholeli and Puso," she said, sitting up straight in her chair. "Would you like the stew on my plate? I do not think I am going to eat it."

Puso nodded quickly and pushed out his plate for the extra portion, and his sister soon followed his lead. Mr J.L.B. Matekoni, though, looked at Mma Ramotswe in astonishment. He lowered his fork to his plate and let it lie there.

"Are you not feeling well, Mma Ramotswe?" he asked. "I have heard that there is something going round the town. People are having trouble with their stomachs."

"I am quite well," said Mma Ramotswe. "I have just decided that from now on I shall eat just a little bit less."

"But you will die," said Puso anxiously. "If you do not eat, then you die. Our teacher told us that."

"I am not going to stop eating altogether," said Mma Ramotswe, laughing at the suggestion. "Don't worry about that. No, it's just that I have decided that I should go on a diet. That is all. I shall eat something, but not as much as before."

"No cake," said Motholeli. "And no doughnuts."

"That is right," said Mma Ramotswe. "Next time Mma Potokwane offers me any of that fruit cake of hers, I shall say, 'No thank you, Mma.' That is what I shall say."

"I shall eat your share of fruit cake," said Mr J.L.B. Matekoni. "I do not need to go on a diet."

Mma Ramotswe said nothing. She was already beginning to feel hungry, and the diet had only been going for a few minutes. Perhaps she should have just a little bit of the stew—there was still some left in the pot in the kitchen. She rose to her feet.

Mr J.L.B. Matekoni smiled. "Is that you going into the kitchen to help yourself to stew in secret?" he asked.

Mma Ramotswe sat down. "I was not going into the kitchen," she said hotly. "I was just adjusting my dress. It's feeling rather loose, you see."

She looked up at the ceiling. She had heard that dieting was not easy. Some time ago, before any question of a diet had arisen, she had seen an article in the paper about how diets encouraged people to become dishonest with others—and with themselves.

There had been a survey conducted at one of the places where people went to diet, and it was revealed that just about everybody who went on the course took with them a secret supply of snacks. She had found that funny; the idea of adults behaving like children and smuggling in sweets and chocolate had struck her as being an amusing one. And yet now that she herself was on a diet, it did not seem so funny after all. In fact, it seemed rather sad. Those poor people wanting to eat and not being allowed to. Dieting was cruel; it was an abuse of human rights. Yes, that's what it was, and she should not allow herself to be manipulated in this way.

She stopped herself. Thinking like that was nothing more than coming up with excuses for breaking the diet. Mma Ramotswe was made of sterner stuff than that, and so she persisted. As the others ate the pudding she had prepared for them—banana custard with spoonfuls of red jam in the middle, she sat as if fixed to her seat, watching them enjoying themselves.

"Are you sure you won't have some of this custard, Mma Ramotswe?" asked Mr J.L.B. Matekoni.

"No," she said. And then said, "Yes. Yes, I am sure that I won't. Which means no."

Mr J.L.B. Matekoni smiled. "It is very good," he said.

This is how we are tempted, thought Mma Ramotswe. But at least some of us are strong.

She closed her eyes. It was easier to be strong, she thought, if one had one's eyes closed; although that would only work to a limited extent. One could not go around indefinitely with one's eyes closed, especially if one was a detective. Quite apart from anything else, that was in direct contradiction of the advice which Clovis Andersen gave in *The Principles of Private Detection*, one chapter of which was entitled "The Importance of Keeping Your Eyes

Open." Had Clovis Andersen ever been on a diet? she wondered. There was a picture of him on the back cover, and although Mma Ramotswe had never paid much attention to it, now that she brought it to mind, one salient feature of it leapt out. Clovis Andersen was traditionally built.

CHAPTER FIFTEEN

MR POLOPETSI TRIES
TO BE HELPFUL

MMA MAKUTSI was already in the office of the No. 1 Ladies' Detective Agency when Mma Ramotswe arrived there the following morning.

"So, Mma," said Mma Ramotswe, after formal greetings had been exchanged. "So, there you are chasing after our friend, Mr Cedric Disani. What have you managed to uncover today?"

Mma Makutsi picked up a piece of paper and brandished it. "There is a small farm down near Lobatse. I have the details here. It is meant to be the property of his brother, but I have already spoken on the telephone to the people down there who sell cattle dip. They say that it is always Mr Cedric Disani who comes to buy the dip and it is always his name on the cheques. The lawyers will be interested to hear this. I think they want to show that he is really the owner."

"They will be very pleased with your work," said Mma Ramotswe, adding, "And Mr Disani will be very displeased."

Mma Makutsi laughed. "We cannot please everybody."

They chatted for a few minutes more before Mma Makutsi offered to make Mma Ramotswe a cup of tea.

"I have brought in some doughnuts," she said. "Phuti gave me

some last night. He has sent one for you and one for Mr J.L.B.
Matekoni."

Mma Ramotswe's face lit up. "That is very kind of him," she
said. "A doughnut . . ." She trailed off. She had remembered
about her diet. She had eaten one slice of toast that morning, and
a banana, and her stomach felt light and empty. A doughnut was
exactly what she wanted; a doughnut with a dusting of coarse
sugar on the outside, enough to give a bit of a crunch and to line
one's lips with white, and a layer of sweetened oil soaked into the
dough itself. Such bliss. Such bliss.

"I don't think that I shall have a doughnut, Mma," she said.
"You may eat mine today."

Mma Makutsi shrugged. "I will be happy to have two," she
said. "Or should I give it to the apprentices to share? No, I don't
think I'll do that. I will eat it myself."

Mma Makutsi rose from her chair and began to walk across
the room towards the kettle. Mma Ramotswe noticed immediately that she was walking in an unusual way. Her steps were
small and she appeared to totter as she put one leg before the
other. The new shoes, of course; she had collected her new shoes
that morning.

Mma Ramotswe leaned forward at her desk and looked.
"Your new shoes, Mma!" she exclaimed. "Those beautiful new
shoes!"

Mma Makutsi stopped where she was. She turned round to
face Mma Ramotswe. "So you like them, Mma Ramotswe?"

Mma Ramotswe did not hesitate. "Of course I do," she said.
"They look very good on you."

Mma Makutsi smiled modestly. "Thank you, Mma. I am just
breaking them in at the moment. You know how that takes a bit
of time."

Mma Ramotswe did know. And she knew too, but did not

say anything, that there were some pairs of shoes that would never be broken in. Shoes that were too small were usually too small for a reason: they were intended for people with small feet. "You'll get used to them," she said. But her voice lacked conviction.

Mma Makutsi continued her journey to the kettle—painfully, thought Mma Ramotswe. Then she went back to her desk and sat down, with relief. Watching this, Mma Ramotswe had to suppress a smile. It was her assistant's one weak point—this interest in unsuitable shoes—but, as failings went, this was not a great one; how much more dangerous was an interest in unsuitable men. And Mma Makutsi did not show any sign of that. In fact, she showed herself to be very sensible when it came to men, even if her last friend had been misleading her. He had not been unsuitable in any way, apart from the fact that he was already married, of course.

Once the kettle had boiled, Mma Makutsi made the tea—Tanganda tea for her and red bush tea for Mma Ramotswe—and she took Mma Ramotswe's cup over to her. Mma Ramotswe suppressed the urge to offer to help her by getting the tea herself, in view of the obvious pain which walking now caused Mma Makutsi. It would not be helpful, she thought, for Mma Makutsi to know that she realised how uncomfortable she was. It would be difficult enough for her to acknowledge her mistake to herself, let alone to others.

The doughnuts were then produced from a grease-stained paper bag, and Mma Makutsi began to eat hers.

"This is very delicious," she said as she chewed on a mouthful. "Phuti says that he knows the baker at that bakery up in Broadhurst, and he always gives him the best doughnuts. They are very good, Mma. Very good." She paused to lick the sugar off her fingers. "You must have had a big breakfast today, Mma Ramotswe. Either that or you're getting sick."

"We don't have to eat doughnuts all day," said Mma Ramotswe. "There are other things to do."

Mma Makutsi raised an eyebrow. It was a bit extreme of Mma Ramotswe to suggest that doughnuts were being consumed all day. Two doughnuts in one morning was not excessive, surely, and Mma Ramotswe would not normally turn up her nose at the possibility of a couple of doughnuts. Unless . . . Well, that would be an extraordinary development. Mma Ramotswe on a diet!

Mma Makutsi looked across at Mma Ramotswe. "You'd never go on a diet, would you, Mma Ramotswe?" The question was asked casually, but Mma Makutsi knew immediately that she had guessed correctly. Mma Ramotswe looked up sharply, with exactly that look of irritation mixed with self-pity that people in the early stages of a diet manifest.

"As a matter of fact, Mma, I am on a diet," said Mma Ramotswe. "And it doesn't make it any easier for me if you eat doughnuts like that in front of me."

It was an uncharacteristically sharp retort from Mma Ramotswe, who was normally so kind and polite, and for that reason Mma Makutsi did not take it to heart. Short temper was a known hazard of dieting—and who could blame people for being a bit irritable when they were constantly hungry? But at the same time, normal life had to go on around dieters, and doughnuts were just a part of normal life.

"You can't expect everybody else to stop eating, Mma Ramotswe," Mma Makutsi pointed out.

Nothing more was said on the subject, but it occurred to Mma Ramotswe that this was exactly the sort of question one should put to Aunty Emang. She imagined the letter: "Dear Aunty Emang, I am on a diet and yet the lady in the office with me insists on eating doughnuts in front of me. I find this very difficult. I do not want to be rude, but is there anything I can do about this?"

Aunty Emang would come up with one of her rather witty responses to that, thought Mma Ramotswe. She reflected on Aunty Emang. It must be strange having people write to one about all sorts of problems. One would end up being party to so many secrets . . . She stopped. An idea had come to her, and she noted it down quickly on a scrap of paper so that it might not be lost, as was the fate of so many ideas, brilliant and otherwise.

SHORTLY BEFORE LUNCH, Mr Polopetsi knocked on the office door. They had not seen him that morning, but this was not unusual. Mr J.L.B. Matekoni had discovered that Mr Polopetsi was a safe driver—unlike the apprentices, who broke the speed limit at every opportunity—and he had decided to use him to collect spares and deliver the cars of customers who could not manage to get in to the garage to collect them. Mr Polopetsi did not mind walking back from the customers' houses, or taking a minibus, whereas the apprentices insisted on being collected by Mr J.L.B. Matekoni in his truck. But all this was time-consuming for him, and sometimes Mr Polopetsi would be out of the garage for hours on end.

"Mr Polopetsi!" said Mma Ramotswe. "Have you been off on one of your long errands, Rra? All over the place? Here and there?"

"He is known all over the town," said Mma Makutsi, laughing. "He is the best-known messenger. Like Superman."

"Superman was not a messenger," said Mma Ramotswe. "He was . . ." She did not complete her sentence. What exactly did Superman do? She was not sure if that was ever made clear.

Mr Polopetsi ignored this talk of Superman. He had noticed that sometimes these ladies got into a silly mood and talked all sorts of nonsense, which was meant to be funny. He did not find it particularly amusing. "I have been collecting some spare parts for Mr J.L.B. Matekoni," he explained patiently. "I had to get some fuses and we had run out of fan belts and . . ."

"And blah blah blah," said Mma Makutsi. "All this garage business. It is of no interest to us, Mr Polopetsi. We are interested in more serious matters on this side of the building."

"You would find fan belts serious enough if yours broke halfway to Francistown," retorted Mr Polopetsi. He was about to continue with an explanation of the importance of mechanical matters, but he stopped. Mma Makutsi had risen from her desk to take a file back to the filing cabinet, and he now saw her new blue shoes. And he noticed, too, the odd way in which she was walking.

"Have you hurt yourself, Mma?" he asked solicitously. "Have you sprained an ankle?"

Mma Makutsi continued on her tottering journey. "No," she said. "I have not hurt myself. I am fine, thank you, Rra."

Mr Polopetsi did not intercept the warning glance from Mma Ramotswe, and continued, "Those look like new shoes. My! They are very fashionable, aren't they? I can hardly see them, they're so small. Are you sure they fit you?"

"Of course I am," mumbled Mma Makutsi. "I am just breaking them in, that's all."

"I would have thought that your feet were far too wide for shoes like that, Mma," Mr Polopetsi went on. "I do not think that you would be able to run in those, do you? Or even walk."

Mma Ramotswe could not help but smile, and she peered down at her desk with intense interest, trying to hide her expression from Mma Makutsi.

"What do you think, Mma Ramotswe?" asked Mr Polopetsi. "Do you think that Mma Makutsi should wear shoes like that?"

"It is none of my business, Rra," said Mma Ramotswe. "Mma Makutsi is old enough to choose her own shoes."

"Yes," said Mma Makutsi defiantly. "I don't comment on your shoes, and you should not comment on mine. It is very rude for a man to comment on a woman's shoes. That is well known, isn't it, Mma Ramotswe?"

"Yes, it is," said Mma Ramotswe loyally. "And anyway, Mr Polopetsi, did you want to see us about something?"

Mr Polopetsi walked across the room and sat in the client's chair, uninvited. "I have something to show you," he said. "It is out at the back. But first I will tell you something. You remember when we went out to Mokolodi? There was something wrong there, wasn't there?"

Mma Ramotswe nodded, but was non-committal. "I do not think that everything was right."

"People were frightened, weren't they?" pressed Mr Polopetsi. "Did you notice that?"

"Maybe," said Mma Ramotswe.

"Well, I certainly noticed it," said Mr Polopetsi. "And while you were talking to people, I did a bit of investigating. I dug a bit deeper."

Mma Ramotswe frowned. It was not for Mr Polopetsi to dig deeper. That was not why she had taken him down to Mokolodi. He was a perceptive man, and an intelligent one, but he should not think that he could initiate enquiries. Not even Mma Makutsi, with her considerable experience in the field, initiated investigations without first talking to Mma Ramotswe about it. This was a simple question of accountability. If anything went wrong, then it would be Mma Ramotswe who would have to bear responsibility as principal. For this reason she had to know what was going on.

She composed herself to talk firmly to Mr Polopetsi. She did not relish doing this, but she was the boss, after all, and she could not shirk her duty.

"Mr Polopetsi," she began. "I do not think . . ."

He cut her off, brightly raising a finger in the air, as if to point to the source of his inspiration.

"It was all to do with a bird," he said. "Would you believe it, Mma Ramotswe? A bird was responsible for all that fear and worry."

Mma Ramotswe was silenced. Of course it was to do with a bird—she had found that out eventually, had winkled the information out of that girl in the restaurant. But she had not expected that Mr Polopetsi, who had no contacts there, would have found out the same thing.

"I did know about the bird," she said gravely. "And I was going to do something about it for them."

Mr Polopetsi raised another finger in the air. "I've done it already," he said brightly. "I've solved the problem."

Mma Makutsi, who had been listening with increasing interest, now broke into the conversation. "What is all this about a bird?" she asked. "How can a bird cause all this trouble?"

Mr Polopetsi turned in his chair to face Mma Makutsi. "It's not just any ordinary bird," he explained. "It's a hornbill— a ground hornbill."

Mma Makutsi gave an involuntary shudder. There were ground hornbills up in the north, where she came from. She knew that they were bad luck. People avoided the ground hornbill if they could. And they were wise to do so, in her view. One only had to look at those birds, which were as big as turkeys and had those great beaks and those old-looking eyes.

"Yes," went on Mr Polopetsi. "This bird had been brought to

the Mokolodi animal sanctuary. Somebody had found it lying on the road up north and brought it down. It had a broken wing and a broken leg, and they bound these up and kept it there to recover. And everybody was very frightened because they knew that this bird would bring death. It would just bring death."

"So why did they not say something?" asked Mma Makutsi.

"Because they were embarrassed," said Mr Polopetsi. "Nobody wanted to be the one to go and tell Neil that the people did not want that bird about the place. Nobody wanted to be thought to be superstitious and not modern. That was it, wasn't it, Mma Ramotswe?"

Mma Ramotswe nodded, somewhat reluctantly. Mr Polopetsi had reached exactly the same conclusion as she had. But what had he done about it? She had considered the issue to be of such delicacy that she would have to think very carefully about what to do. Mr Polopetsi, it would seem, had blundered right in.

"You said that you had solved the problem," she said. "And how did you do that, Rra? Did you tell the bird to fly away?"

Mr Polopetsi shook his head. "No, not that, Mma. I took the bird. I took it away at night-time."

Mma Ramotswe gasped. "But you can't do that . . ."

"Why not, Mma?" asked Mr Polopetsi. "It's a wild creature. Nobody owns wild birds. They had no right to keep it there."

"They would release it once it was healed," said Mma Ramotswe, a note of anger showing in her voice.

"Yes, but before that, what would happen?" Mr Polopetsi challenged. "Somebody could kill the bird. Or some awful thing might happen out there and everybody would then blame Neil for allowing the bird to come. It could have been a terrible mess."

Mma Ramotswe thought for a moment. What Mr Polopetsi said was probably right, but it still did not justify his taking matters into his own hands. "Where did you let it go, Rra?" she asked. "Those birds don't live down here. They live up there." She pointed northwards, in the direction of the empty bush of the Tuli Block, of the Swapong Hills, of the great plains of Matabeleland.

"I know that," said Mr Polopetsi. "And that is why I have not let it go yet. I have asked one of the truck drivers to take it up there when he drives up to Francistown tomorrow. He will let it go for us. I have given him a few pula to do this. And some cigarettes."

"So where is this bird now?" interjected Mma Makutsi. "Where are you hiding it?"

"I am not hiding it anywhere," said Mr Polopetsi. "It is in a cardboard box outside. I will show it to you."

He rose to his feet. Mma Ramotswe exchanged a glance with Mma Makutsi—a glance which was difficult to interpret, but which was a mixture of surprise and foreboding. Then the two of them followed him out of the office and round to the back of the building. Against the wall, unprotected from the sun, was a large cardboard box, air holes punched into the top.

Mr Polopetsi approached the box cautiously. "I will open the lid just a little bit," he said. "I do not want the bird to escape."

Mma Ramotswe and Mma Makutsi stood immediately behind him as he gently tugged at one of the flaps of the box. "Look inside," he whispered. "There he is. He is resting."

Mma Ramotswe peered into the box. There at the bottom lay the great shape of the ground hornbill, its unwieldy bill lying across its chest, half open. She stared for a moment, and then she stood up.

"The bird is dead, Rra," she said. "It is not resting. It is late."

SHE WAS GENTLE with Mr Polopetsi, who was too upset to help them bury the bird in the bush behind Tlokweng Road Speedy Motors. She did not point out to him the foolishness of leaving the bird for several hours out in the hot sun, in a box in which the temperature must have climbed too high for the bird to survive. She did not say that, and a warning glance to Mma Makutsi prevented her from pointing it out either. Instead she said that anybody could make a mistake and that she knew that he was trying to be helpful. And then, as politely as she could, she told him that he should in future get her agreement to any proposed solutions he might have to problems. "It's better that way," she said quietly, touching him gently on the shoulder in an act of reassurance and forgiveness.

She and Mma Makutsi carried the lifeless form of the bird out into the bush. They found a place, a good place, under a small acacia tree, where the earth looked soft enough to dig a hole. And Mma Ramotswe dug a hole, a grave for a bird, using an adze borrowed from a man who had a plot of land next to the garage. She swung the adze high and brought it down into the ground in much the same way as women before her, many generations of women of her family and her tribe, had done in years gone past as they readied the soil of Botswana, the good soil of their country, for the crops. And Mma Makutsi scraped the soil away and prepared the bird for its grave, lowering it in gently, as one may lay a friend to rest.

Mma Ramotswe looked at Mma Makutsi. She wanted to say something, but somehow she could not bring herself to say it. *This bird is one of our brothers and sisters. We are returning it to the ground from which it came, the ground from which we came too. And now we put the soil upon it . . .* And they did that, breaking the soil gently upon the bird, on the great beak, on the large, defeated body, so unfortunate in its short life and its ending, until it was covered entirely.

Mma Ramotswe nodded to Mma Makutsi, and together they walked back to the garage, barefoot, in simplicity, as their mothers and grandmothers had walked before them across the land that meant so much to them, and which was the resting place of us all—of people, of animals, of birds.

CHAPTER SIXTEEN

DR MOFFAT MAKES A DIAGNOSIS

MR POLOPETSI, mortified by what he had done, was now anxious to do anything to make up for the awful outcome of his venture. The next morning he put his head round the door of the No. 1 Ladies' Detective Agency several times, asking if there was anything Mma Ramotswe wanted him to do. She replied politely that there was nothing very much that needed doing, but that she would call on him if something arose.

"Poor man," said Mma Makutsi. "He is feeling very bad, don't you think, Mma?"

"Yes, he is," said Mma Ramotswe. "It cannot be easy for him."

"You were very kind to him, Mma," said Mma Makutsi. "You didn't shout. You didn't show that you were angry."

"What's the point of being angry?" asked Mma Ramotswe. "When we are cross with somebody, what good does that do? Especially if they did not mean to cause harm. Mr Polopetsi was sorry about it —that's the important thing."

She thought for a moment. It was clear that Mr Polopetsi wanted some sign from her, some sign that she still trusted him in the performance of occasional tasks. He dearly wanted to do more detective work—he had made that much very plain—and he was no doubt concerned that this debacle would put an end to that. She would find something. She would give him a sign that she still respected his abilities.

Mma Ramotswe thought about her list of tasks. The Mokolodi matter had been resolved—in a very unfortunate way, of course, but still resolved. That left the matter of the doctor and the matter of Mma Tsau's being blackmailed. She already had an idea of what to do about the doctor, and she would attend to that soon, but the blackmail affair still had to be dealt with. Could she use Mr Polopetsi for that? She decided that she could.

Mma Makutsi summoned Mr Polopetsi into the office, and he sat down in the client's chair, wringing his hands anxiously.

"You know, Mr Polopetsi," began Mma Ramotswe. "You know that I have always respected your ability as a detective. And I still do. I want you to know that."

Mr Polopetsi beamed with pleasure. "Thank you, Mma. You are very kind. You are my mother, Mma Ramotswe."

Mma Ramotswe waved the compliment aside. *I am nobody's mother,* she thought, *except for my little child in heaven. I am the mother of that child.*

"You were asking earlier on for something to do, Rra. Well, I have something for you to look into. There is a young woman called Poppy who came to see us. She works for a lady who had been stealing government food to feed to her husband. This lady, Mma Tsau, has received a blackmail threat. She thought it came from Poppy, because Poppy was the only one who knew."

"And was she?" asked Mr Polopetsi.

"I don't think so," said Mma Ramotswe. "I think that she must have told at least one other person."

"And if we can find out who that person is, then that will be the blackmailer?"

Mma Ramotswe smiled. "There you are!" she said. "I knew that you were a good detective. That is exactly the conclusion one should draw." She paused. "Go and speak to this Poppy and ask her this question. Ask her this: Did you write to anybody, anybody about your troubles? That is all you have to ask her. Use those exact words, and see what she says."

She explained to Mr Polopetsi where Poppy worked. He could go there immediately, she said, and ask to see her. He could tell them that he had a message for her. People were always sending messages to one another, and she would come to receive it.

After Mr Polopetsi had left, Mma Ramotswe smiled at Mma Makutsi. "He is a good detective, that man," she said. "He would be a very good assistant for you, Mma Makutsi."

Mma Makutsi welcomed this. She relished the thought of having an assistant, or indeed anybody who was junior to her. She had done a course in personnel management at the Botswana Secretarial College and had secured a very good mark in it. She still had her notes somewhere and would be able to dig them out and read them through before she started to exercise actual authority over Mr Polopetsi.

"But now," said Mma Ramotswe, glancing at her watch, "I have a medical appointment. I mustn't miss it."

"You aren't ill, are you, Mma Ramotswe?" enquired Mma Makutsi. "This diet of yours . . ."

Mma Ramotswe cut her off. "My diet is going very well," she said. "No, it is nothing to do with the diet. It's just that I thought I should go and have my blood pressure checked."

IT HAD BEEN EASY to find out which doctor Boitelo had been talking about. She had let slip, without thinking, that he was Ugandan, and that his clinic was close enough to where she lived for her to walk to work. She had Boitelo's address and that meant a simple trawl of the list of medical practitioners in the telephone book. The Ugandan names were easily enough spotted—there were a number of them—and after that it was a simple matter to see that Dr Eustace Lubega ran a clinic just round the corner from the street in which Boitelo lived. After that, all that was required was a telephone call to the clinic to make an appointment.

It had been Boitelo who answered the telephone. Mma Ramotswe announced who she was, and there was a silence at the other end of the line.

"Why are you phoning this place?" said Boitelo, her voice lowered.

"I want to make an appointment—as a patient—with your good Dr Lubega," said Mma Ramotswe. "And don't worry. I shall pretend not to recognise you. I shall say nothing about you."

This reassurance was followed by a brief silence. "Do you promise?" asked Boitelo.

"Of course I promise, Mma," said Mma Ramotswe. "I will protect you. You don't need to worry."

"What do you want to see him about?" asked Boitelo.

"I want my blood pressure checked," said Mma Ramotswe.

Now, parking the tiny white van in front of the sign that announced the clinic of Dr Eustace Lubega, MB, ChB (Makerere), she made her way through the front door and into the waiting room. The clinic had been a private house before—one of those old Botswana Housing Corporation houses with a small verandah, not unlike her own house in Zebra Drive—and the living room was now used as the reception area. The fireplace, in which many wood fires would have burned in the cold nights of winter, was still there, but filled now with an arrangement of dried flowers and seed pods. And on one wall a large noticeboard had been mounted, on which were pinned notices about immunisation and several large warnings about the care that people should take now in their personal lives. And then there was a picture of a mosquito and a warning to remain vigilant about stagnant water.

There was another patient waiting to see the doctor, a pregnant woman, who nodded politely to Mma Ramotswe as she came in. Boitelo gave no sign of recognising Mma Ramotswe and invited her to take a seat. The pregnant woman did not seem to need long with the doctor, and so now it was Mma Ramotswe's turn to go in.

Dr Lubega looked up from his desk. Gesturing for Mma Ramotswe to sit down beside his desk, he held out a card in front of him.

"I don't have any records for you," he said.

Mma Ramotswe laughed. "I have not seen a doctor for a long time, Dr Lubega. My records would be very old."

The doctor shrugged. "Well, Mma Ramotswe, what can I do for you today?"

Mma Ramotswe frowned. "My friends have been talking to me about my health," she said. "You know how people are. They said that I should have my blood pressure taken. They say that because I am a bit traditionally built . . ."

Dr Lubega looked puzzled. "Traditionally built, Mma?"

"Yes," said Mma Ramotswe. "I am the shape that African ladies are traditionally meant to be."

Dr Lubega started to smile, but his professional manner took over and he became grave. "They are right about blood pressure. Overweight people need to be a little careful of that. I will check that for you, Mma, and give you a general physical examination."

Mma Ramotswe sat on the examination couch while Dr Lubega conducted a cursory examination. She glanced at him quickly as he listened to her heart; she saw the spotless white shirt with its starched collar, the tie with a university crest, the small line of hair beneath the side of his chin that his razor had missed.

"Your heart sounds strong enough," he said. "You must be a big-hearted lady, Mma."

She smiled weakly, and he raised an eyebrow. "Now, then," he said. "Your blood pressure."

He started to wrap the cuff of the sphygmomanometer around her upper arm, but stopped.

"This cuff is too small," he muttered, unwrapping it. "I must get a traditionally built cuff."

He turned away and opened a cabinet drawer from which he extracted a larger cuff. Connecting this to the instrument, he wound it round Mma Ramotswe's arm and took the reading. She saw that he noted figures down on a card, but she did not see what he wrote.

Back at the side of the doctor's desk, Mma Ramotswe listened to what he had to say.

"You seem in reasonable shape," he said, "for a . . . for a traditionally built lady. But your blood pressure is a bit on the high side, I'm afraid. It's one hundred and sixty over ninety. That's marginally high, and I think that you will need to take some drugs to get it down a bit. I can recommend a very good drug. It is two drugs in one—what we call a beta-blocker and a diuretic. You should take these pills."

"I will do that," said Mma Ramotswe. "I will do as you say, Doctor."

"Good," said Dr Lubega. "But there is one thing I should tell you, Mma. This very good drug is not cheap. It will cost you two hundred pula a month. I can sell it to you here, but that is what it will cost."

Mma Ramotswe whistled. "Ow! That is a lot of money just for some little pills." She paused. "But I really need it, do I?"

"You do," said Dr Lubega.

"In that case I will take it. I do not have two hundred pula with me, but I do have fifty pula."

Dr Lubega made a liberal gesture with his hands. "That will get you started. You can come back for some more, once you have the money."

ARMED WITH HER SMALL BOTTLE of light blue pills, Mma Ramotswe went that evening to the house of her friend Howard Moffat. He and his wife were sitting in their living room when she called at their door. Dr Moffat's bad-tempered brown dog, of whom Mma Ramotswe had a particular distrust, barked loudly but was silenced by his master and sent to the back of the house.

"I'm sorry about that dog," said Dr Moffat. "He is not a very friendly dog. I don't know where we went wrong."

"Some dogs are just bad," said Mma Ramotswe. "It is not the fault of the owners. Just like some children are bad when it is not the fault of the parents."

"Well, maybe my dog will change," said Dr Moffat. "Maybe he will become kinder as he grows older."

Mma Ramotswe smiled. "I hope so, Doctor," she said. "But I have not come here to be unkind about that dog of yours. I have come to ask you a quick favour."

"I am always happy to do anything for you, Mma Ramotswe," said Dr Moffat. "You know that."

"Will you take my blood pressure, then?"

If Dr Moffat was surprised by the request, he did not show it. Ushering Mma Ramotswe into his study at the back of the house, he took a sphygmomanometer out of his desk drawer and began to wrap the cuff round Mma Ramotswe's proffered arm.

"Have you been feeling unwell?" he asked quietly as he inflated the instrument.

"No," said Mma Ramotswe. "It's just that I needed to know."

Dr Moffat looked at the mercury. "It's a tiny bit higher than would be wise," he said. "It's one hundred and sixty over ninety. In a case like that we should probably do some other tests."

Mma Ramotswe stared at him. "Are you sure about that reading?" she asked.

Dr Moffat told her that he was. "It's not too bad," he said.

"It's exactly what I thought it would be."

He gave her a curious look. "Oh? Why would you think that?"

She did not answer the question, but reached into her pocket and took out the bottle of pills which Dr Lubega had sold her. "Do you know these pills?" she asked.

Dr Moffat looked at the label. "That is a well-known pill for high blood pressure," he said. "It's very good. Rather costly. But very good. It's a beta-blocker combined with a diuretic."

He opened the bottle and spilled a couple of pills out onto his hand. He seemed interested in them, and he held one up closer to examine it.

"That's a bit odd," he said, after a moment. "I don't remember this drug looking like that. I seem to recall it was white. I could be wrong, of course. These are . . . blue, aren't they? Yes, definitely blue."

He replaced the pills in the bottle and crossed the floor of his study to reach for a volume from the bookshelf. "This is a copy of the *British National Formulary,*" he said. "It lists all the proprietary drugs and describes their appearance. Let me take a look."

It took him a few minutes to find the drug, but when he did he nodded his agreement with what he read. "There it is," he said, reading from the formulary. "White tablets. Each tablet contains fifty milligrams of beta-blocker and twelve point five milligrams of diuretic." He closed the book and looked at Mma Ramotswe over the top of his spectacles.

"I think you're going to have to tell me where these came from, Mma Ramotswe," he said. "But would it be easier to do so over a cup of tea? I'm sure that Fiona would be happy to make us all a cup of tea while you tell me all about it."

"Tea would be very good," said Mma Ramotswe.

At the end of the story, Dr Moffat shook his head sadly. "I'm afraid that the only conclusion we can reach is that this Dr Lubega is substituting a cheap generic for a costly drug but charging his patients the full cost."

"And that would harm them?" she asked.

"It could," said Dr Moffat. "Some of the generics are all right, but others do not necessarily do what they're meant to. There's an issue of purity, you see. Of course, this doctor may have thought that everything would be all right and that no harm would come to anybody, but that's not good enough. You don't take that sort of risk. And you definitely don't commit fraud on your patients." He shook his head. "We'll have to report this, of course. You know that?"

Mma Ramotswe sighed. That was the trouble with getting involved in these things; one got drawn in. There were reports. Dr Moffat sensed her weariness. "I'll have a word with the ministry," he said. "It's easier that way."

Mma Ramotswe smiled her appreciation and took a sip of her tea. She wondered why a doctor would need to defraud his patients when he could already make a perfectly comfortable living in legitimate practice. Of course, he could have hire-purchase payments or school fees or debts to pay off; one never knew. Or he could need the money because somebody was extorting money out of him. Blackmail drove people to extremes of desperation. And a doctor would be a tempting target for blackmail if he had a dark secret to conceal . . . But it seemed a little bit unlikely to her. It was probably just greed, simple greed. The desire to own a Mercedes-Benz, for example. That could drive people to all sorts of mischief.

CHAPTER SEVENTEEN

WAITING FOR A VISIT

THE NEXT MORNING when Mma Ramotswe arrived at the shared premises of Tlokweng Road Speedy Motors and the No. 1 Ladies' Detective Agency, she found Mr Polopetsi with his head under a car. She was always wary of calling out to a mechanic when he was under a car, as they inevitably bumped their heads in surprise. And so she bent down and whispered to him, "Dumela, Rra. Have you anything to tell me?"

Mr Polopetsi heaved himself out from under the car and wiped his hands on a piece of cloth. "Yes, I do," he said keenly. "I have some very interesting news for you."

"You found Poppy?"

"Yes, I found her."

"And you had a word with her?"

"Yes, I did."

Mma Ramotswe looked at him expectantly. "Well?"

"I asked her whether she had written a letter to anybody about what had happened. That is exactly what I asked her."

Mma Ramotswe felt herself becoming impatient. "Come on, Mr Polopetsi. Tell me what she said."

Mr Polopetsi raised a finger in one of his characteristic gestures of emphasis. "You'll never believe who she wrote to, Mma Ramotswe. You'll never guess."

Mma Ramotswe savoured her moment. "Aunty Emang?" she said quietly.

Mr Polopetsi looked deflated. "Yes. How did you know that?"

"I had a hunch, Mr Polopetsi. I had a hunch." She affected a careless tone. "I find that sometimes I have a hunch, and sometimes they are correct. Anyway, that's very useful information you came up with there. It confirms my view of what is happening."

"I do not know what is happening," said Mr Polopetsi.

"Then I will tell you, Rra," said Mma Ramotswe, pointing to her office. "Come inside and sit down, and I will tell you exactly what is going on and what we need to do."

BOTH MMA MAKUTSI and Mr Polopetsi listened attentively as Mma Ramotswe gave an account of where she had got to in the blackmail investigation.

"Now what do we do?" asked Mma Makutsi. "We know who it is. Do we go to the police?"

"No," said Mma Ramotswe. "At least, not yet."

"Well?" pressed Mr Polopetsi. "Do we go and talk to Aunty Emang, whoever she is?"

"No," said Mma Ramotswe. "I have a better idea than that. We get Aunty Emang to come and talk to us. Here in our office. We get her to sit in that chair and tell us all about her nasty ways."

Mr Polopetsi laughed. "She will never come, Mma! Why should she come?"

"Oh, she will come all right," said Mma Ramotswe. "Mma Makutsi, I should like to dictate a letter. Mr Polopetsi, you stay and listen to what I have to say."

Mma Makutsi liked to use her shorthand, which had been

described by the examiners at the Botswana Secretarial College as "quite the best shorthand we have ever seen, in the whole history of the college."

"Are you ready, Mma?" asked Mma Ramotswe, composing herself at her desk. She was aware of being watched closely by Mr Polopetsi, who appeared to be hanging on her every word. This was a very important moment.

"The letter goes to," she said, ". . . to Aunty Emang, at the newspaper. Begin. Dear Aunty Emang, I am a lady who needs your help and I am writing to you because I know that you give very good advice. I am a private detective, and my name is Mma Ramotswe of the No. 1 Ladies' Detective Agency (but please do not print that bit in the paper, dear Aunty, as I would not like people to know that I am the person who has written this letter)."

She paused, as Mma Makutsi's pencil darted across the page of her notebook.

"Ready," said Mma Makutsi.

"A few weeks ago," dictated Mma Ramotswe, "I met a lady who told me that she was being blackmailed about stealing food and giving it to her husband. I wondered if this lady was telling the truth, but I found out that she was when she showed me the letter and I saw that it was true. Then I found out something really shocking. I spoke to somebody who told me that the blackmailer was a lady who worked at your newspaper! Now I do not know what to do with this information. One part of me tells me that I should just forget about it and mind my own business. The other tells me that I should pass on this name they gave me to the police. I really do not know what to do, and I thought that you would be the best person to advise me. So please, Aunty Emang, will you come and see me at my office and tell me in person what I should do? You are the only one I have spoken to about this, and you are the one I trust. You can come any day before five o'clock, which is when we go home. Our office is part of Tlokweng Road Speedy Motors, which you cannot miss if you drive along the Tlokweng Road in the direction of Tlokweng. I am waiting for you. Your sincere friend, Precious Ramotswe."

Mma Ramotswe finished with a flourish. "There," she said. "What do you think of that?"

"It is brilliant, Mma," said Mr Polopetsi. "Shall I deliver it right now? To the newspaper office?"

"Yes, please," said Mma Ramotswe. "And write 'urgent' on the envelope. I think that we shall have a visit from Aunty Emang before we go home from work today."

"I think so too," said Mma Makutsi. "Now I will type it and you can sign it. This is a very clever letter, Mma. Perhaps the cleverest letter you have ever written."

"Thank you, Mma," said Mma Ramotswe.

HOW SLOWLY the hours can pass, thought Mma Ramotswe. After the writing of the letter to Aunty Emang, the letter that she was confident would draw the blackmailer from her lair, she found it difficult to settle down to anything. Not that she had a great deal of work to do; there were one or two routine matters that required to be worked upon, but both of these involved going out and speaking to people and she did not wish to leave the office that day in case Aunty Emang should arrive. So she sat at her desk, idly paging through a magazine. Mma Ramotswe loved magazines, and could not resist the stand of tempting titles that were on constant display at the Pick-and-Pay supermarket. She liked magazines that combined practical advice (hints for the kitchen and the garden) with articles on the doings of famous people. She knew that these articles should not be taken seriously, but they were fun nonetheless, a sort of gossip, not at all dissimilar to the gossip exchanged in the small stores of Mochudi or with friends on the verandah of the President Hotel, or even with Mma Makutsi when they both had nothing to do. Such gossip was fascinating because it dealt with day-to-day life; the second marriage of the man who ran the new insurance agency in the shopping centre; the unsuitable boyfriend of a well-known politician's daughter; the unexpected promotion of a senior army officer and the airs and graces of his wife, and so on.

She turned the pages of the magazine. There was Prince Charles inspecting his organic biscuit factory. That was very interesting, thought Mma Ramotswe. She had her strong likes and dislikes. She liked Bishop Tutu and that man with the untidy hair who sang to help the hungry. She liked Prince Charles, and here was a picture of a box of his special biscuits, which he sold for his charity. Mma Ramotswe looked at them and wondered what they would taste like. She thought that they would go rather well with bush tea, and she imagined having a packet of them on her desk so that she and Mma Makutsi could help themselves at will. But then she remembered her diet, and her stomach gave a lurch of disappointment and longing.

She continued to page through the magazine. There was a picture of the Pope getting into a helicopter, holding on to the round white cap that he was wearing so that it should not blow away. There were a couple of cardinals in red standing behind him, and she noted that they were both very traditionally built, which was reassuring for her. If I ever see God, she thought, I am sure that he will not be thin.

At midday, Charlie, the older apprentice, came in and asked Mma Makutsi for a loan. "Now that you have a rich husband," he said, "you can afford to lend me some money."

Mma Makutsi gave him a disapproving look. "Mr Phuti Radi-phuti is not yet my husband," she said. "And he is not a very rich man. He has enough money, that is all."

"Well, he must give you some, Mma," Charlie persisted. "And if he does, then surely you can lend me eight hundred pula."

Mma Makutsi looked to Mma Ramotswe for support. "Eight hundred pula," she said. "What do you want with eight hundred pula? That is a lot of money, isn't it, Mma Ramotswe?"

"It is," said Mma Ramotswe. "What do you need it for?"

Charlie looked embarrassed. "It is for a present for my girl-friend," he said. "I want to buy her something."

"Your girlfriend!" shrieked Mma Makutsi. "That's interesting news. I thought you boys didn't stay around long enough to call anybody your girlfriend. And now here you are talking about buy-ing her a present. This is very important news!"

Charlie glanced resentfully at Mma Makutsi and then looked away.

"And what are you thinking of buying her?" asked Mma Makutsi. "A diamond ring?"

Charlie looked down at the ground. He had his hands clasped behind his back, like a man appearing on a charge, and Mma Ramotswe felt a sudden surge of sympathy for him. Mma Makutsi could be a bit hard on the apprentices on occasion; even if they were feckless boys for much of the time, they still had their feelings and she did not like to see them humiliated.

"Tell me about this girl, Charlie," said Mma Ramotswe. "I am sure that she is a very pretty girl. What does she do?"

"She works in a dress shop," said Charlie. "She has a very good job."

"And have you known her long?" asked Mma Ramotswe.

"Three weeks," said Charlie.

"Well," said Mma Makutsi. "What about this present? Is it a ring?"

Her question had not been intended seriously, and she was not prepared for the answer. "Yes," said Charlie. "It is for a ring."

Silence descended on the room. Outside, in the heat of the day, cicadas screeched their endless mating call. The world seemed still at such a time of day, in the heat, and movement seemed pointless, an unwanted disturbance. This was a time for sitting still, doing nothing, until the shadows lengthened and the afternoon became cooler.

Mma Makutsi spoke softly. "Isn't three weeks a bit early to get somebody a ring? Three weeks . . ."

Charlie looked up and fixed her with an intense gaze. "You don't know anything about it, Mma. You don't know what it is like to be in love. I am in love now, and I know what I'm talking about."

Mma Makutsi reeled in the face of the outburst. "I'm sorry . . . ," she began.

"You don't think I have feelings," said Charlie. "All the time you have just laughed at me. You think I don't know that? You think I can't tell?"

Mma Makutsi held up a hand in a placatory gesture. "Listen, Charlie, you cannot say . . ."

"Yes, I can," said Charlie. "Boys have feelings too. I don't want eight hundred pula from you. I do not even want two pula. If you offered to give it to me, I would not take it. Warthog."

Mma Ramotswe rose to her feet. "Charlie! You are not to call Mma Makutsi a warthog. You have done that before. I will not allow it. I shall have to speak to Mr J.L.B. Matekoni."

He moved towards the door. "I am right. She is a warthog. I do not understand why that Radiphuti wants to marry a warthog. Maybe he is a warthog too."

BY THREE O'CLOCK in the afternoon, Mma Ramotswe had taken to looking at her watch anxiously. She wondered now whether the premise upon which she had based her letter to Aunty Emang was entirely wrong. She had no proof that Aunty Emang was the blackmailer—it was no more than surmise. The facts fitted, of course, but facts could fit many situations and still not be the full explanation. If Aunty Emang was not the black-mailer, then she would treat her letter simply as any other one which she received from her readers, and would be unlikely to put herself out by coming to the office. She looked at her watch again. The excitement of Charlie's outburst earlier on had dissipated, and now there was nothing more to look forward to but a couple of hours of fruitless waiting.

Shortly before five, when Mma Ramotswe had reluctantly decided that she had been mistaken, Mma Makutsi, who had a better view from her desk of what was happening outside, hissed across to her, "A car, Mma Ramotswe, a car!"

Mma Ramotswe immediately tidied the magazines off her desk and carefully placed her half-finished cup of bush tea into her top drawer. "You go outside and meet her," she said to Mma Makutsi. "But first tell Mr Polopetsi to come in."

Mma Makutsi did as she was asked and walked out to where the car was parked under the acacia tree. It was an expensive car, she noticed, not a Mercedes-Benz, but close enough. As she approached, a remarkably small woman, tiny indeed, stepped out of the vehicle and approached her. Mma Ramotswe, craning her neck, saw this from within the office, and watched intently as Mma Makutsi bent to talk to the woman.

"She's very small," Mma Ramotswe whispered to Mr Polo-petsi. "Look at her!"

Mr Polopetsi's jaw had opened with surprise. "Look at her," he echoed. "Look at her."

Aunty Emang was ushered into the office by Mma Makutsi. Mma Ramotswe stood up to greet her, and did so politely, with the traditional Setswana courtesies. After all, she was her guest, even if she was a blackmailer.

Aunty Emang glanced about the office casually, almost scornfully.

"So this is the No. 1 Ladies' Detective Agency," she said. "I have heard of this place. I did not think it would be so small."

Mma Ramotswe said nothing, but indicated the client's chair. "Please sit down," she said. "I think you are Aunty Emang. Is that correct?"

"Yes," said the woman. "I am Aunty Emang. That is me. And you are this lady, Precious Ramotswe?" Her voice was high-pitched and nasal, like the voice of a child. It was not a voice that was comforting to listen to, and the fact that it emanated from such a tiny person made it all the more disconcerting.

"I am, Mma," said Mma Ramotswe. "And this is Mma Makutsi and Mr Polopetsi. They both work here."

Aunty Emang looked briefly in the direction of Mma Makutsi and Mr Polopetsi, who was standing beside her. She nodded abruptly. Mma Ramotswe watched her, fascinated by the fact that she was so small. She was like a doll, she thought; a small, malignant doll.

"Now this letter you wrote to me," said Aunty Emang. "I came to see you because I do not like the thought of anybody being worried. It is my job to help people in their difficulties."

Mma Ramotswe looked at her. Her visitor's small face, with its darting, slightly hooded eyes, was impassive, but there was something in the eyes which disturbed her. Evil, she thought. That is what I see. Evil. She had seen it only once or twice in her life, and on each occasion she had known it. Most human failings were no more than that—failings—but evil went beyond that.

"This person who says that she knows somebody who is a blackmailer is just talking nonsense," went on Aunty Emang. "I do not think that you should take the allegation seriously. People are always inventing stories, you know. I see it every day."

"Are they?" said Mma Ramotswe. "Well, I hear lots of stories in my work too, and some of them are true."

Aunty Emang sat quite still. She had not expected quite so confident a response. This woman, this fat woman, would have to be handled differently.

"Of course," Aunty Emang said. "Of course you're right. Some stories are true. But why would you think this one is?"

"Because I trust the person who told me," said Mma Ramotswe. "I think that this person is telling the truth. She is not a person to make anything up."

"If you thought that," said Aunty Emang, "then why did you write to me for my advice?"

Mma Ramotswe reached for a pencil in front of her and twisted it gently through her fingers. Mma Makutsi saw this and recognised the mannerism. It was what Mma Ramotswe always did before she was about to make a revelation. She nudged Mr Polopetsi discreetly.

"I wrote to you," said Mma Ramotswe, "because you are the blackmailer. That is why."

Mr Polopetsi, watching intently, swayed slightly and thought for a moment that he was going to faint. This was the sort of moment that he had imagined would arise in detective work: the moment of denouement when the guilty person faced exposure, when the elaborate reasoning of detection was revealed. *Oh, Mma Ramotswe,* he thought, *what a splendid woman you are!*

Aunty Emang did not move, but sat staring impassively at her accuser. When she spoke, her voice sounded higher than before, and there was a strange clicking when she started talking, like the clicking of a valve. "You are speaking lies, fat woman," she said.

"Oh, am I?" retorted Mma Ramotswe. "Well, here are some details. Mma Tsau. She was the one who was stealing food. You blackmailed her because she would lose her job if she was found out. Then there is Dr Lubega. You found out about him, about what happened in Uganda. And a man who was having an affair and was worried that his wife would find out." She paused. "I have the details of many cases here in this file."

Aunty Emang snorted. "Dr Lubega? Who is this Dr Lubega? I do not know anybody of that name."

Mma Ramotswe glanced at Mma Makutsi and smiled. "You have just shown me that I was right," she said. "You have con-firmed it."

Aunty Emang rose from her chair. "You cannot prove any-thing, Mma. The police will laugh at you."

Mma Ramotswe sat back in her chair. She put the pencil down. And she thought, How might I think if I were in this woman's shoes? How do you think if you are so heartless as to blackmail those who are frightened and guilty? And the answer that came back to her was this: hate. Somewhere some wrong had been done, a wrong connected with who she was perhaps, a wrong which turned her to despair and to hate. And hate had made it possible for her to do all this.

"No, I cannot prove it. Not yet. But I want to tell you one thing, Mma, and I want you to think very carefully about what I tell you. No more Aunty Emang for you. You will have to earn your living some other way. If Aunty Emang continues, then I will make it my business—all of us here in this room, Mma Makutsi over there, who is a very hard-working detective, and Mr Polo-petsi there, who is a very intelligent man—we shall all make it our business to find the proof that we don't have at the moment. Do you understand me?"

Aunty Emang turned slightly, and it seemed for a moment that she was going to storm out of the room without saying anything further. Yet she did not leave immediately, but glanced at Mma Makutsi and Mr Polopetsi and then back at Mma Ramotswe.

"Yes," she said.

"YOU LET HER GO," said Mma Makutsi afterwards, as they sat in the office, discussing what had happened. They had been joined by Mr J.L.B. Matekoni, who had finished work in the garage and who had witnessed the angry departure of Aunty Emang, or the former Aunty Emang, in her expensive car.

"I had no alternative," said Mma Ramotswe. "She was right when she said that we had no proof. I don't think we could have done much more."

"But you had other cases of blackmail," said Mr Polopetsi. "You had that doctor and that man who was having an affair."

"I made up the one about the man having an affair," said Mma Ramotswe. "But I thought it likely that she would be blackmailing such a person. It's very common. And I think I was right. She didn't contradict me, which confirmed that she was the one. But I don't think that she was blackmailing Dr Lubega. I think that he is a man who needed money because he liked it."

"I am very confused about all this," said Mr J.L.B. Matekoni. "I do not know who this doctor is."

Mma Ramotswe looked at her watch. It was time to go home, as she had to cook the evening meal, and that would take time. So they left the office, and after saying goodbye to Mr Polopetsi, she and Mr J.L.B. Matekoni gave Mma Makutsi a ride home in Mr J.L.B. Matekoni's truck. The tiny white van could stay at the garage overnight, said Mma Ramotswe. Nobody would steal such a vehicle, she thought. She was the only one who could love it.

On the way she remarked to Mma Makutsi that she was not wearing her new blue shoes that day. Was she giving them a rest? "One should rotate one's shoes," said Mma Ramotswe. "That is well known."

Mma Makutsi smiled. She was embarrassed, but in the warm intimacy of the truck, at such a moment, after the emotionally cathartic showdown they had all just witnessed, she felt that she could speak freely of shoes.

"They are a bit small for me, Mma," she confessed. "I think you were right. But I felt great happiness when I wore them, and I shall always remember that. They are such beautiful shoes."

Mma Ramotswe laughed. "Well, that's the important thing, isn't it, Mma? To feel happiness, and then to remember it."

"I think that you're right," said Mma Makutsi. Happiness was an elusive thing. It had something to do with having beautiful shoes, sometimes; but it was about so much else. About a country. About a people. About having friends like this.

THE FOLLOWING DAY was a Saturday, which was Mma Ramotswe's favourite day, a day on which she could sit and reflect on the week's events. There was much to think about, and there was good reason, too, to be pleased that the week was over. Mma Ramotswe did not enjoy confrontation—that was not the Botswana way—and yet there were times when finding oneself head-to-head with somebody was inevitable. That had been so when her first husband, the selfish and violent Note Mokoti, had returned unannounced and tried to extort money from her. That moment had tested her badly, but she had stood up to him, and he had gone away, back into his private world of bitterness and distrust. But the encounter had left her feeling weak and raw, as arguments with another so often do. How much better to avoid occasions of conflict altogether, provided that one did not end up running away from things; and that, of course, was the rub. Had she not faced up to Aunty Emang, then the blackmail would have continued because nobody else would have stood up to her. And so it was left to Mma Ramotswe to do so, and Aunty Emang had folded up in the same way that an old hut made of elephant grass and eaten by the ants would collapse the moment one touched its fragile walls.

Now she sat on her verandah and looked out over her garden. She was the only one in the house. Mr J.L.B. Matekoni had taken Puso and Motholeli to visit one of his aunts, and they would not be back until late afternoon, or, more likely, the evening. That particular aunt was known for her loquaciousness and had long stories to tell. It did not matter if the stories had been heard before—as they all had—they would be repeated that day, in great detail, until the sun was slanting down over the Kalahari and the evening sky was red. But it was important, she thought, that the children should get to know that aunt, as there was much she could teach them. In particular, she knew how to renew the pressed mud floor of a good traditional home, a skill that was dying out. The children sometimes helped her with this, although they would never themselves live in a house with a mud-floored yard, for those houses were going and were not being replaced. And all that was linked to them, the stories, the love and concern for others, the sense of doing what one's people had done for so many years, could go too, thought Mma Ramotswe.

She looked up at the sky, which was empty, as it usually was.

In a few days, though, perhaps even earlier, there would be rain. Heavy clouds would build up and make the sky purple, and then there would be lightning and that brief, wonderful smell would fill the air, the smell of the longed-for rain, a smell that lifted the heart. She dropped her gaze to her garden, to the withered plants that she had worked so hard to see through the dry season and which had lived only because she had given them each a small tinful of water each morning and each evening, around the roots; so little water, and so quickly absorbed, that it seemed unlikely that it would make a difference under that relentless sun. But it had, and the plants had kept in their leaves some green against the brown. When the rains came, of course, then everything would be different, and the brown which covered the land, the trees, the stunted grass, would be replaced by green, by growth, by tendrils stretching out, by leaves unfolding. It would happen so quickly that one might go to bed in a drought and wake up in a landscape of shimmering patches of water and cattle with skin washed sleek by the rain.

Mma Ramotswe leaned back in her chair and closed her eyes. She knew that there were places where the world was always green and lush, where water meant nothing because it was always there, where the cattle were never thin and listless; she knew that. But she did not want to live in such a place because it would not be Botswana, or at least not her part of Botswana. Up north they had that, near Maun, in the Delta, where the river ran the wrong way, back into the heart of the country. She had been there several times, and the clear streams and the wide sweeps of Mopani forest and high grass had filled her with wonder. She had been happy for those people, because they had water all about them, but she had not felt that it was her place, which was in the south, in the dry south.

No, she would never exchange what she had for something else. She would never want to be anything but Mma Ramotswe, of Gaborone, wife of Mr J.L.B. Matekoni of Tlokweng Road Speedy Motors, and daughter of the late Obed Ramotswe, retired miner and fine judge of cattle, the man of whom she thought every day, but every day, and whose voice she heard so often when she had cause to remember how things had been in those times. God had given her gifts, she thought. He had made her a Motswana, a citizen of this fine country which had lived up so well to the memory of Sir Seretse Khama, that great statesman, who had stood with such dignity on that night when the new flag had been unfurled and Botswana had come into existence. When as a young girl she had been told of that event and had been shown pictures of it, she had imagined that the world had been watching Botswana on that night and had shared the feelings of her people. Now she knew that this was never true, that nobody had been at all interested, except a few perhaps, and that the world had never paid much attention to places like Botswana, where everything went so well and where people did not squabble and fight. But slowly they had seen, slowly they had come to hear of the secret, and had come to understand.

She opened her eyes. The old van driven by Mma Potokwane had arrived at the gate, and the matron had manoeuvred herself out of the driver's seat and was fiddling with the latch. Mma Potokwane had been known to come to see Mma Ramotswe on a Saturday morning, usually to ask her to get Mr J.L.B. Matekoni to do something for the orphan farm, but such visits were rare. Now, the gate unlatched and pushed back, Mma Potokwane got back into the van and drove up the short driveway to the house. Mma Ramotswe smiled to herself as her visitor nosed her van into the shady place used by Mr J.L.B. Matekoni to park his truck. Mma Potokwane would always find the best place to park, just as she could always be counted upon to find the best deal for the children whom she looked after.

"So, Mma," said Mma Ramotswe to her visitor after they had greeted one another. "So, you have come to see me. This is very good, because I was sitting here with nobody to talk to. Now that has changed."

Mma Potokwane laughed. "But you are a great lady for thinking," she said. "It does not matter to you if there is nobody around, you can just think."

"And so can you," replied Mma Ramotswe. "You have a head too."

Mma Potokwane rolled her eyes upwards. "My poor head is not as good as yours, Mma Ramotswe," she said. "Everybody knows that. You are a very clever lady."

Mma Ramotswe made a gesture of disagreement. She knew that Mma Potokwane was astute, but, like all astute people, the matron was discreet about her talents. "Come and sit with me on the verandah," she said. "I shall make some tea for us."

Once her guest was seated, Mma Ramotswe made her way into the kitchen. She was still smiling to herself as she put on the kettle. Some people never surprised one, thought Mma Ramotswe. They always behave in exactly the way one expects them to behave. Mma Potokwane would talk about general matters for ten minutes or so, and then would come the request. Something would need fixing at the orphan farm. Was Mr J.L.B. Matekoni by any chance free—she was not expecting him to do anything immediately—just to take a look? She thought about this as the kettle boiled, and then she thought: And I'm just as predictable as Mma Potokwane. Mma Makutsi can no doubt anticipate exactly what I'm going to do or say even before I open my mouth. It was a sobering thought. Had she not said something about how I liked to quote Seretse Khama on everything?

Do I really do that? Well, Seretse Khama, Mma Ramotswe told herself, said a lot of things in his time, and it's only right that I should quote a great man like that.

Mma Makutsi, in fact, cropped up in the conversation after Mma Ramotswe had returned to the verandah with a freshly brewed pot of red bush tea.

"That secretary of yours," said Mma Potokwane. "The one with the big glasses . . ."

"That is Mma Makutsi," said Mma Ramotswe firmly. There had been a number of minor clashes between Mma Potokwane and Mma Makutsi—she knows her name, thought Mma Ramotswe; she knows it.

"Yes, of course, Mma Makutsi," said Mma Potokwane. "That is the lady." There was a pause before she continued, "And I hear that she is now engaged. That must be sad for you, Mma, as she will probably not want to work after she is married. So I thought that perhaps you would like to take on a girl who comes from the orphan farm but who has now finished her training at the Botswana Secretarial College. I can send her to you next week . . ."

Mma Ramotswe interrupted her. "But Mma Makutsi has no intention of giving up her job, Mma," she said. "And she is an assistant detective, you know. She is not just any secretary."

Mma Potokwane digested this information in silence. Then she nodded. "I see. So there is no job?"

"There is no job, Mma," said Mma Ramotswe. "I'm sorry."

Mma Potokwane took a sip of her tea. "Oh well, Mma," she said. "I shall ask some other people. I am sure that this girl will find a job somewhere. She is very good. She is not one of those girls who think about boys all the time."

Mma Ramotswe laughed. "That is good, Mma." She looked at her visitor. One of the attractive things about Mma Potokwane was her cheerfulness. The fact that she had failed in her request did not seem to upset her unduly; there would be plenty of other such chances.

The conversation moved on to other things. Mma Potokwane had a niece who was doing very well with her music—she played the piano—and she was hoping to get her a place in David Slater's music camp. Mma Ramotswe heard all about this and then she heard about the troubles that Mma Potokwane's brother was having with his cattle, which had not done well in the dry season. Two of them had also been stolen, and had appeared in somebody's herd with a new brand on them. That was a terrible thing, did Mma Ramotswe not agree, and you would have thought that the local police would have found it easy to deal with such a matter. But they had not, said Mma Potokwane, and they had believed the story offered up by the man in whose herd they had been found. The police were easy to fool, Mma Potokwane suggested; she herself would not have been taken in by a story like that.

Their conversation might have continued for some time along these lines had it not been for the sudden arrival of another van, this time a large green one, which drove smartly through the open gate and drew to a halt in front of the verandah. Mma Ramotswe, puzzled by this further set of visitors, rose to her feet to investigate as a man got out of the front of the van and saluted her cheerfully.

"I am delivering a chair," he announced. "Where do you want me to put it?"

Mma Ramotswe frowned. "I have not bought a chair," she said. "I think that this must be the wrong house."

"Oh?" said the man, consulting a piece of paper which he had extracted from his pocket. "Is this not Mr J.L.B. Matekoni's house?"

"It is his house," said Mma Ramotswe. "But . . ."

"Then this is the right place after all," said the man. "Mr J.L.B. Matekoni bought a chair the other day. Now it is ready. Mr Radiphuti told me to bring it."

So, thought Mma Ramotswe, Mr J.L.B. Matekoni has been shopping, and she could hardly send the chair back. She nodded to the man and gestured to the door behind her. "Please put it through there, Rra," she said. "That is where it will go."

As the chair was carried past them, Mma Potokwane let out a whistle. "That is a very fine chair, Mma," she said. "Mr J.L.B. Matekoni has made a very good choice."

Mma Ramotswe did not reply. She could only imagine the price of such a chair, and she wondered what had possessed Mr J.L.B. Matekoni to buy it. Well, they could talk about it later, when he came back. He could explain himself then.

She turned to Mma Potokwane and noticed that her friend was studying her, watching her reaction. "I'm sorry," said Mma Ramotswe. "It's just that he did not consult me. He does that sort of thing from time to time. It is a very expensive chair."

"Don't be hard on him," said Mma Potokwane. "He is a very good man. And doesn't he deserve a comfortable chair? Doesn't he deserve a comfortable chair after all that hard work?"

Mma Ramotswe sat down. It was true. If Mr J.L.B. Matekoni wanted a comfortable chair, then surely he was entitled to one. She looked at her friend. Perhaps she had been too hard in her judgement of Mma Potokwane; here she was selflessly supporting Mr J.L.B. Matekoni, praising his hard work. She was a considerate woman.

"Yes," said Mma Ramotswe. "You are right, Mma Potokwane. Mr J.L.B. Matekoni has been using an old chair for a long time. He deserves a new chair. You are quite right."

There was a brief silence. Then Mma Potokwane spoke. "In

that case," she said, "do you think that you could give his old chair to the orphan farm? We would be able to use a chair like that. It would be very kind of you to do that, Mma, now that you no longer need it."

There was very little that Mma Ramotswe could do but agree, although she reflected, ruefully, that once again the matron had managed to get something out of her. Well, it was for the orphans' sake, and that, she felt, was the best cause of all. So she sighed, just very slightly, but enough for Mma Potokwane to hear, and agreed. Then she offered to pour Mma Potokwane a further cup of tea, and the offer was quickly accepted.

"I have some cake here," said Mma Potokwane, reaching for the bag she had placed at her feet. "I thought that you might like a piece."

She opened the bag and took out a large parcel of cake, carefully wrapped in greaseproof paper. Mma Ramotswe watched intently as her visitor sliced the slab into two generous portions and laid them on the table, two pieces of paper acting as plates.

"That's very kind of you, Mma," said Mma Ramotswe. "But I think that I'm going to have to say no thank you. You see, I am on a diet now."

It was said without conviction, and her words faded away at the end of the sentence. But Mma Potokwane had heard, and looked up sharply. "Mma Ramotswe!" she exclaimed. "If you go on a diet, then what are the rest of us to do? What will all the other traditionally built ladies think if they hear about this? How can you be so unkind?"

"Unkind?" asked Mma Ramotswe. "I do not see how this is unkind."

"But it is," protested Mma Potokwane. "Traditionally built people are always being told by other people to eat less. Their lives are often a misery. You are a well-known traditionally built person. If you go on a diet, then everybody else will feel guilty. They will feel that they have to go on a diet too, and that will spoil their lives."

Mma Potokwane pushed one of the pieces of cake over to Mma Ramotswe. "You must take this, Mma," she said. "I shall be eating my piece. I am traditionally built too, and we traditionally built people must stick together. We really must."

Mma Potokwane picked up her piece of cake and took a large bite out of it. "It is very good, Mma," she mumbled through a mouth full of fruit cake. "It is very good cake."

For a moment Mma Ramotswe was undecided. *Do I really want to change the way I am?* she asked herself. *Or should I just be myself, which is a traditionally built lady who likes bush tea and who likes to sit on her verandah and think?*

She sighed. There were many good intentions which would never be seen to their implementation. This, she decided, was one of them.

"I think my diet is over now," she said to Mma Potokwane.

They sat there for some time, talking in the way of old friends, licking the crumbs of cake off their fingers. Mma Ramotswe told Mma Potokwane about her stressful week, and Mma Potokwane sympathised with her. "You must take more care of yourself," she said. "We are not born to work, work, work all the time."

"You're right," said Mma Ramotswe. "It is important just to be able to sit and think."

Mma Potokwane agreed with that. "I often tell the orphans not to spend all their time working," she said. "It is quite unnatural to work like that. There should be some time for work and some for play."

"And some for sitting and watching the sun go up and down," said Mma Ramotswe. "And some time for listening to the cattle bells in the bush."

Mma Potokwane thought that this was a fine sentiment. She too, she said, would like to retire one day and go and live out in her village, where people knew one another and cared for one another.

"Will you go back to your village one day?" she asked Mma Ramotswe. And Mma Ramotswe replied, "I shall go back. Yes, one of these days I shall go back."

And in her mind's eye she saw the winding paths of Mochudi, and the cattle pens, and the small walled-off plot of ground where a modest stone bore the inscription *Obed Ramotswe*. And beside the stone there were wild flowers growing, small flowers of such beauty and perfection that they broke the heart. They broke the heart.

africa
africa africa
africa africa africa
africa africa
africa

ABOUT THE AUTHOR

Alexander McCall Smith is the author of the huge international phenomemon The No. 1 Ladies' Detective Agency series, and of The Sunday Philosophy Club and 44 Scotland Street series. He was born in what is now known as Zimbabwe and was a law professor at the University of Botswana and at Edinburgh University. He lives in Scotland.